Blue Earth River

A novel

William Loving

Early Praise for Blue Earth River

"With William Kent Krueger's heart and eye for Midwest detail, William Loving has crafted not only a love letter to the small-town residents of the region, but a hopeful and uplifting page-turner."

~ J. Ryan Stradal, author of *Saturday Night at the Lakeside Supper Club*

"In *Blue Earth River*, Bill Loving takes the macrocosm of divided America and masterfully shrinks it to the small-town stage. Loving's latest is large-hearted and timely—a worthy addition to the Americana canon."

~ Ivy Pochoda, author of *Sing Her Down*

"By turns comic and tragic, this keenly observed novel illuminates the ways in which members of a community rally to care for one another, even as others squabble and scheme for power. A bold and enthralling tale."

~ Omolola Ogunyemi, author of *Jollof Rice and Other Revolutions*

Blue Earth River

Text copyright © 2025 **William Loving**

Edited by Kelly Ottiano

Published in North America and Europe by Running Wild Press.
Visit Running Wild Press at www.runningwildpublishing.com.
Educators, librarians, book clubs (as well as the eternally curious), go to www.runningwildpublishing.com.

Paperback ISBN: 978-1-963869-88-0

eBook ISBN: 978-1-963869-35-4

As always, for Rhonda

Contents

July

The ice cube trays in the microwave were his first inkling that something was amiss with his wife. At first, he suspected she was playing a joke on him. That would be just like Molly Peterson and her whimsical sense of humor. In their forty-five years of marriage, Gus Peterson had grown from annoyance to acceptance to fondness for her manic-pixie-dream-girl antics. The little surprises, the giggles, the poems and dried flowers in his pockets, the smiley face, pink lips, and eyelashes painted on the front of their Toro riding mower. But this time, no giggles. When he asked her about the trays, she claimed to have no knowledge of how they got there and peevishly suggested he was the one playing a practical joke. What might have been a moment of genial levity ended in an awkward standoff. "Pffft," Molly said as she departed the kitchen for the dining room, where she stood in front of the oak sideboard for a long moment studying her menagerie of little painted Swedish horses as if pondering what to do next. She flicked a stray lock of gray hair from her face, wiped her hands on her Gold Medal Flour apron, and cleaned her glasses lenses with her handkerchief, as if the ritualized sequence would jog her memory.

The radio next to the toaster filled the small kitchen with neighborly AM chatter about the weather and ads for lumber yards and car dealers. Gus wondered what was going on in that mysterious head of hers. Bring her back to the present moment. "Did you send the column in?" he called to her.

"Of course I sent the column in," she said. "Do you think I'm senile?"

"I didn't mean it like that." He approached her in the dining room and gently stroked her hair. She snapped her head away and pushed his hand off.

"How *did* you mean it?" She stared at him, her green eyes squinting as if assessing the trustworthiness of a complete stranger.

"I just..." He fumbled, unsure he wanted to get drawn into another of these interrogations. "It's okay, Molly. Sugar. All good."

"Sure it is." She brushed past him and strode into the bedroom. She closed the door hard. Not quite a slam, but loud enough. He knew the signal. No entry allowed until the door was opened from inside.

Gus turned toward the kitchen door and from the hook grabbed his car keys, distinguishable from Molly's by the purple-and-gold Vikings bottle opener dangling from the chain. Outside he walked to the old Ford parked by the barn, his work boots crunching the gravel driveway, a familiar aroma arriving on the breeze from one of the neighbor's hog barns. In moments such as this, it was his custom to retreat to the VFW Post in town where a couple of Grain Belts or three and some masculine conversation would reliably ease his troubled mind. It occurred to him as he turned the key in the ignition, bringing the Cobra V-8 roaring to life, that he might have noticed the signs earlier if he'd been paying closer attention. Molly had seemed a bit off in recent weeks. Maybe months, now that he thought about it. Not quite her usual sunny disposition, more frequent episodes of cranky contrariness. He'd chalked it up to some kind of female life-stage thing.

He tuned the radio to a classic rock station—no Twins game till later—backed out of the driveway onto County Road 4, and followed a flatbed semi piled high with fresh hay bales stacked like sandstone-colored blocks. The road was freshly blacktopped and rifle straight as it cut through the yard-tall corn and foot-tall beans on either side. The land was flat as a placid lake, and Gus could see to the horizon in all directions, a sun-dappled expanse of bright green dotted by an archipelago of dark green shelter-belt trees in clusters obscuring the farmsteads. Here and there a gleaming new silo, barn roof, or grain elevator peeked through the treetops. The recent farm economy had been very good, a situation many of his neighbors gullibly credited to the con artist in Washington while overlooking the fact that things were not so great in their own hometown. He often wondered if he'd have been better off as a farmer rather than a high school teacher and baseball coach.

As it was, they lived among the farmers, outside of town in a one-story rambler on a two-acre lot that Molly had once dreamed of turning into a small chicken farm with goats and rabbits. Gus would have preferred to live in town, on one of those lovely oak-lined streets west of the square where the grand old homes eventually yielded to the wooded valley of the river. In any case, Molly's dislike for actual chickens, goats, and rabbits was exceeded only by their dislike for her, leaving the Petersons with an acre of lawn to tend and an acre-sized vegetable patch, the produce from which Molly sold at her roadside stand.

He left the semi when he made the turnoff onto 242nd Avenue, which would take him straight into town. The tiny burg of Newfield lay nestled alongside the Blue Earth River, which snaked lazily through the south-central part of the state on its way north to meet the Minnesota River. To get there, you take Highway 169 south from Mankato. Don't blink or you'll miss the county road turnoff. If you get to Winnebago, you've gone too far. Deep in the corn belt, the locals would tell you, is found some of the richest farmland in the world. Corn, soybeans, and hogs had sustained the town of some two-thousand remaining souls and the surrounding farmsteads for well over a century. The town was settled in the 1890s by farmers from Bavaria, who called it Neuesfeld then changed it to Newfield in 1918 amid anti-German sentiment in the United States.

The radio station's endless run of commercials gave way to the opening strains of The Rolling Stones' "Gimme Shelter." Gus cranked up the volume as he drove past the old corn syrup processing plant just outside of town, still operating but strangely quiet with few cars in the parking lot. He thought of the people he'd known from high school who had worked there for years. Some of those laid off had left town in search of opportunity; others had stayed and drifted into pointless days of minimum-wage jobs and endless nights of soothing alcohol. The corn plant was once the largest employer in town, originally run by the Steinbach family, now by a mysterious entity called Invex LLC, a private equity group of some sort. The geniuses at Invex apparently were using the old plant in some sort of tax-dodging, commodities-trading algorithm that nobody in town understood. The one thing they did understand was the algorithm required only a dozen employees at the plant as opposed to the hundreds who worked there in Newfield's better days, when the entire town was redolent of the cloying aroma of fructose.

For a few years there were jobs at the ethanol plant in Winnebago, but the ethanol market proved volatile, and that plant had recently closed. That left the Green Giant cannery down in Blue Earth the lone remaining large employer south of Mankato, but those jobs were mostly already taken by Mexican, Central American, and Asian immigrants, who were known to be willing to work harder and for less money than the locals, a source of no small amount of animosity in some quarters, such as the Newfield VFW Post.

Dark and cool it was inside Post 5433, named in honor of local war hero Arne Thorvaldsen, who was posthumously awarded the medal of honor in 1945 after he hijacked a German army fuel truck in the wee hours and, apparently passed out drunk on blackberry schnapps, crashed it into an enemy command post, immolating everyone inside, including himself. The bar was a welcome respite from the muggy heat of mid-July. The smell of Lysol and stale beer filled the space, where three stout men in ball caps—one Twins, one Gophers, one Pioneer Hybrid—sat at the bar nursing longnecks. The room was dimly lit by neon beer signs on the walls. Schell's. Leinenkugel's. Grain Belt. Hamm's. Bud Light. A flat-screen TV over the bar silently displayed a golf tournament. An electronic dartboard machine sat neglected in a corner, luring customers with a siren's call of flashing lights and murmured beeps and boops. Its very existence was an affront to Gus, who in his younger days had won more than his share of beers and dollar bills at real cork dartboards in bars from Minneapolis to Honolulu to Saigon.

"You still faking that limp, Peterson?" came the usual greeting from John Berg. He had turned on his barstool at the sound of the squeaking front door opening and letting in a brief shaft of sunlight. A pile of torn paper lottery tickets sat on the bar next to his Leinenkugel's.

"You still wasting money on pull tabs and Wisconsin goat piss?" Gus replied.

"When you gonna stop defrauding the VA with that old war-wound scam?" said Carl Larsen from under his dingy yellow seed cap with the curled visor pulled low over his bloodshot eyes and capillary-map of a nose.

"On the day you turn yourself into AA, you walking beer keg," said Gus. He settled his slender frame on the stool next to Berg and lifted his Reapers ballcap to allow the indoor air to cool his shiny pate. Though he'd been outside only a few minutes, his faded Newfield Athletic Dept. t-shirt had sweated through, leaving dark stains on his chest, back, and underarms.

"Are you still driving that old piece of shit?" chimed in Harry Kugelman. "When are you gonna get a new car? Or better yet, a big manly truck?" As the Minnesota Twins were still in first place, Kugelman hadn't yet ditched his blue and red TC hat for his purple Vikings hat, a seasonal wardrobe change whose timing was determined by the American League Central Division standings.

"My car is worth more than you three clowns put together,"

said Gus. He gestured to Cindy Smith behind the bar for his usual Grain Belt Premium, straight from the ice chest not the leaky refrigerator.

The ritual hazing of Gus Peterson by his three pals, all Vietnam veterans like himself, was a form of indirect tribute reserved for the only one among them who had seen action and suffered a serious wound. The insult fest continued for several more minutes, until the foursome grew weary of it and clinked their bottles together and traded arm punches.

"We were having ourselves a debate before you came in," said Berg. "Maybe you can settle it."

"What is it this time?" Gus said after taking a long swig.

"TikTok versus YouTube. Which platform is better for establishing your influencer brand and monetizing your unique value proposition?"

Gus stared at the three of them in succession, waiting for a conspiratorial wink or stifled chuckle. Three stone faces. Apparently, they were serious.

"I say YouTube," said Larsen. "Berg here, a Chinese-loving commie if ever there was one, says TikTok. And Kugelman, dialing in via modem from the year 2002, says MySpace."

Berg and Larsen laughed and clinked their bottles together. Kugelman shrugged and said, "What do I know? I only use a computer to check email."

"Liar," said Larsen. "I see you checking Facebook on your phone all the time."

"That's different," said Kugelman. He scanned their faces for confirmation. "Isn't it?"

They shook their heads sadly and lifted their beers.

"What say you, oh distinguished educator of young Newfield minds? YouTube or TikTok?" said Berg.

"*Retired* educator, I remind you, and I say leave me out of this, you nutjobs. You've been listening to your grandkids too much.

Why don't you debate something important, like … I dunno … Bud versus Miller." Gus took a swig of his beer.

"How's Molly?" said Berg after a brief pause in the conversation.

"Fine," Gus lied, startled by the sudden change of subject. "The love of my life." He raised his bottle for another round of clinking glass, then drained his and ordered another.

"To the Advice Queen of Minnesota," said Berg, holding his bottle high then taking another swig.

"To the Tomato Queen of Minnesota," slurred Larsen.

"The Lager Queen of Minnesota," said Kugelman.

"No, that's a book, dummy," said Gus.

"A good one, too," said Larsen. "All about beer. Mmmmmmm. By some guy named Strudel."

"Stradal," Gus corrected.

The door squeaked open again, the shaft of light slicing the barroom in two like a laser scalpel, and in walked Chester Greenfield, the largest pork producer in the county, and possibly the largest man in the county at six-feet-five and about three hundred pounds. Unlike the other regulars in their jeans and t-shirts, Greenfield wore a pale blue seersucker suit with red tie, a white goatee, and a red MAGA hat atop his sunburned head. He ordered a beer at the bar—a Budweiser—nodded to the foursome on the stools, who nodded back politely, then took a table in the corner rather than joining them and stared at his cellphone. After a few minutes his phone rang and he walked outside leaving the half-full beer, as if his business were too important to be overheard.

"That fucking Chester, with his goddam Trump hat. Wears it in here just to piss me off," said Berg.

"Seems to work, because you let it," said Gus.

"It ain't just Chester pissin' you off. Lotta people in town like Trump," said Kugelman. "I bet he carries this county by twenty points again."

"Lotta people in town like their taxes cut … and don't like Mexicans," said Berg, casting a side eye at Kugelman.

"Mexicans are okay with me, they're hard-working, church-going people, at least the ones I know," said Larsen. He was the only one of the foursome who was an actual farmer, with three hundred acres just east of Highway 169. "Lower taxes are okay with me, too, and getting the government out of my personal business. But there's something wrong with that guy. He wasn't raised right. A liar and a cheat, he is. Why folks around here thought a New York rich boy with mob ties would make a good president is beyond me."

"They overlook the lying and cheating part so they can get their taxes cut and stick it to the liberals," said Kugelman. He drained his Bud Light and signaled to Cindy for another. "And they like what he says. It's what they think but are afraid to say out loud. He's like a naughty stand-up comedy act. Ain't that right, Cindy?"

The tattoos and piercings-festooned bartender, listening from the other end of the bar while drying and stacking beer mugs, said, "You already know what I think about Trump. Bernie woulda whupped his ass." She slid a bottle of Bud Light down the bar where it stopped precisely in front of Kugelman like a perfectly placed shuffleboard disc, as if she had done it a hundred times before, because she had.

"What do you say, Gus?" said Berg. "You're always quiet when the subject of Trump comes up."

Gus took another pull on his beer but said nothing.

"I know how you feel about the military and all that fake patriotic bullshit," Berg continued. "After what happened …"

"It's not the military and you know it," said Gus. "It's American foreign policy..."

"Trump said he'll get us out of all these endless wars," said Kugelman.

"That draft-dodging sonofabitch will say anything to get himself re-elected," said Gus.

"Might as well get used to the idea," said Kugelman. "Trump's gonna get re-elected. On account of the economy."

"Don't listen to him," said Cindy as she poured herself a draft. "You watch. Bernie's going to kick his ass."

"You voted for Trump last time," Berg said to Kugelman. "So did you," he said to Larsen. "You guys gonna do it again?"

Larsen shrugged and took a long swig from his Hamm's.

"I ain't saying," said Kugelman. "Anyway, the election's more than a year off. Let's see what happens."

Gus drank the last of his beer, left a ten spot on the bar, and spun his stool toward the door. "I will leave you gentleman to the eternal questions of YouTube versus TikTok versus Trump. I have business to conduct. So long, Cindy. Don't be afraid to eighty-six these clowns when they start drooling."

The midday sun nearly blinded him as he left the bar and groped his way toward his 1975 Gran Torino, drawn to the still-gleaming chrome trim and candy-apple-red paint job he'd so lovingly preserved for forty-four years. He was angle parked on East Main, right in front of the tan Kasota-stone façade of the bar, next to Chester Greenfield's enormous black Ford F-250 crew cab jacked up on big tires, inside of which he could make out the bulk of the owner through the tinted glass talking animatedly on his phone with the engine running and air conditioning going full blast.

Gus gazed across the town square at the Bird Song Café, just visible below the canopy of maples that lined the park, and wondered if he should drop in to say hi to Mavis. Maybe later. Mavis Birdsong's café was the last restaurant still open on the square, where empty storefronts gaped like missing teeth in a once-brilliant smile. He paused to admire the old Schmerz brewery next to the town hall, which closed in the late 1960s after seventy years employing generations of Newfielders serving up reliably mediocre lagers. "Schmerz: The Beer That Flirts" the billboards used to say confusingly; "Schmerz: So Bad It Hurts" the teenagers would reply, riffing on the founding family's name, the German word for pain. The old brewery's wine-red Romanesque castle survived, first as a hotel, which failed, then an outlet mall, which failed, and finally a home for the town's skimpy historical society. It was the grandest building on Newfield's town square, a two-block-long by one-block-wide grassy rectangle surrounded by Victorian-era limestone and red brick store fronts, punctuated in the center by a white-washed bandstand and a war memorial's gray antique ship cannon pointed ominously at the offices of the local weekly newspaper, *The Newfield Clarion*, as if in unsubtle warning from the town burghers.

The truck window lowered, expelling a blast of cold air in Gus's face, breaking his thoughts. Greenfield turned to him with a smile and said, "Hey, Gus. Remind me, which one are you supposed to be? Starsky? Or Hutch?" He snickered and the darkened window slid up again. Gus ignored the lame joke, which he'd heard a hundred times over the years, and climbed into his car with a notion to swing by the offices of the *Clarion* on the north end of the square—too far to walk on his gimpy ankle—to see his old friend the editor and publisher, Jim Tomlinson, and confirm that Molly really had sent in next week's advice column. "Dear Molly" was the most popular feature in the paper, more even than the crossword puzzles and horoscopes. For Tomlinson, it was one of the few things, along with high school sports, still drawing enough readers and advertisers to justify keeping the hundred-and-one-year-old tabloid going, at least until that inevitable day when he'd have to cancel the press run and go strictly online, which would break his father's heart down there on the Florida Gulf Coast.

Gus found Tomlinson ensconced in his glassed-in office at the rear of the cramped little newsroom with its four desks empty and no one minding the reception area. The phone was ringing, no one to pick it up. Lunchtime, he guessed. The editor was tapping at his computer keyboard with both index fingers, glasses perched atop his balding head. He looked up and smiled. "Hey. I was just thinking about you."

Gus sat in the chair facing Tomlinson, who resumed pecking at the keyboard. "Phone's ringing," Gus observed.

"I know," said Jim.

"What if it's a whistleblower with the scandal of the century?"

"Yeah, like that's going to happen at the *Clarion*. Anyways—voicemail."

The *Clarion* newsroom was not quite up to Gus's impressions from *The Front Page* and *All the President's Men*. It seemed a sleepy operation, as evidenced by the tidy desks and lack of anything that smelled like news. Then again, Newfield was a sleepy town.

"Let me finish this editorial and I'll buy you a cheeseburger at the Post. And a beer or six."

"You're not drinking. I hope." Gus raised an eyebrow of concern.

"I meant a beer or six for you."

"Thanks, but I just came from there," said Gus. He belched out the evidence. "Chester Greenfield came in, so I left."

Tomlinson shook his head. "Did you know Chester thinks he can get Trump to make a campaign stop in Newfield?"

"No way."

"He thinks because he's a big donor he can get the Trump Train to make a whistle stop in our fair city. As if."

"Dream on, Chester," Gus said with a chuckle. "So, what's the editorial? Trump?"

"Nah. The high school again. I know since you retired, oh great one, there's no reason to keep it open, but I still cling to the Quixotic hope we can keep Newfield High going a while longer and put off the inevitable slide into ghost town. And keep our kids from getting bused all the way to Blue Earth."

Gus turned and glanced across the newsroom through the picture window overlooking the town square where the black circle of the war memorial cannon's muzzle gazed at him impassively like the lens of a surveillance camera. "Doesn't that cannon give you the creeps?" he said. "After the way you took down Jack White, it wouldn't surprise me if he loaded a shell in there and fired it right through that window."

"Don't worry about old Jack. We're pals again, ever since I endorsed his wife for mayor."

"For which Cindy will never forgive you."

"You know I love Cindy to death, but let's be honest, she's not exactly mayor material. Bartender material, yes."

"Anyway, I just stopped in to see if you have any new letters for Molly and if you got her column this week. I proofed it like usual but I'm never sure what Molly does to it before she sends it in."

"No new letters yet. I haven't seen the column and I was wondering if everything's okay. It was due yesterday and she's almost never late."

"Everything's fine," Gus lied again, his voice catching involuntarily. "I'll remind her when I get home." He looked at the ceiling, trying to hide the truth on his face from the newsman's prying eyes.

"Thanks. So, what are the Miss Lonelyhearts and dysfunctional clans of southern Minnesota whining to Molly about this week?"

"One guess."

Dear Molly,
I love my big brother, honest I do. Which is why I am so heartbroken. We were always close, and we still get together once a month with our kids for hot dish or brats on the grill. But now I'm not sure we'll ever speak again. It's all because of this Trump business. For the last few years, we've tried to avoid politics, but at our July

4th cookout last week it all blew up and I am so angry and heartbroken. Maybe I had a little too much Chablis when I let it slip that I thought the president ought to be in jail instead of in the White House four more years. My brother, who as usual had been hitting the Long Island iced teas pretty hard, went into a rage and called me names I'd never heard come out of his mouth. My husband, God love him, stuck up for me and the two men almost came to blows. My sister-in-law, who has always been sweet and ladylike, started screaming about Hillary Clinton and pedophiles and dumped a bowl of potato salad all over our patio. I just snapped. Somehow she ended up covered in Buffalo wings sauce. That might have been my fault. The Weber got knocked over and the coals set the dead grass on fire. My husband's Crocs melted when he tried to stamp it out. Somebody called the fire department. My brother and his family piled into their truck and left. I am so embarrassed and ashamed. How can I ever patch this up?
Signed,
Heartbroken.

Dear Heartbroken,
Oh my. That does not seem like adult behavior, now does it. Sorry to say, I've been getting too many letters like this for the last few years. So many that I stopped printing them. But this story of yours tells me things are getting worse. It makes me sad to see politics turning level-headed, civic-minded Minnesotans into petulant children. If I had a paddle big enough, I'd spank the lot of you.
As for patching things up, you need to decide how important family ties are to you, specifically with your brother and his wife. They are family

to you, like it or not. Your children and their
children are cousins. Are you prepared to break
off those relationships over something as fleeting
as politics?

Surely you have enough shared history and
memories to tie you together, leaving politics
aside. You and your brother managed to avoid
that subject for years, and you can do it again.
You just need to call a truce. One of you has to
be the grown-up and swallow your pride. Since
you are the one asking, I suggest that it be you.
Have your brother meet you on neutral ground.
Just you and he, no spouses. Take the high road
and apologize for the Buffalo wings sauce (which
"might have been" your fault? First you need
to own your own behavior). Chances are he'll
apologize, too, and you'll be on your way to
reconciliation. There is no fracture so deep
that it can't be healed over a slice of pie.
Also, next barbecue, go easy on the Chablis.

Hugs,
Molly

Gus awoke from a recurring nightmare in which he was being
chased through a burning jungle by panicked fleeing animals—
water buffalo, Komodo dragons, white tigers, pythons, monkeys.
He wasn't sure if they were after him or just trying to escape the
flames, but he kept running. He sat up in bed and realized he'd been
yelling again, an occasional occurrence that Molly usually halted
by wrapping him in her arms. This morning however, no Molly.
The covers on her side of the queen bed were tossed aside. Anxiety
began its gradual creep to the surface. Odd for her to be up before
him, he thought. The clock radio on the nightstand said six-thirty.

He threw on his Hombre cowboy robe and wandered into
the kitchen, hoping she'd put the kettle on for coffee. No kettle,

no Molly. He shuffled over to the sink and gazed out the window into the back yard where the morning sun cast long shadows across the grass. The old white barn, sagging a bit and needing a fresh coat, was lit up by the low angled rays like a rustic painting. He scanned the vegetable beds then saw her, off toward the side yard among the tomatoes, wearing her faded 1980s Emmylou Harris t-shirt. (Where and when was that concert? Mankato? Rochester?) There was something not quite right about this tranquil tableau. He blinked, thinking he was imagining things, but no, he was not: she was wearing nothing else, naked from the waist down, bending over to pick an Early Girl tomato. If anyone happened to drive by on County Road 4 and glanced into the yard, the full moon might have sent them into the ditch. Gus tried to suppress his rising sense of alarm and focused on rectifying the situation before it brought shame upon the house. He hustled back to the bedroom as fast as his gimpy leg would take him and grabbed Molly's pink chenille robe off the hook on her closet door. He approached her discreetly from behind, not wanting to make a big deal out of it, and wrapped the robe around her scrawny shoulders. She turned and smacked him square on the nose with her closed fist, watering his eyes.

"Ow!" he said.

"Who do you think you are, sneaking up on me like that?" she said.

"I think I'm Gus Peterson," he said. He gingerly felt his nose, which throbbed but didn't seem broken.

"Go away, Gus Peterson. You bother me." She turned back to her tomatoes. "You have a nosebleed," she added matter-of-factly, as if she'd had nothing to do with it.

Gus felt the warm trickle run down to his lips and covered it with his hand. He walked back to the house, thoroughly chastened. "No good deed…," he muttered to himself. As he pressed a damp paper towel to his nose, he checked on her from the kitchen window to make sure she remained covered. She stood facing the road, looking down at her nakedness showing through the open robe, and hurriedly wrapped it closed and tied the belt, glancing around as if checking for gawkers, her elfin face stricken with a look of panic and fear.

Satisfied that he'd stanched the nosebleed, Gus retreated to the bedroom to get dressed. In the two weeks since the ice cube trays incident, Molly had seemed more like her old self, with no troubling behaviors outside of the time she whacked him on the shoulder with a soup ladle when he accused her, perhaps undiplomatically, of forgetting to send in her column. He made a mental note to himself to tread lightly around Molly, hoping these recent incidents, coming atop several months of increasing crankiness, did not mean what he feared they meant. Her gradual personality change he had regarded at first with irritation then with a dollop of admiration as she seemed to be evolving from the younger woman's desire to be liked to the older woman's desire to not give a shit. He'd initially been embarrassed by her verbal floggings of townsfolk who'd failed to live up to her exacting standards, such as the waitress at Denny's who tried to take her plate before she was done eating and her fellow customers in line who were rude to the shy, awkward night clerk at Kwik-Mart. But eventually he had come to enjoy them as a sort of impromptu street theater. Molly had long been loved and respected as the town's locus of moral authority and now had added a soupçon of intimidation.

He tossed his robe on the bed and pulled on a clean pair of Wranglers over his plaid boxers. Atop his bird's-eye-maple dresser, collecting dust (had Molly stopped dusting? She used to be fanatical about it) was the shrine to his youth, when his dreams were still arrayed before him. He picked up the yellowing baseball, autographed by his teammates from Newfield High School's Southern Minnesota District champions of 1968. He rotated it in his fingers to recreate the forkball grip that had made him All-State. Next to the ball was the framed letter of confirmation from the Pittsburgh

Pirates congratulating him for being their tenth player drafted that same year. Next to that was an empty space, now occupied by his wallet, that formerly displayed his Selective Service draft notice and his Purple Heart, which had put an end to his field of dreams and which he had discarded years ago along with his honorable discharge papers when his pride in serving his country dissolved. On the far end of the dresser stood the framed portrait of a young man in uniform, frozen in time, which Gus never failed to tap lightly with his index fingertip before he started his day.

Tap.

While Molly remained outside fertilizing the tomatoes, Gus wandered into the spare bedroom used as her office and sat at the little gray metal desk, a converted sewing table. He opened the notebook computer and typed in her password "HuGs&KiSsEs," bringing the screen to life. Molly got testy when he proofed her columns for typos and spelling, even though she'd agreed to the arrangement years ago, so he was more frequently doing it on the sly. And more frequently finding errors to fix. Her latest column was already up on the screen.

```
Dear Molly,
I've always taken great pride in my pies.
Especially my strawberry-rhubarb pie, on account
of which I have many ribbons from county fairs.
I've also tried to be generous and share my
recipes with family, friends and neighbors.
Recently I learned that one of my friends has
been entering my pie recipes at fairs in counties
near mine where she lives. And apparently she
has a blue ribbon from one of them.
Now I hear through the grapevine that she's
entered "her" strawberry-rhubarb pie in the
Minnesota State Fair. The gall! I feel like I
should confront her about it, but she is one
of my oldest friends, from all the way back in
high school, and I'd hate to lose a friend over
```

something as small as pie recipes.

Still, this feels like theft to me, or at the very least a betrayal of friendship. Am I overreacting? I'm entering the State Fair pie contest, too. Should I confront her, or just let it pass and hope for the best?

Signed,

The Pie Lady

Dear Pie Lady,

Gosh, this is a sticky one. On the one hand, it does seem dishonest of her to enter a strawberry-rhubarb pie made with someone else's recipe. On the other hand, you did give her the recipe, with no strings attached I assume, so she has a right to do with it as she pleases, no? And how do you know she hasn't customized your recipe and added a few flourishes of her own, making it truly her recipe now?

You must ask yourself what's more important, the years-long friendship you've enjoyed with her, or winning a pie contest? And what if she does win? Wouldn't you derive some satisfaction knowing that you contributed to your friend's moment of triumph?

If you feel you must do something, I suggest talking to her about it first. Mention that you heard she's entering the State Fair and ask her about her entry. Be conversational not confrontational. Maybe she'll fess up and ask your permission. If not, ask her about the recipe. Give her a chance to see the error of her ways without putting her on the defensive. If she still seems disingenuous, then it's up to you to decide whether to confront or let it go. If it were me, I'd let it go.

By the way, I read the State Fair's rules and regulations for baking contests, and it says nothing about entering "borrowed" recipes. There

```
is, however, a procedure for filing a protest.
But I certainly hope it wouldn't come to that.
Hugs,
Molly
```

After he finished his edits and corrections, Gus managed to contort his face into a smile under furrowed brow at the same time. He smiled at Molly's lovely, common-sense outlook on life, always reasonable, always assuming the best in people, always the adult in the room. He worried about the alarming rise in errors and typos. She'd misspelled or mistyped several words and wrote apple pie where it should have been strawberry-rhubarb. As a woman who had begun her newspaper career taking classified ads over the phone, Molly had learned the importance of scrupulous accuracy, which had carried over to her writing. Until recently.

He heard Molly enter the house and he closed the laptop and quietly slipped out of the room. Molly was in the bedroom, putting shorts on under her t-shirt.

"Did you send the column to Jim?" he asked her from the hallway.

"No not yet," she said. "You don't have to keep reminding me. I'm not senile you know."

"Of course you aren't."

"I'm finished with it. Did you look at it?"

"Yup. Looks good. Same old Molly. Best advice in town."

"Whatever."

Gus returned to the office to retrieve his reading glasses, which he'd left on the desk next to the laptop. He noticed a stack of papers in the trash can underneath and, his curiosity piqued, grabbed a handful and thumbed through them. Submissions to "Dear Molly" that she had discarded, several of them containing little more than recipes and household tips, which Molly sometimes saved if they were any good. Not these, apparently. One letter, hand-written, caught his eye.

Dear Molly,

Why are people around here so rude? I used to think Minnesotans, especially down here in farm country, were the nicest people in the world. What happened?

I grew up here. Then I went away. When I came back, I hardly recognized the place. People won't talk to you on the street. They won't even make eye contact. Somebody I thought I recognized from the old days crossed the street to the other side when I approached her just to say hi.

Am I that ugly and strange? I do not think so. I seen myself in the mirror. I am not so bad. What's wrong with everybody? I hope you put this in the paper because I'd like to know what you think. And maybe people will read it and think on their own behavior.

Sincerely

Fed up

Gus shook his head and tossed the pile back into the trash can. That's an odd one. Takes all kinds. He could see why Molly threw it out. No real problem to solve or advice to give. Just an inchoate whine.

That Early Girl tasted a little mealy. Did I remember to fertilize? Who does that jackass think he is? Old whatshisname. I got him good, though. Laid him out. What was it I was going to do? I walked in here for a reason. Nobody saw my bare ass. It was six o'clock in the morning. I can show my bare ass if I want. It's my yard. Can't open a magazine anymore without seeing someone's bare ass hanging out. The prude. Gus, that's his name. Augustus, like he's a Roman emperor or something. He put the ice cube trays in the microwave and blamed me. What's that called? Gas lamping?

Gas something. Thinks I'm senile. He's the one, not me. His fault for not fixing the ice maker. Who was that guy did those funny TV ads for that bank? TCF. Bob something. Benchwarmer Bob something. Oh. What was it? Dear Molly. That's it. The column. I can't tell if I make any sense anymore. Jim prints it. Must be fine. There was something wrong with that tomato. A little bit off. More fertilizer, that's it. And more Ladybugs. Is it Ladybugs that eat aphids? Or do aphids eat the Ladybugs? I was thirteen the first time I let a boy kiss me. Kenny Thomas. Whatever happened to him? Did he die in the war? Why can't I remember? Don't let old whatshisname know you're forgetful. He'll never let you hear the end of it. I should go check on the tomatoes. That Early Girl tasted a little mealy.

August

Mavis Birdsong emerged from the back room to the front counter and hung the key on its hook below the cash register. At 6:00 am, the usual cluster of impatient customers was already milling about outside the front door, some pressing their faces against the glass like fish in an aquarium. "Coffee junkies," she muttered under her breath. And where was Travis? The teenager was supposed to be there with her at opening, not too much to ask of a boy with nothing to do over summer vacation but help out at his grandmother's café. He'd had a "sleepover" last night, which was a euphemism for an all-night party in the woods down by the river, so no way to wake him and drag him into work.

Before unlocking the front door of the Bird Song Café she turned the gas grill on to heat the griddle and checked the coffeemaker, on which she'd set the timer yesterday at closing. It was gurgling and steaming promisingly, so she opened the door. "Morning people! Coffee's on," she said with forced joviality.

First through the door, belly barging in like the prow of a ship, was Chester Greenfield in a tan poplin suit and red tie and matching ballcap. Behind him, Jill White, Newfield's recently elected mayor, red pantsuit with silver hair coiffed perfectly, and her husband Jack, Chevrolet dealer and former mayor, blue suit, red tie. The threesome, all with American flag pins on their lapels, took their usual table in the corner window where they could monitor the comings and goings on the street and across the town square. More regulars slid into their favorite booths and sleepily perused the menus, as if they ever ordered anything different. A table of out-of-towners commented on the Native American artwork and crafts that lined the walls and shelves.

After pouring coffee and distributing menus, Mavis heard the back door open and slam shut. She turned to see Travis stumble in. "Be right with you, folks," she said and entered the back doing a slow burn. "What's wrong with you, boy?" she said and reached up to knock the maroon Bulls cap off his head. He picked it up and stood, his six-foot height towering over his diminutive grandmother, and put it on sideways over his shoulder-length jet-black hair, which he knew infuriated her. "I need you here at ten minutes before six, not ten minutes after," she said. "And don't give me that shit about White man time. I've got a business to run, and here we use the White man clock."

"Sorry, Gram. I fell asleep on Jo Jo's couch, and he didn't wake me."

"Jo Jo's couch my ass. You still got leaves and dirt on your jeans. You slept down at the river again. How much did you drink?"

"Only a couple beers."

"Did you smoke? I can smell it on you."

"Only a couple spleefs."

"Spleefs? What, you Jamaican now?"

Travis shrugged and looked at the floor.

"Go in the bathroom and clean up. Put on the apron and get out there and start taking orders."

Mavis washed her hands in the front sink and flicked a few drops of water on the griddle surface. They danced and hissed for a few seconds before disappearing into vapor like tiny ghosts. She pulled a carton of eggs and packages of bacon and sausage out of

31

the fridge and set them on the counter. Travis entered the seating area and handed out menus, suddenly pleasant and articulate as he bantered with customers about prospects for the coming season of Newfield High's football team, on which he was expected to be the star running back, as his grandfather Elvis had been long ago. Mavis watched the boy and wondered if he would be academically eligible this year and drug-free. Worries, always the worries, invading her carefully curated serenity. Her thoughts wandered to her daughter Jeanne, Travis's mother, likely still living in the streets of Minneapolis after eighteen years, ever since she handed her baby to her mother—father unknown—and disappeared from Newfield never to return. Mavis had gone looking for her several times over the years; the last one, eight years back, she found her in the Indian women's shelter, inebriated and incoherent with a swollen black eye, unwilling to be coaxed home. Last thing she and Elvis heard about their daughter was she'd hopped a freight train with a disreputable character named Leroi. Mavis and Elvis raised Travis from infancy. She swore to herself he would not succumb to the lure of drink and drug, the mind haze that soothes the pain of life on the margin. She would see to it. The sunken riverbed's wooded seclusion kept her awake at night, fretting over the biker gangs, meth cookers, and other unsavory souls who hung out there.

Travis returned to the counter with a handful of paper orders and went to the back room to unload the dishwasher. Mavis cracked eggs on the griddle and pulled six strips of bacon from the pack and arrayed them carefully next to the sizzling sunflowers of yolk and white. Even with her back to the tables, she could discern the conversations rising from the clusters of customers. Her bat-like hearing was legendary among her family and members of the Lower Sioux community but largely unknown among the rest of the town, investing Mavis with a secret treasury of town gossip and inside information, rivaled only by that of Cindy Smith, who had the advantage of liquored-up customers in need of someone to talk to.

In the booth closest to the counter, an elderly couple was discussing their adult granddaughter. Grandpa said, "Her only expenses are cigarettes…" "…and losing at the casino," Grandma inserted.

At the corner table, she overheard Chester Greenfield tell the Whites, "I'm telling you, I can get the money, and money talks. Especially with that bunch."

"I can see him coming to Rochester, or Mankato. But Newfield?" said Jack White. "C'mon, Chester. I love our town more than anybody—present company excluded," he said with a wink at his wife the mayor. "But let's be realistic."

Jill White said something sibilant that Mavis couldn't quite make out. It sounded like the hissing of summer lawns.

"Listen," said Greenfield. He lowered his voice and leaned in, gesturing the Whites to lean closer. Mavis couldn't hear the rest of the conversation, now overdubbed by the couple at the counter debating whether to order the Denver omelet or the huevos rancheros.

The back door opened, and Travis greeted Maria Elena Cervantes with her three stacked boxes of the day's order of pastries. Mavis left the grill as Maria Elena deposited the flimsy white boxes in Travis's arms and the two women embraced. "*Gracias*, M'lena," Mavis said, and kissed her on the cheek.

"Get a room, ladies," said Travis.

"Shut up, boy. Go back to work."

He stacked the boxes on a table and left to man the front counter.

"What have we today?" Mavis asked, opening the lid of the top box and taking in the sweet fruity bouquet.

"Sumpin' diff'rent today. I couldn't get no peaches. So. Strawberry," said M'lena. She smiled a hopeful smile, as if needing affirmation, her white teeth, brown skin, and nearly black eyes an almost mirror image of Mavis, as if they could be sisters or mother and daughter.

Mavis closed the lid on the strawberry danishes and stared for a long moment at her best friend and most reliable supplier. "Did Julio come home last night?"

"No. He no come till morning. He thought he sneak in before I'm awake, but I was up early. Worrying."

"Travis, too. They were together, I know it. Down by the river. No doubt."

"I hate that river," M'lena said. Her shoulders slumped and she looked away.

Mavis didn't care to dwell on it and changed the subject. "Julio going out for football?"

"No. I no let him. Too much danger. His head. His knees. I can't watch. He play soccer. Real futbol." She turned toward the back door. "I go now. Miggy wants breakfast."

The two women embraced. "*Vaya con Dios*," Mavis whispered into her ear.

"*Toksa*," M'lena answered.

Mavis smiled. "Your Lakota is improving."

"Your Spanish still sucks," M'lena said with a laugh. Mavis slapped her in the butt with a spatula as she turned to leave the café.

Mavis hurried to the front counter and elbowed Travis back to the kitchen to finish with the dishwasher. More customers had arrived. The morning rush crowd. Busy for early August, a time when some folks left town for their lake cabins. The tiny café filled with the alluring aromas of hot coffee and frying bacon. Someone had fired up the antique Rock-Ola jukebox to play Johnny Cash's "Ring of Fire." The table closest to the door was now occupied by that old drunk farmer, Larsen, in his ubiquitous yellow seed cap, and his buddy the baseball coach, Peterson. Is that a black eye he's got? And a red nose. He a drinker too? Where were the other guys? Berg and whatshisname, Cuckoo-man? If that's not his name, it should be.

She flipped the eggs to over easy and moved the bacon strips around to keep them from sticking. The café was full now, the conversations and music bouncing off the ceiling to form a cheery cacophony, making it hard for Mavis to decipher the words. Hard, but not impossible. Travis made another pass through the tables and returned with three more tickets. She loaded four slices of whole wheat in the toaster and cracked six eggs into a metal bowl for scrambling. From the din she picked out a few phrases from the Larsen-Peterson table. A couple of old Swedes. Maybe one was a Norsky; she could never tell the difference. Peterson was saying "...never seen her like that..." and "...packs a wallop..." Larsen muttered something like "...they all get ornery..."

She wondered who they were talking about, and guessed maybe it was Peterson's wife Molly, the newspaper columnist. "Ornery" didn't sound like her, though. She'd always been kind to her. Mavis was a devotee of the "Dear Molly" column, and even had one of her letters published in the *Clarion*.

Dear Molly, it said. Mavis had memorized every word.
No way I ever thought I'd have to say this. But I got to say it.
Tell your kids: Don't drink ethanol. It's not the same as alcohol. It's poison and it will straight out kill you dead.
I am writing to you in hopes that you will put this in the newspaper and online so folks will see it. You know what I'm talking about. It was in your very own paper. Last month three teens from this county snuck into the ethanol factory and siphoned off some ethanol left in a tank outside the plant. Two boys are now dead. One is still in the hospital. (Only one little story in the Clarion? Because they weren't White?) An urban legend going around among our kids says ethanol will get you high, higher than that grain alcohol they are getting from someplace.

Or someone. It will get you high all right. High enough to meet your maker in the sky. Who will not be pleased to see you.

I know the plant is closed, but they need better security. But mostly what we need is smarter kids. Be smarter, kids. Parents, too.

Signed
Worried Parent

Dear Worried, Molly had responded.

Thank you so much for your heartfelt warning. I agree with you one hundred percent. Parents, please talk to your children.

I understand a lawsuit against the ethanol plant is being contemplated. But we never should have got to this point. There is something deeply wrong in our community if our children are driven to seek ever stronger means of intoxication. Is life in our beautiful, bountiful land so dreary, so hopeless, that drinking or smoking or injecting oneself to death is the only path of escape?

I know being a teenager is no picnic. I was one myself. At that age you're old enough to detect the hypocrisy and disappointing compromises of adulthood, but not yet old enough to see all the choices in front of you and make the right ones. Life has so much to offer in this blessed corner of God's creation. All of us, parents, grandparents, teachers, priests and pastors, have a responsibility to ensure that the next generation sees the beauty and possibilities in life right here.

And I agree that these tragedies deserve more coverage in the news.

Hugs,
Molly

Cindy Smith had just opened the bar at the VFW and was changing the empty keg under the Bud Light tap. Mornings were her favorite, the only time she had to herself to catch up on chores and hear herself think before the daytime drinkers started oozing in. Tending bar for small-town drunks had not been part of her life plan, but there was something calming about the mindlessness of the tasks and the chummy monotony of the clientele. Returning to her hometown after two decades haunting the nightlife of Minneapolis and Brooklyn was just the thing to regroup and recharge. Maybe she would stay. Maybe not. Dull as it was, Newfield offered a wholesome respite from her life as part-time tattoo artist, bartender, bouncer, and DJ in straight dives and dyke bars. Her failed campaign the previous year for mayor of Newfield started as a lark, an anti-Trump protest stunt, but left her with the feeling that maybe if she did hang around, she could make a difference, whip this dreary burg into shape. A decent restaurant, for starters. A gay bar, for sure. And a movie theater, not one of those crappy suburban multiplexes but an old-school single screen, maybe in the empty armory building.

She grabbed the remote and turned on the flat screen, which flashed to a Fox News talk show. She cursed aloud and quickly switched to ESPN before her blood began to boil. She muted the TV and turned on the bar's sound system, tuned to a classic country station. Jerry Jeff Walker's rendition of "LA Freeway" immediately improved her disposition. Though it was a bright and sunny morning outside, the bar was dark inside and Cindy flipped on the lights to better see what she was doing. She had just started Windexing the glass door of the cooler when the barroom door squeaked open, spoiling her quiet time. In walked Pam Strich, the nosy reporter from the *Clarion*. Cindy felt a combination of irritation and anticipation at the interruption. This could be a business call, she thought, as Pam stopped by now and again to vacuum up any wisps of town gossip still lingering in the stale air. Or then again, maybe it was a social call. Pam was a daytime drinker, more than most folks knew, and sometimes seemed to take a rather personal interest in Cindy.

"You're early," Cindy said.

"The early bird, amiright?"

"Catch any worms?"

"No, but I will catch a little something cold and foamy." Pam pulled out a bar stool and sat.

Cindy grabbed a glass, filled it from the Leine's tap, and slid it across the bar. She glanced at the Budweiser clock above the door. "Ten a.m. Kind of soon to start in, no?"

"Just a taste." Pam took a sip. "So," she said, and paused. "What's the word? Watcha heard?"

"Just like that? You're not going to flirt with me first?"

Pam's cheeks turned pink.

"Don't be embarrassed. You're adorable," said Cindy. "But are you here for the gossip? Or something else?"

"Can't it be both?"

Cindy stared at her for a long while. Pam lifted her glass and turned away. Cindy had noticed this woman right after she'd shown up in town, about a year ago. Rumor had it the young reporter had left the St. Paul *Pioneer Press* after an unspecified scandal and landed at the small-town weekly to re-start her career from the bottom rung. Cindy intended to investigate the rumor but hadn't gotten around to it. Her unfailing gaydar blipped loud and fast at the first sight of Pam. The way she dressed and carried herself. Cindy thought Pam's nose ring and spiky short hair, bleached almost white, were a bit much. But she had to admit she was cute, although at least ten years younger than herself. She figured they would likely hook up at some point. There weren't that many lesbians or bisexuals in the area. Cindy believed she knew all of them, including a few women who didn't know it yet.

"One thing at a time," she said. "About that other thing? We'll talk later." Cindy glanced at Pam without smiling. Pam's cheeks were still pink. Cindy grabbed a damp towel and wiped down the bar.

"Okay then," said Pam. "What's the latest?"

"Chester Greenfield is trying to get the Trump campaign to stop in Newfield."

"Tell me something I don't know." Pam took a long pull on her beer, then slammed the empty glass on the bar.

Cindy poured her another. "Where did you hear that?"

"Jim. The editor knows all. Sees all."

The door creaked open, and John Berg and Harry Kugelman waddled in and approached their usual stools at the far end of the bar. Kugelman, wearing his Twins hat backwards like a teenager, glanced at the TV and asked Cindy to turn it to Fox News. She smiled sweetly and gave him the finger.

"Hey, Pammy," said Berg. "How are the Gophers gonna do this year?"

"You always ask me that and I always say the same thing: they're gonna suck." She moved down to take a seat next to Berg.

"Shows what you know," Cindy said. "They went to a bowl game last year."

"Whatever. Just because I'm an alum doesn't mean I give a shit."

Cindy had the men's beers uncapped and served before they'd even sat down.

"Thanks, darlin'," said Kugelman. Cindy winked at him. He winked back and lowered his eyes to admire her formidable chest, where the cleavage just above the scoop-neck of her t-shirt enfolded a tarantula tattoo. She snapped her towel at him and turned away, knowing he would lean over the bar to get a better view of her Spandexed posterior.

"You're gross, you know that?" Pam told him. "Does your wife know you come in here to ogle the bartender?"

Cindy emitted an audible snicker.

"Hell, yes. She always says, 'Give her tits a squeeze for

me.'"

"Where are the other two Musketeers?" said Cindy, eager to change the subject.

"They'll be along," said Berg. "Probably getting breakfast at Mavis's."

The barstool banter continued for another hour until Pam apparently gave up hope of landing any useful gossip and departed for the *Clarion* newsroom to check in with the boss, taking care to disguise her beer breath with chewing gum.

"Pammy's kind of cute," said Berg after she left. "If she'd just grow her hair out and put on some makeup."

"She's a lezzie, I hear," said Kugelman. "Ain't that right, Cindy?"

"None of my business," she said. "None of yours, either."

"Thought maybe you would know," he said with a wink. She ignored him.

"Maybe she swings from both sides of the plate," said Berg. "She's flirted with me a few times. All sexy like."

"Don't flatter yourself, Bergy" Cindy interjected. "She's just softening you up so she can squeeze some gossip out of you."

Gus Peterson and Carl Larsen strolled in around noon and took up their usual positions at the bar alongside Berg and Kugelman. Cindy opened them each a bottle and asked where they'd been all morning. They reported the doings at the Bird Song Café, where there seemed to be a conspiracy of sorts brewing with Chester Greenfield and the Whites. Peterson opined that it was about Chester's preposterous idea of bringing Trump to Newfield, while Larsen suggested there was something more diabolical afoot, no doubt a scheme to leverage Jill White's new power as mayor to fatten the bottom lines of Greenfield Farms, Inc., and Jack White Chevrolet, just the sort of graft that had precipitated the downfall of the Jack White administration two years earlier. Also, Mavis had been hopping mad at her grandson Travis about something, possibly _s. All agreed that Mavis and Elvis had been heroic in raising their grandson after their daughter's sad descent into the tragic cliché of urban Indian hell. The conversation segued from the ravages of drugs and alcohol on local youth to the sinister activities in the densely canopied river valley, where the Blue Hogs motorcycle club congregated for keg parties. The river was also rumored to be the source of the tributary of grain alcohol, opioids, and crystal meth that flowed into town, which the underfunded and undermanned county sheriff's department had been unable to either confirm or stanch.

When Gus returned home for lunch, Molly was in the garden again, fully dressed, thankfully, tending to her seven varieties of tomatoes, along with her pole beans, peppers, cucumbers, and squash. Soon it would be time to set up her "Mollywood" roadside stand on County Road 4. She stood and turned toward him as he parked on the gravel drive in front of the barn next to Molly's old white Chevy pickup and heaved himself out of the seat, grabbing the top of the car door for leverage.

"If you want lunch, you gotta fix it yourself. I'm busy," Molly said preemptively and turned back to her bountiful harvest.

Gus waved to her and limped into the house, hoping he wasn't weaving too obviously from his three beers. Instead of making lunch right away, he went into Molly's office to peek at her progress on the week's column. He moved a pile of needles and yarn off the chair onto the bookshelf and sat. There was nothing on her computer screen and no word processing apps running. He checked the "Recent Documents" folder and saw nothing new since last week's column. He opened her *Clarion* email account and scanned for fresh submissions to "Dear Molly." Nothing since he'd last checked.

A pile of snail mail sat next to the computer, about a dozen letters unfolded, their ripped envelopes in the trash can. He started reading. A few of them offered more recipes to share with Molly's readers; she published the best of them—tested herself—four times a year, timed to the changes of seasons. One letter asked for advice on dog training, which he was pretty sure she knew nothing about, as they'd never had one due to Molly's allergies. Another lamented a Millennial son who had been camping on his parents' couch for two years, rarely looking up from his phone; Gus had seen variations of that theme in Molly's columns for at least a decade. Still another writer suspected her husband was being unfaithful with the UPS driver, gender unspecified. At the bottom of the pile was a letter with an opening line that grabbed his attention. It was handwritten and looked familiar.

Dear Molly,

I am writing to you again because I am fed up. I am fed up with my so called friends, my so called neighbors, this whole so called country. Everybody. Enough. That's it.

I want to say something about gratitude. I hope you will put this in your column because everybody needs to hear this. There is no gratitude in this world. Nobody cares about anybody else. Nobody even knows what other people do for them because they're so wrapped up in their own shit pardon my French (you don't have to print that part.)

Nobody knows what I done for them. Nobody even knows who I am. People see me on the street and they look away like I wasn't even there.

What does a person have to do to get some gratitude around here? Sometimes I think I need to holler out loud who I am and what I done. Or maybe do something big to get people's attention. Like walk down Mill Street with one of them ad boards hanging on me with the words You're Welcome! on it. Or something even bigger.

What would you do Molly? How do you get what's coming to you?
Fed Up

Gus read it twice, then three times. Another strange letter. It had to be the same author. That one had been thrown out, so he couldn't compare the handwriting. But he was pretty sure it was the same. And like the first one, this had no specific problem for Molly to solve, just a general sense of grievance. And over what? Maybe he was imagining it, but the words sounded vaguely like a threat. He wondered if Molly had read it yet and what she thought of it. He searched through the envelopes in the trash to see if he could match one to that letter. None of them had return addresses; nearly all of Molly's correspondents preferred to remain anonymous, difficult in a small, tight-knit community, which is why Molly, Gus, and Jim tried to edit out any potentially identifying details. All had postmarks from USPS offices around the region—Newfield, Amboy, Good Thunder, Lake Crystal, Vernon. Except one—no stamp or postmark, probably hand delivered to the *Clarion* office.

He put the letter back at the bottom of the pile, returned the envelopes to the trash can, put the needles and yarn back on the chair to cover his tracks, and went into the kitchen to make himself a fried Spam sandwich.

Chester Greenfield perched in the air-conditioned, tinted-glass cab of his three-hundred-thousand-dollar John Deere tractor like a monarch on his throne. As usual, his cellphone was glued to the side of his face, where his wife Rosalita often joked the damn thing should be surgically attached to save him time. When he was in his cab, diesel engine idling pointlessly, satellite radio tuned to The Highway country hits, he truly felt like a king, a lord of the manor, master of two-thousand acres of corn, beans, and hog barns. The ever-present noxious stench from the barns was temporarily masked by the acrid odor of diesel exhaust.

To folks in Newfield, Chester was indeed a lord of the manor, a larger-than-life figure in town affairs and the principal fundraiser for the Republican Party in this county and several others nearby. What most people didn't know was that Chester was not technically the owner of Greenfield Farms, Inc. Rather, he was the managing partner of an investor group of moneymen scattered across the Upper Midwest, from Sioux Falls to Des Moines to Minneapolis. This arrangement, had it been widely known, would have come as a surprise to Newfielders, given that corporate ownership of farmland was technically illegal in Minnesota. But there were loopholes in the Family Farm Preservation Act, and what was Chester paying all those lawyers, lobbyists, and pols up in St. Paul for if not to find those holes and keep them open? In any case, the less people knew the better. Chester's investors were silent partners, city people, not farmers. He talked with them on a weekly basis, sharing updates on corn and bean prices, pork belly futures, interest rates, land values, and so forth. Unspoken in their conference calls was the knowledge that any disappointments in return on investment could result in Chester being ousted as managing partner, forced to leave the estate that had been in his family for four generations, replaced by "professional farm management." This knowledge loomed over him like a dangling sword, a constant presence feeding daily anxieties that required medication to remain functional. He knew this was a possibility when he agreed to clandestinely sell the family farm to this corporation after his father died, an act of rebellion launched once he was out from under the oppressive filial thumb, but his outsized ego and inherited avarice would not allow for self doubts. He used his windfall from the sale to invest in real estate development while holding onto twenty-five percent of the farm ownership and profits for himself. Modern farming on two-thousand acres was a complex, high-tech business, involving things like GPS, GIS, and other acronyms he'd long forgotten, something the city folk investors knew little about. Chester was confident he could keep the cash flowing, and his partners didn't need to know every little detail.

From his position in the big green machine, outside the equipment shed on a rise near his house, he could see an endless verdant expanse punctuated by the roofs of enormous animal holding pens. It filled him with a sense of calm and indescribable joy. In this space, he liked to say, no one can hear you scheme. Today's phone call was not with his investors. It was with the Minnesota chairman of the Trump 2020 campaign, a man named Wally Johnson, a billionaire from Wayzata who had made his fortune in home medical supplies. Wally "The Bedpan King" Johnson was a hard man to reach, and Chester had been on hold for twenty minutes. It was one of the humiliations one had to endure, even as a big fundraiser, when one was from a nowhere burg like Newfield.

Rosalita came out of the house and hurried toward her fire-engine red Dodge Ram pickup, parked on the sweeping circular drive in front of the pillared entrance. Where's she off to now? Anxiety and lust mixed into the usual cocktail of unease that comes with being married to the hottest woman in the county. Chester admired his tall, raven-haired wife and the way her high-heeled cowboy boots shaped her calves and her tight skinny jeans accentuated her butt. It gave him that familiar swelling feeling in his trousers. With Cassandra heading off to Tampa soon for her freshman year at USF, Chester looked forward to an empty house where he and Rosie could get up to all kinds of mischief.

"Chester!" Wally Johnson's booming voice startled him out of his fantasy, and he jerked his phone away from his ear then recovered his composure.

"Hey, hey, Wally! What's shakin' up there at Lake Minnetonka?"

"I'm on my boat right now!" Johnson announced, as if to the world. Chester could tell Wally was shouting to be heard above the twin diesel engines. "Not much shakin' goin' on. The water's calm today. Typical August. You ought to come up sometime and take a ride on Lady of the Lake III."

The insincerity oozed through the cell connection like a viscous fluid. An invitation to board the sixty-five-foot yacht would never happen, not in a million years.

"You bet! Love to!" he said.

"So, what can I do for you, Chester?"

"I want to go over the Trump campaign's plans in Minnesota next year. The whole itinerary, etcetera."

"Chester, we've had this conversation. You know I can't make any promises."

"I know, I know. You can't blame a guy for trying. After all, I've delivered quite a pile of cash for the campaign."

"Yes, you have, Chester, and believe me that has not gone unnoticed. But seriously, Newfield? We're hoping he makes two visits, probably Duluth and St. Cloud, then maybe Rochester and Mankato. Even that might be a tough ask. To get the president to go to a small town nobody's ever heard of, there has to be some kind of unique story, with great optics. Something amazing going on there that would align with the vision for Donald Trump's America, know what I'm saying? Plus, you've got to have a secure venue for a huge crowd, ten thousand or more."

"Let me work on that, Wally."

"You do that, Chester. Meantime, how's the fundraising going? We're looking for another big bundle of checks from you. Sooner the better."

The money, always the money. Chester knew the big kahunas in Minneapolis saw him as some kind of bumpkin ATM, a reliable source of cash, but nobody they'd invite to their VIPs-only victory parties.

"It's going great, Wally," he lied. "We've got an event 'p that should be a bonanza."

"Sounds good, Chester. Gotta go. The wife's waving at me. Bye."

The lord of the manor sat on his throne, swelling gone down, and wondered what kind of bonanza he could squeeze out of this bloodless rock of a county. And what kind of "unique story with great optics" he could concoct to put Newfield on the political map. Could they crowbar ten thousand people into the old armory?

He grabbed the vial of magic pills from his suitcoat pocket and popped one into his mouth. Better make it two.

When Gus Peterson returned from Vietnam in the spring of 1972, it wasn't his high school sweetheart Frieda Stanicek who was waiting for him; she had run off to Minneapolis with Eddie Sloan, a man ten years her senior who had passed through Newfield in his tricked-out Ford Econoline with the airbrushed Rocky Mountains scenes on the sides, promising the sort of nomadic bohemian life Frieda could never have hoped for in her hometown. Instead, Gus found waiting for him the shy girl he'd barely acknowledged in school and around town, Molly O'Rourke, who unbeknownst to him had been pining since junior year, waiting out Frieda Stanicek for her opportunity, which had finally arrived in the form of Eddie Sloan's van.

Gus had moved home to his parents' house, squeezing himself in between his mother's hanging macrame projects and his father's endless beer can collection, just temporarily until he sorted things out and planned his next move, possibly the college career he'd stupidly passed up to answer the call of the Selective Service lottery. After high school, he'd considered declining the Pirates' contract offer and accepting a baseball scholarship to the U of M, which also could have deferred his draft status. But his father, a World War II veteran of the U.S. Navy, made it abundantly clear that in his family, duty to country came before personal ambition. In this his mother dissented, but as usual his father's will had carried the day, as it had when Gus's older brother Marcus had opted for the Air Force. When Gus returned, his father assured him, both the Pirates contract and the college scholarship would be waiting. Unspoken in this assurance was the missing word "if" he returned. As it happened, he did return, however not quite in one piece: with imperfectly repaired ankle and shin bones that had been shattered by shrapnel from the landmine that had separated his platoon leader's legs from his torso. So it could have been worse. He was alive and back home, but with his baseball dreams left behind in an Army field hospital outside Da Nang. Subsequent surgeries at various VA hospitals eventually modified his debilitating stagger into a mild limp.

After his parents broke the news of Frieda's escape from Newfield—she hadn't even bothered to write him a Dear John letter—they mentioned that the quiet, red-haired O'Rourke girl had been dropping by the house to inquire after Gus's health and expected return. He later learned, from both Molly and his parents, that they had been pleasant to her but not encouraging, as she was Catholic and they were Lutherans—not just Lutherans but Missouri Synod Lutherans who viewed the Papacy with suspicion if not outright paranoia, the Pope as the anti-Christ, the whole shebang. Molly managed to work around this polite but obvious diversion by studying Gus's movements about town upon his return—"like a stalker," he later teased her—and arranging to bump into him at the Dairy Queen on Mill Street, where he often stopped for a vanilla milkshake. She had cleverly ordered the same thing, and something about the way the white foam sat on her upper lip when she smiled broke him in places he didn't know he had. That milky smile had opened a door into the shy girl he'd scarcely noticed before and who

.hs of grace, wisdom, and love he'd never imagined.

memories flooded Gus's mind like a bittersweet elixir the empty sterile waiting room, mindlessly thumbing x-month-old *Sports Illustrated*, while Molly was seen by Dr. Mollenhoff, the same Mankato gerontologist who had ministered to his mother's final years a decade before. Except his mother was in her eighties then, not her sixties like Molly.

It had taken several weeks of gentle persuasion followed by more insistent cajoling to get Molly to agree to the appointment. The turning point came in late August, an incident that shocked them both and sent Molly spiraling further into depression and hostility. They had ventured north to Falcon Heights to catch the opening day of the Minnesota State Fair, an annual tradition they'd seldom missed for over forty years. Gus had felt some trepidation, given Molly's recent erratic behavior, but she'd seemed calm and lucid when she closed her produce stand the day before they drove north. She'd planned to re-open it for a few more weeks when they got back, depending on the size and quality of her final harvest.

The first hours at the fair had been pleasant. Cool for August but humid, low 70s with a gentle breeze. The usual opening-day massive crowd, nearly two-hundred thousand. They left Newfield in the Gran Torino at ten and made it to the remote parking lot at the U of M in just over two hours and rode the shuttle bus to the fairgrounds. Gus normally avoided activities that required long or arduous walking, but he made an annual exception for the fair. As long as they maintained a leisurely pace, took frequent breaks to sample food and drink and watch the river of sweaty, t-shirted humanity flow by, and rode the gondola when necessary, they could make a full day of it and be home before midnight. Over the years their circumambulations had narrowed into ever tighter arcs; they'd long ago stopped visiting the northeast corner with its farm machinery displays and kiddie amusement park (which elicited unwelcome memories) and the southwest corner with its cavernous animal barns (which they found foul-smelling and depre... livestock on display like zoo animals, reminding them they we... not cut out for the farming life). They usually started with a stroll through West End Market and its rows of stalls selling handmade leather goods and rustic wood carvings, then a "Sky Ride" gondola trip to the southeast corner where they would spend most of the day, starting with the octagonal Agriculture-Horticulture building, "Ag-Hort" as Molly called it, her favorite spot at the fair. Then the usual route: the Department of Natural Resources building (next to the best public restrooms); the International Bazaar to gawk at handmade goods from the global supply chain; the Creative Activities building where Molly could kill hours among the quilts and crafts (while Gus cruised the concession stands outside in search of the latest preposterous fried foods on a stick, which he would devour with gusto then ridicule when rejoining Molly); ending with a nighttime stroll through the Mighty Midway to bathe in the chiaroscuro of flashing lights, spinning machinery, head-pounding rock music, carnival barkers, crooked games of skill and chance, and hordes of screaming teenagers.

On this day, everything was fine until they entered the Ag-Hort building. Molly seemed in a good mood, regaling Gus with descriptions of the elaborate dollhouses she'd seen in Creative Activities. First they waited in line to see the crop art displays (the State Fair version of queuing up at the Louvre to see the Mona Lisa), where artists created "paintings" made solely of seeds. Next Gus sought out the Minnesota Craft Beer pavilion, where ten bucks could buy a flight of local IPAs or lagers or stouts. Molly said she needed to visit the ladies' room and would meet him at the exit facing the gondola station.

Gus found a concrete wall on which to perch while watching the cranky family dramas (exasperated dad to twin tykes in a retro Radio Flyer wagon: "If anybody pees their pants, they're going to sit in their wet undies the rest of the day!"). He balanced the flimsy cardboard carrier of four beers in tiny plastic cups on his lap, sampling each one in turn. He'd finished the last one, a Göse sour ale, when it occurred to him that Molly was taking an especially long time in the ladies' room. He went back inside to stand watch by the bathrooms. Ten minutes passed. He tried calling her cellphone, but it went straight to voicemail. He sent her a text. Where R U ? No reply. He asked an elderly woman coming out of the restroom in pink high-top tennies and a tie-dyed t-shirt declaring her the "World's Coolest Grandma," if she would mind going back in and asking if there's a Molly Peterson in the room. She was happy to oblige, and Gus winced in embarrassment when the little woman's voice boomed loud enough to be heard out in the hall. Passersby stopped and smiled. When she emerged with the sad news, no Molly Peterson in there, he thanked the World's Coolest Grandma and started searching through the dense crowds in all eight wings of the Ag-Hort octagon. Another call went to voicemail. Another text unanswered. The prospect of wandering around the fairgrounds trying to spot Molly's pink sunhat among tens of thousands of people seemed as ridiculous as it was hopeless. She wasn't answering her phone, possibly had let the battery die again, as she was doing more often these days. He wondered if she did it on purpose to cut herself off from his nosy intrusions into her whereabouts. He remembered there was a State Fair Police Department station across from the gondola stop at the other end, so he bought a ticket and rode back.

The officer who greeted him outside the station listened patiently as Gus recounted the events of the last hour and offered a description of Molly along with a photo of her on his phone. She advised him that this was a common occurrence at the fair, reported several times each day, usually a confused grandparent or adventuresome child getting separated and temporarily lost among the multitudes. No one ever disappeared at the fair, she said. She smiled encouragingly. This did not mollify him. Gus added the detail that his wife might be having a "senior moment" and could be lost and confused, with no apparent cellphone service. He texted her photo to the officer, who said she would share it with other officers and fair officials and commence a search. She advised him to wait at the station; they would bring Molly in when she was found. He located a bench outside where he could people watch while keeping an eye peeled for her.

As the families and gaggles of teenagers thronged past, his mind wandered back to the dozens of fair visits he had made with Molly over the years, including several in which they'd towed a toddler in a wagon, and a few more years trying to keep up with a hyperexcited little boy, too soon turned into a teenager who wanted nothing to do with them once they passed through the fair gates and eventually stopped going with them at all. The images made him smile: a boy astonished by thousand-pound hogs; enormous bright green farm machinery; dizzying rides; games of chance; and the endless supply of deep-fried foods that inevitably ended with a stomachache. The happy memories soon washed away on a tide of grief, and his mind shut the images down, corralling them back into the compartment where they were safely kept.

His thoughts turned to Molly, and he imagined her confused and lost, wandering in a vast kaleidoscope of sights and sounds. Or maybe she was merely pissed off at him for something and decided to ditch him for the rest of the day. She'd been doing a lot of that lately. He hoped it was only that.

Just after eight, an officer driving a golf cart pulled up to the station. Seated next to him was Molly, looking scared and angry. She'd been missing for four hours. Gus approached her as she stepped out of the cart and tried to hug her. She pushed him away and followed the officer straight into the police station. Gus followed. Inside there was an awkward moment when the officers tried to verify Molly's identity and relationship to Gus. Her cellphone was indeed dead, and she had no ID on her; she'd locked her wallet in the glove box of the car for fear of pickpockets. Molly offered scant assistance. She didn't seem to recognize Gus. The officer who brought her in pulled Gus aside and told him he'd found her at the far west end of the Midway, standing still, looking up at the Ferris wheel, as if transfixed by a vision. When he approached and asked if she was Molly Peterson, she was uncooperative and refused to confirm her identity. She said she was waiting for someone to come down from the Ferris wheel. The officer told her her husband was not on the wheel, he was waiting for her back at the station. She became indignant and threatened to make a scene. After a tense standoff, as a crowd began to form around them, a cop seeming to harass an old lady, he finally persuaded her that he could take her to the person she was waiting for, if only she would come along.

Gus convinced the police with photos on his phone that they were in fact a married couple. They were allowed to sit together on a bench and work things out while the officers calmly observed. "Molly," he said, and touched her hand. The contact of skin on skin seemed to trigger an electric charge of recognition; she raised her eyes and looked at Gus for the first time since she'd arrived in the cart.

"Oh, Gus," she said in weak voice, and lay her head on his shoulder. The officers turned away, satisfied.

Gus led Molly out of the station and toward the gate where they could catch the shuttle back to their car. She got as far as the West End Market before collapsing onto a bench in shuddering tears. Gus sat with her and put an arm around her trembling shoulder.

"I didn't know who I was, or where I was," she said, sobbing quietly.

"It's okay, Molly. We all have days like that. I walk into rooms all the time and can't remember what I was looking for."

"No, no, it wasn't like that. I wandered through the fair, for hours I think, lost, not sure what I was doing or where I was going. I found myself in the horse barn. Their big brown heads terrified me. I thought they were talking to me. It was like a nightmare. I wandered toward the bright lights and loud noises. All that noise, those lights. I was so confused. Then I saw the Ferris wheel. I went over there and waited…" she sobbed and blew her nose with a napkin. "I waited for … Augie … to come down off that Ferris wheel. Oh, God, Gus." She collapsed onto his lap, body shaking, sobs coming louder, attracting concerned looks from passersby, some of whom stopped and made a circle around them.

"Are you folks okay?" said a tall heavyset blonde woman wearing a red Make America Great Again t-shirt.

Gus managed a weak smile. "Thank you, we're fine, just a little tired."

The crowd lost interest and turned away.

"Oh, Gus, I thought it was Augie, up there on the wheel."

The mention of the name pried open the compartment where he stored all the painful memories, and they burst forth as if from a breached dam. He started to cry as well, and leaned over Molly, resting his head on hers to hide their tears from the passing gawkers.

He knew why Molly thought Augie was on the Ferris wheel. In her confused state she was reliving a traumatic event from years ago, when Augie was six. Molly had taken him to the fair, just the two of them, as Gus was recuperating at home from another ankle surgery. As usual, they had ended their day in the Mighty Midway, where the floodlights overpowered the evening's darkness and cast an otherworldly glow on the garish attractions, which to Augie seemed a magical kingdom. He insisted on riding the Ferris wheel by himself, after a few years of being told he wasn't old enough. He wore Molly down with his persistence, and she capitulated. As if directed by a capricious fate, the wheel malfunctioned and stopped, with Augie alone in his swaying cage at the very top. Molly watched in horror from the ground far below. She tried to call to Augie, but her voice was lost in the laughter and noise from the nearby crowds. Minutes rolled by. Ten. Twenty. The wheel remained frozen as the attendant waited for mechanics to arrive. The riders became bored and quiet. There was a break in the blaring music and crowd noise from the adjacent rides, and Molly could make out the faint sounds of a boy sobbing far above. She called to him. He called for his mommy. Molly ran to the mechanics when they arrived and begged them to hurry. In another few minutes the wheel's motor sparked to life and the slow rotation resumed. When Augie's cage reached the bottom, he was near hysterical and had to be helped out by the attendant. He had been trapped up there for more than thirty minutes. He was fine by the time they got home in the wee hours and in the morning was able to recount his little horror story to his father with enthusiasm and humor. But he refused to ride the Ferris wheel for years thereafter, until he was a cocky teenager.

After Molly's troubling episode, she and Gus were mostly silent on the long drive home. Molly slept intermittently. In the morning, after a long conversation in the kitchen over coffee, Gus called Dr. Mollenhoff's office to make an appointment.

A nurse in pale blue scrubs poked her round head into the waiting room, where the flat screen TV on the wall blared the strident voice of a man on Fox News, and summoned Gus to follow her. He was led to the doctor's office, where Mollenhoff was waiting at his desk, picture window behind him overlooking Mankato's towering grain elevators painted with colossal murals along the Minnesota River, Molly in a facing chair. Gus sat next to her and placed his hand on her arm. She didn't respond, looking at her shoes.

"Thank you for coming, Gus," the doctor said. They had been on a first-name basis for years—Gus called him Doc—going back to his mother's long decline. After some brief small talk, Mollenhoff leaned back in his swivel chair and said, "I'm going to need to order some tests. I still have a lot of questions. But based on my preliminary examination, I'm seeing some definite signs of dementia, possibly early onset Alzheimer's."

The "A" word Gus had avoided and dreaded hearing. He looked over at Molly, who continued to stare impassively at her shoes. "She's only sixty-seven," he said, as if bargaining.

"That's why we call it 'early onset.' But let's wait for the tests before we jump to any conclusions. There might be other explanations. Blood clots, mild strokes, possibly even allergic reactions."

Armed with faint hopes, Gus and Molly drove home to Newfield, Molly seeming to spiral deep into depression, Gus following not far behind.

What the heck. I read this letter three times. I don't understand it. What's wrong with me? Or maybe it's not me. It's the letter. Badly written. No good. Delete it. On to the next one. Oh damn. What happened? Where's my email? Damn computer. Hate it hate it hate it. Ought to only answer snail mail. I'm gonna do this later. Check on the tomatoes. This kitchen. So sad. Needs paint. New linoleum. That cheap bastard whatshisname won't do it. Wish I knew how. How hard could it be? What's the big deal about getting lost at the fair? Happens all the time. That's what the nice police lady said. I wasn't lost. Waiting for Augie. Waiting. Wait. What was I doing? This always happens. He said Alzheimer's. No way. I'm too young. Just a girl. Married that boy came home from the war. What happened to that boy who died in the war? I can't remember his name. But I married that other one. Old whathisname, the ballplayer. There was something I was supposed to do. What was it? Dear Molly? That's it. Go to the computer and check for new letters. That pile of mail had nothing good in it. What's wrong with people? Why so much stupid whining and poor me? I hate them. Hate them all. When is Augie coming home? I miss my boy.

September

Pam Strich woke with a mouth full of cotton and a violent storm raging in her head. She sat up in bed and recognized the familiar feeling: a savage hangover. Saharan dry mouth, a typhoon of a headache. She was naked, not her usual sleeping ensemble of t-shirt and gym shorts. And it was not her bed. Not her apartment. This wasn't the first time she'd awakened hungover in a stranger's bed, although it had been a few months. A dry spell. Who was it this time? She looked around the room for clues. Nothing looked familiar. It was a Victorian house; she could tell by the two tall skinny windows and the white-painted wainscoting on the white walls. No art or anything she could get a handle on. A faint odor of marijuana lingered in the air. Also, something that smelled like fresh coffee. And maybe … cat litterbox? Quite a heady brew, eye watering. She tried to recall the preceding night, but it was beyond reach, nothingness. Another blackout drunk. Way to go, Pam.

"Are you alive in there?" someone called from another room.

"Mmmph," was all the response she could muster.

"I've got coffee on. Looks like you'll need it," said Cindy Smith, now standing in the bedroom doorway, leggings and a Bernie 2020 t-shirt, short blonde hair still wet from a shower, head tilted, a look of concern on her face. "I have to go to work. Stay in bed if you want. The bathroom is through the kitchen if you have to puke."

Cindy fucking Smith!

"Oh, god," said Pam. The bacchanalia scenes of last night emerged through the fog.

"Oh, come on, I wasn't that bad, was I?"

"Sorry, I didn't mean you. I mean I've got to get to work, too, and I'm a fucking zombie."

Cindy sat on the bed and cupped a hand on Pam's right breast. She leaned in to kiss her. Pam turned away. "My breath. I must taste like a dumpster." Cindy kissed her on the cheek and gave her nipple a gentle pinch. "You can shower here. Help yourself to some breakfast. There's cereal and milk in the kitchen. And coffee. Drink lots of coffee. You'll be fine."

"Shit. I'm gonna be late."

"Tell old Jimmy Boy you're late because you banged the town gossip and future mayor and got leads on juicy stories."

"Did I?"

"Did you what? Bang the town gossip? Or get juicy leads?"

"You tell me."

"You don't remember?"

"Honestly, no."

"Some reporter you are. I gotta go. See ya later."

"What did you tell me, Cindy?!" Pam called to her retreating back, perhaps too loudly.

Cindy stopped at the door and turned around. "I guess you'll have to bang me again to find out." And she was gone.

Pam sat in bed and tried to collect herself enough to stand and walk to the kitchen. Or maybe the bathroom first. Images from last night flooded her aching head. It started at the Labor Day fish fry at St. Stephen's. Followed by wine. Lots of wine. They killed at least three bottles. She lost track. A couple of joints. Why did Cindy seem so chipper this morning? Didn't she get hangovers?

She swung her legs around and put her feet on the floor. Her head was still spinning, her clothes strewn about the room. An empty wine bottle. Handcuffs. Sex toys. Oh, right. That. They'd gone at it for hours. Cindy was gymnastic. A blur of skin and tattoos and piercings and tongues and…. Pam hocked up a pubic hair lodged in her throat. She smiled. It had been months since she'd gotten off with someone other than herself. She groaned as her head throbbed. She had told herself she was done with hookups. And blackout drunks.

What did Cindy say last night? Something about the Whites? Or was it Greenfield? She stood unsteadily, gathered her clothes, and staggered toward the general direction of the shower. As she crossed the cramped living room packed with mismatched found furniture, a furry black object darted in front of her and disappeared under the couch. She remembered that Cindy has a cat. Betsy? Bobby? She couldn't recall its name, still too much brain fog. After she toweled off and dressed, she downed two full glasses of tap water. The coffee was still hot and tasted good black. She checked her phone. It was after ten o'clock. Two missed calls and three texts. All from her boss, starting at seven am, the last one at nine-fifteen. Shit. She texted him back: Not feeling good this morning. Will be in soon. Whas up?

Had a meeting with Jill White at 8

Went ahead without you

We'll talk more

"Oh, shit," she said. The mayor, a conservative Republican, had been bad mouthing Pam around town, saying her leftist and anti-Trump bias skewed her reporting. She asked for a face-to-face meeting with Pam and her boss. And Pam overslept and missed it. She wasn't there to defend herself. She hoped Jim had stood up for her.

Pam was grateful to Jim for this job and looked up to him as a kindly avuncular figure. After her debacle in St. Paul, when she needed a job, she heard about the feisty little paper down south that had investigated the mayor and forced his resignation. The story was carried all over the state. The *Clarion* reporter who broke the story had been snatched away by the *Des Moines Register*. When she sat in Tomlinson's office interviewing for the job, she was up front about her departure from the *Pioneer Press*. The *contretemps* was something Pam preferred to think of as an affair among consenting adults. Others viewed it as sexual harassment. With an intern. Human resources got involved, and the matter quickly resolved when it was determined it would be in the best interest of all parties if Pam quietly resigned. That seemed to satisfy the intern, who dropped her threat of legal action and was eventually promoted into Pam's old job.

Tomlinson was silent for a moment while he absorbed this tale.

"Well, we don't have interns at the *Clarion*," he said finally. "Can't afford them, and kids won't work for free anymore. Look, Pam, I worked at papers all over this state before I came home to take over my dad's paper. And in every newsroom it seemed like everybody was screwing everybody else. If the HR departments knew about all of them, there would be no one left to get the papers out. So, if I hire you, I'm not going to care about how you spend your free time. All I ask is that you be discrete, avoid conflicts, and not tarnish the good name of the *Clarion*."

Pam said she understood. Tomlinson said her reporting and writing at the *Pioneer Press* was impressive. He offered her the job as local news reporter. The *only* local news reporter, covering city government, schools, crime, business—everything except sports. Her beat would cover the entire county, not just Newfield. At least one story every day for the website, plus daily posts with iPhone photos or videos on Facebook, Instagram, and Twitter, plus five or more stories for the weekly print edition. For a little over half her salary in St. Paul.

She stared at her boss's texts and contemplated what to say about her latest fuck-up. She could lie and say she was sick. She did say she wasn't feeling well in her text; didn't say it was a hangover. But no, she would not lie to Jim. She had overslept. She would promise not to do it again. It was that simple. Except she probably should leave Cindy out of it.

She walked out of Cindy's apartment and saw in the early September daylight what she vaguely remembered from the night before. It was an enormous Queen Anne-style Victorian mansion on West Elm Street, painted bright yellow and subdivided into apartments. Cindy's one-bedroom was one of two on the first floor. The neighborhood, once grand, was now a little less grand. From the sagging front porch, she could see the tops of the trees peeking up from the river valley to the west and the verdant farmland rising on the other side. Pam looked for her car; she couldn't remember where she'd parked. Eventually she found her green Subaru Outback in the driveway at the rear of the property and headed into the office to face the music.

As she drove, her thoughts turned from her cover story for her boss to the erotic scene from last night. Pam had always thought of herself as an alpha female. In her mind she was Carol from *The Price of Salt,* or even Patricia Highsmith herself, Pam's favorite author, notorious seducer of women married and unmarried. When she was aroused by a woman, she made the first move, and she liked to dominate in bed. She'd learned those moves long ago, as a pre-teen, in the back of a van, pinned in the muscled arms of her sixth-grade school nurse Mrs. Cameron. Cindy Smith ate her alive. When she was naked, her biceps and washboard abs rippled under all those tattoos. It was the first time Pam had been dominated in bed. And she had to admit she *really* liked it. Was Cindy a one-hit wonder, was last night merely a notch on her bedpost? Or could this be a regular thing? Cindy did say "you'll have to bang me again," so there's an implied opening. She found herself hoping for it. On the down low, of course. Cindy was planning to run for mayor again next year and having an affair with a reporter could be bad news for both of them. A lesbian affair at that, although people didn't seem to care as much about that anymore. They surely *would* care about a blatant conflict of interest. That would be the end of Pam's journalism career, at twenty-eight, and probably Cindy's political aspirations. Pam took solace in the fact that she hadn't slept with Cindy to wheedle scoops from her. She'd gotten plenty of those across the polished oak bar at the VFW. The truth was, she was lonely and horny and had begun to obsess about Cindy after their many barroom *tete-a-tetes*. She found herself constantly fantasizing about what lay south of that tarantula tattoo. She pondered this as she arrived at her parking spot behind the *Clarion* office, torn between her ambition and this newly tapped vein of lust.

The icy stare of Jill White from across her desk, with her perfectly coifed silver hair in an updo and her signature red suit with matching pumps, bathed in a miasma of Black Opium perfume, was enough to make Chester Greenfield's testicles seek shelter. Chester searched those cold blue eyes for signs of remembrance of their shared history so long ago but saw only the dead-eyed gaze of a great white shark. No dice. She'd made it clear once she'd launched her political career that their youthful dalliance was to be erased from memory, never to be spoken of again.

The mayor's office in town hall had been repainted and tidied up under the new administration. Chester recalled what a disheveled mess it had been in the Jack White regime. Her Honor Jill White had redecorated all traces of her husband out of existence, lining the walls with framed photos of herself with various Minnesota and national GOP figures, the ex-mayor strangely absent.

Chester's prepared monologue about his current situation and proposed remedies, sounding more pathetic with each passing minute, drew not even an eye blink of acknowledgment.

"How did you manage to get your balls caught in this particular steel trap?" she asked calmly.

Chester's "balls" consisted of four million dollars in bank loans tied up in his various land and development deals (having squandered his legacy from selling the farm and subsequently leveraging himself to the hilt) and the "steel trap" was the terms of said loans. Unfortunately, cash flow from those projects needed to service the loans appeared inadequate to the task, leaving him with only one option: secretly divert funds from Greenfield Farms, Inc., to Greenfield Enterprises, LLC, a risky scheme that could result in his ouster, lawsuits, and possibly criminal fraud charges and prison. Worst of all, Rosalita would surely leave him.

Unless he could come up with another source of funds.

"You know damn well how, Jill," he said, trying to summon some semblance of gravitas. "Your Honor. Madam Mayor," he added weakly. "Your husband knows, too. His balls got caught in the same trap."

"Jack paid the price for his hubris. He knows that. But he didn't put millions of dollars at risk. He's too savvy for that. If you ask me, you simply got greedy. I don't know what you think *I* can do about that." She checked her Movado wristwatch and turned to her computer screen, as if dismissing a naughty schoolboy.

He felt the old beast waking within, that blood-red rage, and he wanted to reach across the desk and slap that smirk off her face. But no, he was done with hitting women. He'd made a promise to God. And to himself. He'd gotten away with a lot of rough stuff in high school, back when football players were excused with a "boys will be boys" shrug and eyeroll. No more. He'd hit Rosalita only once, and she vowed to apply a butcher knife to his manhood if he tried it again.

He counted to three and took a deep breath. "Do I have to remind you," he said, feeling his confidence returning, his testicles descending, "that you need me in this town as much as I need you?" His eyes wandered to the portrait of the president on the wall behind her walnut desk, an unsubtle reminder where the power came from in this new world order and who in this room had access to that power. The fact that his access might be rather exaggerated did not concern Chester Greenfield, who was not one to quibble over such details, what with his balls caught in a steel trap, as Jill White so elegantly framed it.

"We're not done here," he said, and walked out without saying another word before the mayor could verbally tear him a new asshole in retreat, as only Jill White could do. He paused in the hall outside her office and fumbled in his coat pocket for his vial of pills, "allergy pills" he called them. Not finding it, he left town hall through the rear entrance with his anxiety level rising.

Jim Tomlinson sat alone in his office as the staffers who happened to be in at the moment tried not to make eye contact with him. Lexie Sanderson, the receptionist, stared out the window as if expecting someone to come bounding across the town square. Connie Nelson, the news/copy editor and webmaster, had just arrived and busied herself at her computer. The photographer Katie Tran was taking her Nikon apart for cleaning. The sportswriter Tommy Trecanelli wouldn't be in till noon as he had a high school football game to cover that night. Pam Strich supposedly was on her way, two hours late. Again. Her excuse likely a whopper. He knew the convoluted tales and twisted logic of alcoholics, being one himself, although sober now for seventeen years, three months, and nineteen days. He could have—should have—fired her months ago. But something about her held him back, as if hoping for a redemption of sorts, for Pam, and maybe for himself.

The reason no one in the office would make eye contact was their stunned embarrassment after Jill White's blistering, paint-peeling diatribe earlier in the morning. Her stream of piercing invective seemed to echo still off the walls of the tiny office. It was a shock how such an elegant woman could morph so suddenly into a fire-spewing dragon lady.

Jill White is one piece of ... *work*, he thought. He could handle her husband, full of gassy bravado, a glad-handing cliché of a car salesman. Straight out of Sinclair Lewis. George Babbitt made flesh. So dim and full of himself he thought he could slip zoning easements past the town council and county land office that would have benefitted his own expansion plans for Jack White Chevrolet, not to mention land grabs eagerly anticipated by Chester Greenfield and several other slick operators, all of whom were donors to politicians like Jack White and who envisioned a new big-box shopping center on County Road 4 at Highway 169, which likely would have rung the death knell for Newfield's charming but fragile downtown.

Jack White's wife, however, was another matter entirely. A terrifying presence. Dangerously smart and absolutely ruthless. A born politician. Her nickname around town was the Princess of Darkness, a label she wore with pride. She intimidated the hell out of Tomlinson. His paper had endorsed Jill White for mayor despite the fact she was a Republican, while the *Clarion* had long ties to the old Farmer-Labor party, mostly because, as former school board chair, she was the only candidate with any government experience— running against a bartender—and she had managed to steer well clear of her husband's shenanigans. But he really had no choice. If he didn't back Jill, she would have made his life a living hell. Like she had just done this morning, even so.

Pam Strich slinked in through the backdoor and quietly went to her desk, as if hoping no one would see her. In a small room with only four other people.

"Pammy," Tomlinson called from his office. Calmly, not too authoritarian sounding.

She finished logging into her computer and hooked her shoulder bag over the back of her chair and death marched into the boss's office, head down.

"Close the door," he said.

65

She sat.

"Your eyes are bloodshot. You look like hell."

"Am I fired?" she asked. She looked away and seemed unable to make eye contact, locking her gaze on the topographical map of the county framed on the wall in which the river looked like a coiled blue phone cord.

"That depends on you, Pam. Like a cat with nine lives, you're on number nine. This has got to stop. Starting today. No more oversleeping with hangovers, no more missed assignments. Or that's it. Are we clear?"

Pam choked back a sob. She wiped her eyes with her sleeve and sniffed. She looked him in the eye and nodded.

"Yes?"

"Yes, Jim, I understand."

"As for this morning's meeting, Jill White wants you fired. She's got it in for you. I told her I would keep an eye out for any bias in your reporting, which frankly I don't see, but I am not firing any reporters just because the mayor doesn't like them."

Pam managed a weak smile of relief, as if for a death sentence commuted.

"She asked me why we don't do more positive stories about Newfield. I didn't have a good answer for her. Would it kill you to do a few features on the businesses in town that are thriving, like we talked about?"

"Thriving? Is that what you call it?" Her smile morphed into a scowl of outrage. "Look around this town that she's supposedly mayor of. There are no good jobs, not anymore. They've all been shipped overseas or wiped out by some corporate raiders. Empty storefronts around the square. All the young people are leaving, those who can anyway. And what is she doing about it?"

Jim held his hands up, as if in surrender. He wasn't in the mood for this debate at the moment. There was a more pressing matter at hand. "What I'm saying is, you have to be more conscientious, Pam. Professional and reliable."

"I know."

"I've been on to your drinking problem for some time, which you chose not to disclose when I offered you this job. But I know what it's like. I'm an alcoholic and I know all the shame and denial that comes with that. You need to get help, Pam. I can't make you. It doesn't work that way. You have to want to get sober. You need a buddy, a sponsor to help you. It can't be me, obviously, I'm your boss. But I can recommend some folks who've been through AA. It worked for me. Maybe it'll work for you."

She blew her nose, then shook her head. "I went to a meeting once. In St. Paul. Drug rehab. I couldn't stand it. Being around all those losers made me want to go out and get wasted. So I kicked the habit by myself."

Jim stared at her and folded his arms across his chest.

"It was meth. I used for about six months. But I quit when I saw where that shit ends up."

More undisclosed information. A surge of anger welled up inside him and he had an urge to fire her on the spot. But he'd promised her one more chance, and he would keep the promise. In any case, she hadn't lied about her drug and alcohol abuse. He simply hadn't asked her and didn't believe in drug tests. So that was on him. He sort of loved this troubled young woman, in a paternal sense. He saw a bit of himself in her, in his wild drinking days as a young reporter in New Ulm, Red Wing, and Rochester. He took a deep breath and let his anger out with an audible exhale.

"If meetings aren't your thing, a good one-on-one sponsor, or a therapist, who will hold you to account, can work. If you ask me, I will refer you to some people. But you have to ask."

"Okay."

"Yes?"

"Yes. I'm asking."

Jack White stood next to the bed in just his undershirt, wondering where he'd left his boxers and pants. Little Willie was standing at attention, rubbed raw but ready for another go. Jack gave up on that idea when he heard the snores emanating from the lump under the blanket. Anyway, no time.

"Down, Willie," he said. He again noticed the faint whiff of stale cigarette smoke in the carpet and curtains, vaguely reminiscent of body odor, and wondered why they hadn't got the non-smoking room as requested. He made a mental note to lodge a complaint with the stringy-haired, gap-toothed misfit manning the desk at the Shady Rest Inn.

Now, those pants. Where? They had attacked each other with such urgency once they closed the motel room door. They'd stripped each other's clothes off, limbs and lips entangled, as they stumbled across the suite toward the king-sized bed.

Ah. There. On the floor outside the bathroom door. He gathered the rest of his clothes and dressed. He leaned over the bed and pulled the covers back. She opened her eyes. "Time to go already?" she said, and then yawned.

Jack took in the glorious sight of the naked Rosalita Greenfield, black hair wild as a conspiracy of ravens. "You can stay, baby," he said. "I have to get back to the office. Jill keeps me on a short leash these days. She'll no doubt stop by the dealership this afternoon just to say hi."

"You see the irony, here, right?" She leveled that smirk at him with those collagen lips and dark brown eyes that annoyed and aroused him at the same time.

"Tell me. What *isn't* ironic about this whole set up?"

"You know who Chester's with this very moment, don't you?"

"I'm guessing Jill."

"Mmmhmm. He's got some scheme cooked up and needs the mayor's buy-in."

"You think they're fucking?"

Rosie cackled. "You must not think very highly of your wife, to think she might be screwing that tub of lard."

"Well, she used to."

"A long time ago, before Chester swelled up like a dirigible."

Jack had noticed in the latest resumption of their decades-long, on-and-off affair that Rosie preferred now to take her men from on top, in the "reverse cowgirl" position, like riding a horse facing backwards. He liked doing it this way, so he didn't complain. When he asked her about it, she said it had become a habit when Chester had grown so fat his enormous belly was crushing her in the missionary position. Jack suspected the real reason was she didn't want to look at her lovers' faces. When he was screwing Rosie, he had the distinct feeling that men were interchangeable to her, that she preferred not to be reminded of which stallion she was riding at any given moment. In earlier, less enlightened times, Rosalita Greenfield would be known as the town slut. Jack preferred to think of her as the coolest/hottest woman in town, in control of her own sexuality, which she dispensed to a few lucky men like a recreational drug. Tongue loosened under the influence of alcohol, she'd once confessed she found Chester repulsive, like having sex with a manatee, but she continued acquiescing to her marital duties to preserve her access to the Greenfield family fortune. Damn that pre-nup. Her pleasure she would seek elsewhere. God, that woman could hump. Exhausting. He pondered this as he climbed into his black Chevy Suburban—dealer plates, all the bells and whistles— turned on the AC full blast, and started the drive back from the Mankato motel where he and Rosie felt relatively sure they would not be recognized.

Gus stared at the computer screen in Molly's home office. A new letter apparently had arrived by email and she had it opened in one window. In another window she had written her reply.

Dear Molly,

I always thought of myself a good mother. A bad wife, maybe. My husband ran off when our two kids were babies. I been a single mom for over 20 years. I never remarried, but I've had a few boyfriends. None I guess considered me wife material.

My children were so loving and sweet when they were small. Now they are filled with hate for me, their own mother. Their abuse of me must be a punishment I deserve. I feel the hand of God's judgment on me.

My failure as a parent, people say, is I never provided them a "proper father figure." Men came and went through our homes. None of them stayed. They were good men, mostly. They hardly ever hit me.

Our social worker said my children lacked a "stabilizing masculine presence" in their lives. Her words, not mine. Lord, Molly, how I tried. One of my boyfriends, I'll call him "Jim," was so fond of my daughter and was always happy to look after her when I had to go to work, which was often. Another one, "Bob," bonded with my son and took him on camping and fishing trips, just like a father and son. Both Jim and Bob left us suddenly after about a year. When I tried to get them to come back, after what the social worker said, my teenagers went crazy and threatened to run away. How could they be afraid of men who showed them so much kindness and attention?

Now my daughter is serving a five-year sentence in federal pen on drug charges. She and her lawyer say she was innocent, a victim of a set-up, and as she is my daughter, I must believe her.

My son is home now. He had been living on the streets of Minneapolis, so I am glad to have him back. I know he is an addict, even though he denies it. I think he is stealing from me. Things go missing, like they just vanished into thin air.

My daughter refuses to let me visit her in prison. My son is all I have left in the world. I know he is taking advantage of me, but I can't bring myself to ask him to leave. Can you tell me what to do, Molly?

Signed,
Bad Mom

Dear Mom

Good gracioua are you letting your grown-up son live rbent free? If he is stealing from you, you should at least charge him for the privilige.

I know you miss your daughter. Five years is not long. She will be home before you know it and the three of you will be together again.

I am glad to hear that you had substitute father figures in your childrens' lives after your rat of a husband ran away. A good boyfriend can be a steading influence. Lots of good boyfriends ios even better. I only hope that at least somne of the m can be father figures in your childrens lives. I agree with the social worker. It sounds like they need it.

My advice to you is to hold on to your son, keep him off the streets, but make him pay rent, until that day when your daughter comes homes and you can all be together, with your home a lively and loving venue for all. And find one of those boyfriends and bring him home.

I know you are a good mom. God has a plan for

you. It may not mnake sense to you now but it
makes sense to God which means all will become
clear on Judgment Day.
Hugs,
Molly

This was terrible, nonsensical advice, even beyond the typos. The woman who wrote that letter was a trailer-park dumpster fire, a menace to her children who may have unwittingly enabled sexual abuse by her boyfriends. Molly seemed unable to read between the lines. He would have to completely rewrite it. Or discard it and find another letter to answer. Jim Tomlinson and the *Clarion's* readers would be none the wiser; Gus had been copyediting Molly's columns for so long that he could mimic her distinctive voice in his sleep.

Gus heard the kitchen door open and close. He stepped away from the computer and went to greet Molly.

"Augie? Is that you?" she said. She had carried in a wicker basket full of freshly pulled carrots and turnips, the wild greens a fragrant canopy above the fat roots, and laid it on the counter.

He entered the kitchen and faced her across the room. Molly reached over to the counter and turned off the Twins game on the radio and stared at him as if he were a Martian. Not a trace of recognition in her eyes. Oh, Jesus, not again. He sensed what was coming and the dread filled him up like poured concrete.

"It's me, Molly. Gus." His voiced wavered, not the calming balm he'd practiced.

"You're not Augie. Who the hell are you?" She placed her hands on her hips and tilted her head.

"Augie's not coming, Molly. Not today."

"Why not? Who are you?"

"Molly. I'm your husband. Gus, remember? We talked about this yesterday."

"You're a liar. Get out." She took a step back.

He softened his tone, and prepared to go there, to the place of pain and regret. He approached her, hoping a gentle touch would break the spell. "You know where Augie is, Molly." He placed his hand on her shoulder. "He's not coming. Not today. Not ever."

"I said get out!" She jerked her shoulder away and stepped back, staring at him with a look of fear and hatred. Then she attacked. She windmilled her arms in rabbit punches, raining blows on his face, head, and shoulders. He raised his hands to protect himself and backed away. She stopped swinging and stared at him again. He thought he saw a flicker of recognition in her eyes and stepped toward her. She stepped back.

"Molly," he said.

She grabbed a metal spatula off the counter and was on him in a second. A blow to the head with the sharp edge. Another and another before he had a chance to react.

"Fuck! Molly! Stop!"

He put his hands up to block the slicing blows, which cut him like a knife. Blood ran down from his bald head into his eyes. His hands and forearms bled. He backed away, tried to escape from the kitchen. She followed, as if crazed, swinging the spatula like a battle ax. He turned and grabbed her wrist, halting the blows. She tried to twist away from him, but he was too strong. He spun behind and wrapped his arms around her, pinning hers to her sides.

"Molly, Molly, for God's sake, stop! It's me Gus." He was crying now, tears mixed with blood. She tried to wriggle out of his grasp. He pulled her down onto the kitchen floor and lay on top of her, still pinning her arms. She had dropped the spatula and after a few seconds stopped struggling. Her body trembled and she let out a piercing, terrifying cry, like an animal howling in distress. She started to sob. Eventually she quieted down and soon they were both softly sobbing. When her body had gone limp and she seemed either to be asleep or just giving up the fight, Gus released her and stood up. She didn't move. What if she'd had a heart attack during the struggle? What if he'd killed her?

"Oh, Molly. Fuck. Fuck. Fuck." He knelt beside her. She was still breathing. Eyes closed. Body lightly trembling. She looked exhausted. Not a threat. He carefully picked her up off the floor and held her in his arms as if she were a sleeping child. He carried her into the bedroom and put her under the white summer quilt and tucked her in. He kissed her on the forehead, leaving a trail of his tears in her hair.

He went to the bathroom to check his injuries in the mirror. Multiple bleeding gashes on his head, arms, and hands. He dampened a hand towel and wiped himself clean of blood. Some of the cuts continued to ooze, others didn't. None of them seemed a life-threatening gusher. They were thin, short slices; he could probably bandage them himself. What if he needed to go to the hospital to get stitches? How to explain what happened? He could not let word get out that Molly was descending into madness and violence. He had to protect her. But he couldn't hide his cuts for long. What would people say? A convincing story would have to be concocted. A lawnmower accident? Not likely. Shattering glass falling on him from above? Maybe. He would have to come up with a believable piece of falling glass. A light fixture? Figure that out later.

After applying a dozen bandages on his cuts, he lay on the living room sofa and wondered what the hell had just happened. It was only the third time she'd hit him, but this was a shocking escalation. Crazy town. Some hard decisions would have to be made in the coming days. Starting with a call to Doc Mollenhoff first thing in the morning.

He thought of her hallucinations about Augie. He'd reminded her many times recently of the truth about their only child, but it was as if she couldn't process it, couldn't retain it.

Augie. Augustus James Peterson, Jr. Gone these sixteen years. A life cut short at age twenty-six. His body was never found, the Army said. All they could tell them was that he disappeared during a firefight outside Fallujah. Missing in action, presumed killed.

Not knowing had torn a hole in two hearts. Still, they held out hope. For five years. Then ten. Then there was no hope. And a light dimmed in Molly's bright eyes and loving smile.

Elvis Birdsong threw open the door to the VFW bar and stood in the sun-splashed frame like a divine silhouette.

"Hooah!" he shouted.

Cindy Smith placed her hands together in prayerful respect and bent slightly from the waist. Four gray eminences spun on their barstools and yelled in unison, "Hooah!"

"Elvis Birdsong in the house!" announced John Berg.

Only Gus knew this was not a spontaneous visit by one of Newfield's most revered citizens. Elvis had told him he would be dropping by, with something important to say. What that something was, he wouldn't tell. Elvis was the only person in town who knew about the scabbed-over gashes hidden under Gus's ballcap and long-sleeved shirts, the only person Gus felt comfortable confiding in about Molly's latest episode, aside from Doc Mollenhoff, of course, who lived twenty-five miles away in Mankato.

The foursome climbed down from their perches, leaving their beers behind, and gathered around the tall, weathered man in the cowboy hat atop a fulsome gray ponytail. Backs were slapped. Fives were highed. Bar patrons turned away from the pool table and dart board machine to admire the spectacle. Cindy turned down the music, silencing Gram Parsons in mid-chorus, and poured Elvis a shot of his go-to, Makers Mark. On the house. Just one. And poured one for herself.

It was a rare appearance for Elvis at Post 5433. He was old school in certain respects, including the conviction that an Indian in a bar was not a good look. He'd seen that look too many times, in the dreary saloons of south Minneapolis, searching for his daughter on Franklin Avenue. It was especially not a good look for the beloved Newfield High School math teacher and track coach, former football star, 1970 state high school decathlon champion, and decorated Vietnam veteran. Gus shared a bond with Elvis unlike any he had with the rest of the VFW crowd. Like himself, Elvis had sacrificed his athletic ambitions to serve his country. And like Gus, Elvis was one of the few who had seen action in the jungles and hamlets of Vietnam. But unlike Gus, he came home physically intact and adorned with military decorations for valor, including a Bronze Star. A true hero, in Gus's eyes, not only because of the medals but mainly because Elvis was still physically able to pursue his dreams after he returned but chose instead to remain in Newfield and dedicate himself to the youth of his hometown.

"Pull up a stool, Elvis," said Larsen. "We were just having ourselves a debate. Maybe you can settle it."

Elvis glanced at Gus and shook his head knowingly.

"Don't listen to these drunks," said Gus. "They've been attending those adult-ed lectures up at State and are showing off."

"Okay, I'll bite," said Elvis. "Try me."

"Debussy versus Stravinsky. Who's more influential on twentieth-century music?" said Larsen. "I say Debussy. Berg here, a commie Russian lover if ever there was one, says Stravinsky..."

"And I say they're both wrong," Kugelman interrupted. "Gotta be Schoenberg."

"You only say that 'cuz you're a kraut," said Larsen.

"I'll have you know Schoenberg was Austrian not German."

"Same diff."

"What say you, oh distinguished educator of young Newfield minds?" said Berg.

"Can I say Scott Joplin? Or W.C. Handy?" said Elvis.

"Touché!" said Berg and raised his bottle in respect.

Elvis downed his shot of Makers Mark, slammed the shot glass on the bar, saluted Cindy, and emitted a sustained ahhhhhh.

"How's the boy?" said Kugelman. "I heard he scored two touchdowns in the home opener. Beat Fairmont for the first time in ten years."

"Not so good," said Elvis. "Caught drinking and smoking after the game. Off the team."

"Oh, shit. I'm sorry, Elvis," said Kugelman.

Travis Birdsong's continuing struggles with drugs and alcohol were a source of constant aggravation for his grandparents. This year, his senior year, was supposed to be when he finally got his act together, graduated, and maybe got an athletic scholarship, hopefully at Minnesota State, the very thing his grandfather had passed up. The whole town, it seemed, was pulling for him, as was the entire Lower Sioux community. Now that dream appeared to be going up in a cloud of marijuana smoke.

"The reason I came by, gents," said Elvis, "is we got a serious drug problem in this town. Trouble in River City, as the song goes. The meth cookers, the biker gangs, the whole pot and pills scene down at the river. The county has its head up its ass, as usual. For some reason they think car thefts and DUIs are the only bad things happening around here. Not that those aren't problems, but they got the same root cause. Alcohol and drugs, coming out of that damn river jungle."

"What are you suggesting, Elvis?" said Gus. He had a pretty good idea of what Elvis was suggesting and hoped he was wrong.

"We're all military men. So what if we're in our sixties? We have guns and tactical skills. Where my people are from, on the rez, we would be a council of elders. It's on us to take charge and protect our community, our kids, our grandkids."

Elvis was right about them, in a technical sense, Gus reflected. They all had received military training. *Fifty years ago.* And they had guns. Gus, for instance, owned a twenty-gauge Remington for bird hunting that he hadn't used in years and was not sure where he'd stored it.

"Holy shit, Elvis. Are you talking about a fight with the Blue Hogs?" said Larsen. "They're armed to the teeth. Sawed-off shotguns, assault rifles. God knows what else. Plus, there's got to be at least a dozen of them. We're only five."

"No, no, no. Not a fight. I'm talking about a show of strength, like one of them militias. And we can get ten, maybe twenty more guys in town to join us. Outnumber them. Make them find another community to pollute with their poison. Remember, these are dumbass, cosplay warriors. Not a single one has military experience that I know of."

Gus admired Elvis's passion, but his bold words did not instill confidence. No military genius was required for some meth-fueled biker to empty the clip of an AR-15 into a gathering of well-intentioned old men.

"The first thing you need to know about me is I don't believe in God. So forget about all that 'higher power' and 'follow Jesus' stuff."

Pam sat facing this woman, her maybe sponsor on the road to recovery, in cheap folding chairs, knees almost touching. They were in the therapist's apartment-slash-office, a second-floor walkup via fire escape at the back of a brick building housing an auto parts store on the ground level about a mile out of town. Her name was Marie Thibodaux, a beautiful French-sounding name although she seemed obviously Native American. Her skin a weathered light brown, like tanned leather. Dark eyes, black hair pulled into a long braid that reached her lower back.

"Me neither," said Marie, after a long pause.

She was not one of Jim's recommended AA buddies. They were all men. Pam insisted on a woman. Word was passed around; a friend of a friend of a friend knew of a woman outside of town who used unorthodox methods but supposedly got results. Pam didn't care about her methods. The woman was a licensed therapist and accepted Pam's health plan. She arranged a meeting right away.

When she arrived, the sketchy-looking apartment in the sketchy end of town out past Highway 169 made her re-think the whole idea. Was she up to it? Also, an Indian alcoholism counselor? Really? What the hell. Why not? It actually made sense. She probably had lots of experience with clients in her own community. While filling out the usual ream of paperwork, Pam scanned the framed diplomas on the wall. One was from South Dakota State University. She couldn't read the other. Pam wondered how long Marie had occupied this space. Unpacked moving boxes were stacked against the walls, which were bare aside from the diplomas. A faint odor of burnt sage or something like it hung in the air.

"How it's going to work is this," said Marie, leaning closer after reviewing the paperwork and setting it aside. "No group meetings, no come-to-Jesus bullshit. You and me are going to be joined at the hip. Like conjoined twins. We will meet once a week. And you will check in with me every day by phone. Every. Goddamn. Day. For six months. Work it into your daily schedule. Mornings. Nights. Whatever. You will give me your cellphone number, and I will not tolerate being ghosted. I am going to be all up in your face. Smelling your breath. Reading your eyeballs. Listening for slurred words. Believe me, I know all the tricks, all the dodges, all the lies."

"Okay," said Pam, completely flummoxed and unsure she meant it.

"Also, I smell weed on you right now. That needs to stop. If you come to our check-ins high, I will know and I will bust your ass."

This is one tough bitch. Maybe a bit too much. Pam felt a surge of resentment and almost told the woman to fuck off. She'd walked out of addiction treatment once before and it turned out okay. She could do it again, get clean and sober on her own, right? Then she remembered her promise to Jim and stifled her anger.

Marie's kind of hot, too, in a rough sort of way, as if she'd had a hardscrabble life but didn't allow herself to go to hell. Pam caught herself imagining Marie naked. Why did older, domineering women always hold this erotic power over her? Pam had never slept with an Indian woman and she fantasized stroking her lovely brown skin. She'd had a Black girlfriend once, in college, Tanya, who broke her heart over coffee in Coffman Union. God, she'd loved her. Pam realized she was probably fetishizing women of color, but honestly, White chicks could be so tiresome at times, so goddamn entitled.

So she stayed and began unspooling her backstory while Marie listened and nodded. When the fifty minutes were up, she handed over her copayment and agreed to check in every evening after she got off work.

Jack White held the handset of his desk phone close to his face, trying to pantomime his end of a jovial business call full of masculine banter. Chester Greenfield was outside his office, rapping on the glass wall and pointing to his watch. Did Chester still wear a watch? He couldn't recall seeing one. But the gesture was universal, as if from a vestigial sign language. On the other end of his phone call, which was real enough, Rosalita Greenfield was berating him about his most recent performance and questioning his devotion. He voiced assurances to her—yes, he loved her, he lied, knowing she knew it was a lie and didn't care—while waving at her husband through a glass barrier. Maintaining the casual smile on his face grew more difficult as she called him "dickless wonder," which was wounding not to mention unfair given his rather vigorous performance, in his opinion. Also, "pussy whipped," she added, for his evident fear of Jill. That one stung the most, as they both knew it to be true.

Rosie was still talking, so he kept her husband waiting

outside. He dared not hang up on her, not in the state she was in. Rosie was volatile and required careful handling. For the umpteenth time, she said maybe they should call it off. She said she was feeling guilty about cheating on Chester. Jack had to stifle a laugh. That was utter bullshit, and they both knew it. She was growing tired of Jack, again, as she had many times over the years, and lately was getting her needs met by the UPS driver, Tony whatshisname, the Italian Stallion, who apparently was carving a swath through the female population of Newfield, married and unmarried, and, according to the rumors, some of the male populace as well, furtive trysts in the back of the big brown van between the stacks of boxes full of crap imported from China.

Jack wondered how long he should keep his old friend waiting. Chester and Jack went way back. Newfield High class of 1989. That was before Jack had met and married Jill. Jack and Jill. A big joke at the time. Still is. The pails of water gags never got old. Their families went way back, too. All the way back to when their surnames were Grunfeld and Weis.

Chester once had a little side thing going with Jill. Years ago. Jack was dating her at the time. They weren't married yet, so technically it was okay in Chester's mind. Jack knew about it and viewed it as manly competition for Jill McKenzie, the hot new girl in town from Decorah, Iowa. Once Jack won the prize, there were no hard feelings. Chester quickly got over his disappointment upon the sudden blossoming of the young Rosie Melendez, daughter of one of his father's farmhands, who seemingly overnight erupted into the Latina bombshell of his dreams. Over the years, though, Jack developed second thoughts about Chester's dalliance with Jill and viewed it as a backstabbing attempt by a friend to steal his woman. That was his justification for screwing Rosie, anyway.

And so the Greenfields and the Whites were a complicated foursome, entangled in so many ways. Jack and Rosie's affair was no secret to Chester and Jill. But Chester deluded himself that it had happened only once and feared losing her if he made too big an issue of it. Jill, on the other hand, held it over her husband like a probationary release that could be revoked at any time. Chester and Jack had also been business partners in numerous real estate developments. Jack assumed it was the financial entanglements between the Greenfields and the Whites that brought Chester to Jack White Chevrolet on this day. He knew Jill had twice shown Chester the back of her hand when he'd asked for political help in allowing some of his underwater investments to come up for air.

Jack had stopped listening to Rosie's rant and didn't notice right away that she'd hung up. He replaced his handset, and waved Chester in.

Chester sat across from him, Jack's absurdly large desk between them, and described his dubious proposition to invest in his latest scheme. Chester leaned forward as he spoke and nervously fingered Jack's Lego farm set on the desk. Jack was annoyed but listened patiently, nodding as if in agreement. He told Chester he'd think about it. A million dollars was a lot of money. Not that he didn't have it. But Chester had a poor track record as a real estate entrepreneur. He should stick to farming, although the rumors had reached Jack that Greenfield Farms, Inc., wasn't doing so hot either, kind of hard to believe in these boom times for agriculture, with the current administration in Washington doling out bales of cash to farmers in a naked ploy to buy votes in the nation's heartland.

Chester seemed to accept Jack's completely insincere promise to think about it and switched the conversation to Republican fundraising projects, a topic on which Chester and Jack were more in alignment. Jack had already heard Chester's preposterous dream to bring the Trump Train to Newfield, an idea that had been harshly shot down by everyone in local GOP circles. So now Chester had a new brainstorm: a big, attention-getting event, a money-maker that would generate national media coverage and interest from the Trump campaign.

"What the hell are you talking about?" said Jack.

"I was thinking maybe a motorcycle rally, next summer, here in Newfield, like the one in Sturgis, South Dakota. Bikers for Trump we could call it, with money raised online for every bike and mile ridden, like one of those walk-a-thons for cancer. Everybody involved would be turned into a fundraiser for Trump. We could get a caravan of hundreds of bikers, maybe thousands, riding hundreds of miles. Newfield to Mankato to Worthington to Albert Lea to Rochester to Owatonna to Mankato and back to Newfield."

Jack almost laughed aloud, but stopped himself, considered it, and had to admit the concept was not without potential, including the potential to skim money off the top, which his old pal Chester no doubt had already calculated. "How much money we talking about?" he said.

"I don't know. Two, maybe three-hundred K. That'd be a nice piece of change for the Minnesota Trump campaign, would it not? Buy a lotta airtime."

Jack said he'd think about it, and really meant it this time. They shook hands and Chester departed. Jill was due to arrive any minute, and Jack needed to erase all thoughts of the naked Mrs. Greenfield from his tumescent brain. Which proved impossible. The harder he tried to not think about the naked Mrs. Greenfield the more indelibly the images burned into his mind's eye. Those long legs, wrapped around him like the jaws of life. The way she kissed, like she could suck his teeth and tongue right out of his head. He started to get aroused. No no no. Bad idea. But that wild jungle of black hair, smelling of jasmine—

"What are you smiling about?" said Jill White, somehow magically appearing before him, as if teleported from town hall, her red power suit a five-alarm presence. It was more a statement than a question. "You look like you just got a blowjob. Under your desk by one of your cute receptionists. Is she under there now? Did I come at a bad time? Did you?" She sat in the chair opposite her husband, the seat still warm from Chester's massive butt cheeks, and smiled a smile that gave him gooseflesh.

"Ummm. I was just thinking about the 2020 models. It's, ah, going to be a banner year. I can feel it in my bones."

"You're a terrible liar. Always were. Probably what you're feeling is a boner, not your bones."

Good one. Landed like a right uppercut. His arousal shriveled. He smiled at her, trying not to display that goofy, dreaming-of-Rosie smile. It seemed to work. Jill shifted in her chair and looked around the room at the framed photos of vintage Chevrolets, a signal that she was about to change the subject, to Jack's relief.

"Did Chester come see you?" she said.

"He just left, a few minutes ago."

"How much did he ask for?"

"The usual ante for a Chester poker game. A mill. I said I'd think about it."

"Don't think too hard."

Jill rehashed Chester's most recent visits to her office, including the direness of his financial straits and his cheeky requests for help in re-zoning some of his underperforming land holdings. As if Her Honor the Mayor Jill White would be stupid enough to participate in the very sort of graft that had brought disgrace on her husband, sitting across from her now in his sad little fishbowl, no longer enthroned at town hall. She didn't put it exactly that way, but Jack caught her drift.

He considered not mentioning Chester's idea for a motorcycle rally, maybe keep it a secret for a while, but remembered it was futile to try to hide anything from Jill White. The woman had built-in radar for secrets and scheming. So he told her. She didn't laugh.

"What's he up to?" she said.

"I think he just wants to play with the high rollers in the Trump campaign. Rub elbows with that crowd."

"Maybe, but I bet there's more to it. He's in a tight spot.

He needs money. I refused to help with the taxes and zoning on his crappy land deals. He's working on a scam. I just know it."

"The question is, how do we get in on it?" Jack said. He was a firm believer in the zero-sum theory of investing. Of life itself, really. None of this win-win Kumbaya for Jack. In order for him to win, someone else, somewhere, didn't matter who or where, had to lose. On that view of life, Jack and Jill White were in complete accord.

"If this Bikers for Trump thing looks like it's got legs, we'll need to step in and manage it, with the backing of the state party," she said. "And if there's any money to be made, we should get our share."

"I agree. The question is, how?'

"We start by giving Wally Johnson a call. He owes me one."

Indeed, he did, as Jack well knew. Of the compromises and humiliations they both had endured to raise money and serve the party elites, well, the less said the better. If anyone in Newfield ever found out, they would have to leave town, change their names.

"What about Chester?" said Jack.

"Fuck Chester."

Elvis Birdsong took in the sorry sight of his assembled militia. Eight men altogether, including himself. They would need at least eight more. But this would do as a start.

Some militia. Gimpy Gus Peterson with his ancient shotgun. Miggy Cervantes brandishing what looked like Wyatt Earp's Colt 45 revolver. Carl Larson shouldering a double-barrel twelve-gauge muzzle pointed to the sky instead of down at the ground like you're supposed to. Was he drunk? His eyes looked a tad unfocused. Great. A sot with a shotgun. A review of basic gun safety would have to be the first order of business. The other regulars from the VFW were there, Berg and Kugelman and a few others Elvis didn't know. Berg had vouched for them. Someone had suggested they invite Cindy Smith, who was widely admired as a badass and known to keep a .357 magnum under the bar when on duty, as if prepping for a rerun of the one time the VFW was robbed in 1979. But no, they voted, no girls allowed in this clubhouse.

A battered old GMC pickup rumbled into the clearing on the Birdsong's wooded land near the river north of town where the militia had gathered for its first training session. Out stepped Tommy Kugelman, Harry's twenty-one-year-old nephew, in full camo, chubby with an unflattering blonde bowl cut under his army surplus helmet. He turned to grab something from the passenger seat and emerged with an AR-15 assault rifle strapped diagonally across his torso. "Hey, Unc." He waved at Kugelman and faced the assemblage with a silly grin. Kugelman regarded his nephew with a raised eyebrow and a who-invited-you stare.

"What the hell?" said Elvis. "Where did you get that?"

"Ordered online. Easy peasy," said Tommy.

This was not good. A collection of concerned citizens with hunting rifles and sidearms was one thing, a relatively low-power show of force. To Elvis, a military-style assault rifle, more lethal than the progenitor he carried in Nam, which elicited long-buried memories he did not wish to exhume, smacked of those racist, right-wing militias. His would be a righteous militia, proud crime fighters, not haters.

"Get that thing out of here," he said.

"What? I thought this was supposed to be a militia."

Elvis noticed the Trump-Pence 2020 bumper sticker on Tommy's truck. It turned his stomach. But he resolved to be open to all sorts of concerned citizens. After all, their mission was nonpartisan, a civic duty. How to keep Tommy in the fold while banning his heinous killing machine? "I appreciate you showing up, Tommy," he said. "We're proud to have you on board. We need more military men like you." (Unspoken was the fact that Tommy had completed basic training but washed out shortly after deployment with a dishonorable discharge, something to do with a sexual assault accusation, which must have been especially egregious to be taken seriously by the U.S. Army.) "But I gotta say, machine guns are not a good look for a citizen crime-fighting patrol."

"It's not a machine gun it's a—"

"I know, it's a semi-automatic. Spare me your NRA talking points. I'm an NRA member. Ex-military. I know the difference. But it's no difference, really. That there strapped on your chest is a weapon of mass destruction, designed for modern warfare. It's got no place in civilian society. You're welcome here, Tommy. But please, take your rifle home, lock it up in a gun safe, and come back with something less lethal. A pistol, a hunting gun."

"Go ahead, Tommy," said Kugelman. "Come back with your dad's thirty-ought-six. And ask him to come along and bring his Glock."

Tommy pulled the AR-15 off and tossed it into the cab of his truck and climbed in. His wheels spun in the mud as he tried too hard to make a dramatic exit.

Elvis was about to start the basic gun safety lesson when Deputy Sheriff Joe Morton arrived in his official black-and-white SUV cruiser. Morton parked next to Gus's Gran Torino and admired its retro perfection before approaching the gathering, walking tall in his knee-high brown boots, tan trousers, olive green shirt, and tan cowboy hat over a fleshy pink face.

"What that hell do you boys think you're doing?" he said, directing his question at Elvis, emphasizing the word "boys." Elvis wasn't used to being called "boy." He'd had plenty of unpleasant run-ins with White law enforcement. He'd been called Tonto and Geronimo and Crazy Horse, but never boy.

"Just a little shooting practice, exercising our Second Amendment rights," he said. "This is my land, private property. Is there a problem?"

"You know what I'm talking about, Elvis. Rumor has it you boys are planning some kind of citizen militia."

"There's no law against that."

"You're right, Elvis. But I'd like to remind you that I am the law in this part of the county, and if there is a crime problem in your community, you need to come to me about it, not take the law into your own hands."

"Who ratted us out? One of our wives?" said Kugelman.

"Maybe. I couldn't say."

Elvis catalogued the numerous occasions when the county sheriff's department had displayed either indifference to problems in the Native American community or outright hostility. Not to mention the county's obliviousness toward the doings in the Blue Earth River valley. But he chose not to mention those things. Instead, he said, "We'll keep that in mind, Deputy Morton. Just think of us as your citizen auxiliary, here to serve."

Morton retreated to his cruiser, apparently with bigger walleyes to fry. Before climbing in, he turned to face the group and said, "All I ask is that you assholes don't shoot anybody, least of all yourselves." Then he drove off.

"Tell me about your sponsor," Jim Tomlinson said. His phone was ringing but he let it go to voicemail.

Pam closed the door to his office and sat. "Marie Thibodaux. She's cool. Native American. Kind of a badass. I couldn't get much info out of her. Whenever I tried my sneaky reporter tricks, she deflected the conversation back on me. All I know is she's from South Dakota. Married then divorced. Got her degree at SDSU. Worked as a counselor on one of those big reservations. Rosebud, maybe. Or Pine Ridge. Came to Newfield about a year ago, right after I did, not sure why."

"She legit? Licensed in Minnesota and all that?"

"Yup. Even takes your crappy insurance coverage. Twenty-five-dollar co-pay."

That's rich, thought Jim. Complaining about her benefits when the only reason she has a job is her boss is a pushover with a soft spot for drunks. "Be happy you have insurance at all. Plenty of people in this town don't."

"Meanwhile," said Pam with a dramatic pause, "guess who I saw coming out of town hall yesterday."

"Jimmy Hoffa."

"Damn, you're good. How did you know?"

"No, really. Who?"

"Chester Greenfield."

"So? Everybody knows he's old friends with the mayor."

"Then why would he slip out the rear entrance, the one marked Employees Only, skulking around like he didn't want to be seen, and walk two blocks away where his truck was parked?"

"So what are you saying? That ol' Chester and Jill are gettin' it on?"

"*That* would be pretty juicy. But what if they're cooking up something corrupt? Like the Jack White scam?"

"You'd love that, wouldn't you?" he said. "A chance to take down Jill White."

"Let me tail them for a while. See where it leads."

Jim regarded his protégé and admired her youthful energy. He knew she was burning with ambition to land a big scoop to jumpstart the rehabilitation of her career. After which she would ditch him for a better job in a bigger town faster than you can say Pulitzer. That day was inevitable anyway. Either she got her act together and resumed her upward path, or she flamed out entirely. Neither scenario likely would involve her continued employment at *The Newfield Clarion*. His Pam Strich project came with an expiration date. Meantime, he worried about her personal issues, her unstable grip on the necessities of adult living. A drug habit supposedly left behind, a drinking problem still hanging over her. He wanted her to succeed, as he had, to overcome her demons, whatever they might be. No, she needed more time to pull herself together before diving into a high-risk investigative boondoggle. If the Whites and Greenfields really were up to something untoward, it would come out soon enough. Newfield was a small town where secrets weren't secret for long. Besides, it wouldn't look good to go after Jill White, Newfield's first female mayor, so soon after exposing her husband's corruption. It could seem like a vendetta and might not play well with everyone in town, some of whom were among the dwindling pool of advertisers. There were already scurrilous rumors that the *Clarion* had gone after Jack White only because he had ceased advertising his car dealership in the paper.

"No, let's not do that right now. I can't afford to have you go off on some wild pheasant hunt. This ain't *The Washington Post*, as you may have noticed."

Pam glared at him with a look of filial defiance and smirking contempt. But she acquiesced, and they moved on to other topics. School board. Zoning commission. He could smell the boredom emanating from her chair.

October

Mavis Birdsong followed the narrow, two-lane road down into the wooded river valley and pulled onto the dirt path just before the crossing. She parked her white van on the pebbled beach under a copse of shading cottonwoods. The van was new. She kept it pure white, unblemished by customization or advertising. Too many previous versions, with the Bird Song Café logo and Native American embellishments, had been broken into, burglarized, or vandalized with racist graffiti. Now her plain white van blended in with a thousand others like it.

She'd closed the café at three, as usual after the lunch rush, and drove to the river without telling anyone. Possibly a stupid idea, but she didn't want to be talked out of it. She climbed out and locked the doors, then walked north along the east bank of the river into the deepening canopy of the wooded valley in search of Travis, missing now for twenty-four hours. The nagging worries that had been her constant companion had erupted into panic as her worst fears seemed to be emerging into view.

Elvis had warned her to stay away from the river and to let his militia patrol the area. To Mavis, Elvis's militia was a joke, an old man's fantasy army, looking for trouble they no doubt would find. A woman alone searching for her missing grandson likely would have better luck than a band of geezers with hunting rifles. She wanted a shot at solving her grandson's disappearance herself before calling in the White man's police, the county sheriff. If they'd lived on the rez, the tribal police would have had him home inside of an hour.

She followed the shore of the meandering river. The water level was lower than normal due to the dry summer, a possible harbinger of things to come. Many of her people, the Mdewakanton Band of Dakota in the Lower Sioux Community, had seen climate change coming for generations, but lacked the influence or will to do anything about it. To the some of elders, it was simply the natural cycles of creation. To others, especially the young, it was a righteous reckoning for the White man's exploitation of the earth.

Mavis was not interested in such debates right now, she was focused on finding her grandson before he began the downward spiral that had swallowed his mother, her daughter. The low water level, whether or not caused by climate change, created wider beaches and afforded Mavis an easier path downstream as she carefully made her way deeper into the woods, senses keen for signs of human activity. Soon she came to a wide sandy section where the river bent. What she found there disgusted her: the detritus of an obvious party spot. Beer cans. Cigarette butts. Fast food wrappers. Used condoms. Charred logs from a spent fire. It was an affront to this beautiful sylvan valley, this gently burbling source of precious water, which was already under assault from farm chemical runoff. She would have to come back with a trash bag and clean it up. But later, not now.

She pressed on. The yellow-tinged woods, smelling of autumn rot and smoke, grew dark and deep, nearly blocking out the early October afternoon sun. After ten more minutes of pushing branches away from her face and wading through shallows where there was no beach, she heard the crack of a broken branch, as if underfoot. She stopped and listened. The river at this spot was lazy and silent, with no surfaced rocks or logs to slap against. She heard the unmistakable sound of footsteps on dry leaves, tentative, as if someone were trying to conceal their presence. Fat chance, she thought, sneaking up on Mavis Birdsong. Her husband and grandson teased her about her preternatural hearing, calling her Miss Indian Rabbit Ears. But her skill had nothing to do with being Native, it was simply a matter of being a listener not a talker, not someone who polluted the silence with their own blather.

She heard another twig snap behind her. As she turned a figure emerged from the thick underbrush. A man, short and stocky, with a scowl on his pockmarked face under a battered black cowboy hat. She reached into her pocket for her small can of mace, and …

"Holy shit, Mavis. What are you doing out here?"

"Oh God, Miggy. You scared me. Why you sneak up on me like that? I almost maced you."

"I been tracking you for five minutes," Miguel Cervantes said. His hands were up, as in surrender, but he was smiling now. "I thought you Indians were supposed to move all silent like through the woods. I could hear you fifty yards away."

She laughed. "I guess I've been living in town too long, forgot all my magic Indian shit."

Miguel's embarrassed smile told her the subtle dig had landed; he'd been caught stereotyping her again. Not that she was immune to such laziness. More than once she had referred to Miggy and M'lena as Mexicans, when in fact only M'lena was from Mexico, an Indigenous woman who considered herself as "Indian" as Mavis; Miguel was of old Spanish stock, from Colombia. *Conquistador,* his wife called him in moments of anger.

"Anyway, why are you here?" he said.

"I'm looking for Travis. Seen him?"

"No. I'm looking for Julio. I guess we had the same idea. You think they're together?"

"When did you see Julio last? Travis has been gone since yesterday morning."

"Same. Yesterday morning. He helped M'lena load the truck,

93

then said he was going over to the high school to kick his soccer ball around."

"That's what Travis said. He was going to the high school to throw the football around."

"How long you been searching?" said Miguel.

"Only twenty minutes or so."

"I've been mucking around over an hour. They're not here. There's nobody here. Not right now. But I got something to show you."

Mavis followed Miguel back into the woods, in the direction he'd come from, away from the riverbank. He led her through the thick undergrowth along what appeared to be a deer path. She reminded herself to strip off her clothes and check for ticks when she got home. They walked for five minutes, the canopy overhead so dense Mavis couldn't make out where the sun was and couldn't tell in what direction they were headed. Finally they reached a clearing, where the undergrowth had been hacked away into a round-ish bare spot of ground, about twenty yards across. In the center sat a small wooden shack, no bigger than a garden shed. A coat of brown paint had faded to a grayish tan, nearly undistinguishable from the weathered wood, the roof shingles warped and covered with moss. A small paned window on the side was covered on the inside with old newspaper. The door, locked.

"Look at that keyhole," Miguel said. "It's still shiny, unlike the rest of this place, so it's been used recently. I can't see anything inside."

"Whose shack is this?"

"I don't know. Could be the Blue Hogs. Like a stash house or party shack."

"Or somebody's fishing shack."

"Not much fishing around here. The river's about a hundred yards away. Fishing's better in the lakes anyway."

"Maybe it's a hunting cabin."

"Could be," he said. He slammed his shoulder against the door, which shook but held firm. "It's reinforced somehow, from inside. We should leave it be for now and ask folks around town what they know about this place."

Mavis snapped a few photos of the shack with her phone to text them to Elvis, but realized she had no cell service.

Molly lay her head on Gus's chest and gently stroked the scabbed-over gashes on his right forearm. Two weeks after the attack, they looked like thin strips of beef jerky. Her hand wandered up to his bald head to repeat the gentle strokes on the places marked by her irrational rage. "I'm so sorry, I'm so sorry," she murmured again and again. In the days since the spatula incident, she had drifted in and out of herself, vacillating between obliviousness and remorse.

They were lying together on the living room couch, limbs entwined, as they listened to Molly's calming music on the CD player, a Chopin nocturne. "It's okay, Sugar," Gus said, repeating his soothing mantra. "You didn't know it was me. You attacked an intruder, defended yourself and our home. I feel better knowing you're such a badass. Pity the fool who tries to come at Molly Peterson." It was false bravado, and he knew it, but he couldn't allow himself to express the fear and dread in his heart.

"Stop trying to make me feel better. I went crazy. I didn't know who you were or what I was doing. What's going to happen to me?"

"We're going to take good care of you. Me and Doc Mollenhoff. Remember, he said there are treatments nowadays that can …" He wasn't sure exactly how to phrase what it was the drugs and other therapies were supposed to do. "Help," he said.

"I'm not going to any mental place."

"Nobody said anything about sending you anywhere. You're staying right here with me." He turned toward her and wrapped her in his arms. He kissed her on the cheek, on the forehead, on the neck, on the mouth. She smiled and giggled, displaying that infatuating Molly face he'd lately seen so rarely.

In truth, Mollenhoff had mentioned the possibility of Molly going to live in a "memory care" facility, probably in Mankato. Gus was adamant in his opposition. He insisted he could care for Molly at home, where she would be comfortable in familiar surroundings. Mollenhoff accepted this arrangement for the time being, but given Molly's rapid decline, he warned Gus that he likely wouldn't be able to handle her, "in her advanced stages." The phrase gave Gus a sunken feeling. "Advanced stages." How could it get worse than when she attacked him with a sharp object? He didn't want to think about it and vowed to keep her at home as long as... well, until the end, whatever that is and whenever it comes.

Soon Molly was asleep, her breath a soothing sibilant rhythm. Gus gently released her from his embrace and lay there, gazing at the ceiling. His thoughts turned from Molly to the strange letter writer who signed his missives as "Fed Up." He, if it was a he, had continued to write to Molly weekly, repeating the same unspecified grievances with vague requests for acknowledgment and redress. Gus found the letters, at least the ones he'd managed to intercept, to be increasingly unhinged and possibly threatening. When he asked Molly about them, she claimed they contained secret messages from Augie, who was alive somewhere, in hiding, and communicating with her *incognito*. For a passing moment, Gus had allowed himself to believe it could be true, then came to his senses and wrote it off as another of Molly's delusions, the product of a failing mind. The pathos of it depressed him. She believed it because she wanted to, needed to. He wanted and needed it to be true, as well. He wished he could exist in a fantasy world in which Augie was still alive.

To drive away disturbing thoughts about what might lie ahead for him, Molly, and Mr. Fed Up, he tried to excavate more pleasant memories. The first images to emerge were of the snowy, windswept campus of the University of Minnesota in Minneapolis. The grandeur of the central mall, bookended by Northrop Auditorium to the north and Coffman Memorial Union to the south, grass blanketed in white, walkways freshly plowed. Molly in her pink woolen beanie and camel hair overcoat, face partially obscured by a tartan plaid scarf wrapped around her head, frost forming where her breath escaped, exposing only her twinkling eyes, which smiled at Gus as they met on their way to get coffee in Stadium Village.

Gus had enrolled at "the U," as locals called it, and planned to double major in American history and education, his eyes already set on teaching high school somewhere, maybe even his hometown. Molly had followed him to Minneapolis three months later with plans for a degree in English. He'd already fallen deeply in love with her, and there was little doubt, although unspoken, that they would end up together even after Gus had left for Minneapolis.

At first, he viewed her arrival with mixed emotions. He'd thought of going off to college as a way to shed the identity the U.S. Army had stamped on him and figure out who he really was. He knew Molly would wait for him. It would be only four years, and Minneapolis was only two hours away; it wasn't like they wouldn't see each other. He liked the idea of being on his own in the big city. But three months alone on the huge, anonymous campus, an older student out of sync with his classmates, was enough to change his mind. Back in Newfield, he'd been greeted as a hero, a wounded vet with a Purple Heart, his limp an outward badge of authenticity. At the U, he kept his military history to himself, as anti-war sentiment in 1973, though waning as the Vietnam War decelerated, was still the dominant vibe on campus. He'd made the mistake in his first week of confiding to a grad student TA over beers at Stub & Herb's that he'd served in Nam. The grad student asked him, in all seriousness, how many Vietnamese peasants he'd napalmed. The fact that the answer was "none," and that Gus had never even fired his rifle, and that the only action he saw was the landmine that killed his platoon leader, which, it turned out, had been placed there by the U.S. Army, the irony of which was not lost on young Corporal Peterson, who was already beginning to grasp the immoral folly of the war, was of no interest to the shaggy-haired grad student, who had escaped the draft with a high lottery number.

Molly's arrival made Gus immediately forget his "single man in the big city" fantasies, and when she got off the Greyhound bus, he embraced her as if she were a flotation device tossed to a drowning man. Her following him to college at first seemed adorable, a loyal puppy running after its master. Eventually he realized the agenda hidden in her sudden interest in a college degree was to keep close tabs on him, as she was not entirely sure he would return to Newfield from a world of thousands of cute and sexually liberated coeds. This being the 1970s. Much as she wanted to keep her boyfriend close (and her enemies closer), Molly made it abundantly clear that they would not be cohabitating. Her Catholic parents, after all, were paying her tuition and living expenses. She took an off-campus apartment in St. Anthony Park over in St. Paul and rode the campus shuttle to class. Gus was living in a hovel full of grad students, an odiferous ramshackle Victorian in Dinkytown. Having Molly nearby centered him and helped clarify his goals in life. She had that effect on people. Even then. A font of stabilizing wisdom, love, and endless patience. After a few months, he knew what he had to do.

He recalled the scene of his proposal to Molly, an indelible memory that made him smile. It was summer, the first one in which Gus hadn't returned home to take a temp job at the corn plant. He and Molly had rented a cabin on the North Shore of Lake Superior in a place with the unlikely but somehow inevitable name of Gooseberry Falls. Hikes by day, bonfires on the rocks at night. It was there that their clumsy efforts at sex ripened into languorous days and ardent nights of extended lovemaking. On the third day Gus suggested a hike in the Tettegouche wilderness, maybe all the way out to Shovel Point, from where the deep blue vastness of Gitchi-gami stretched to the horizon like a boreal ocean. There was a rocky ledge at the end of the point where Gus had planned to hatch his surprise. With the ring in its little clamshell case safely stashed in his jeans pocket, they walked hand in hand along the twisting path through the coastal forest of paper birch, quaking aspen, balsam poplar, and black ash. After an appropriate moment of awed silence honoring the eastward vista toward the not quite visible shore of Wisconsin, Gus knelt on the rocks dappled with orange and pale green lichen and produced the clam shell, like a sacrificial offering to a Greek goddess. Molly stared at him, and it, with a bemused smile.

"Aren't you going to say something?" he asked.

"Aren't *you* going to say something?" she responded.

Gus flushed, embarrassed that he was about to botch the most important moment in his life, at least since the time PFC Maynard Jones carried him and his shattered bleeding leg all the way to the evac chopper through a kilometer of rice paddies, jungle, and dubiously mapped minefields, undoubtedly saving his young life.

"Molly O'Rourke, will you make me the happiest man on planet Earth and marry me?"

She stared at him for a long moment. His dodgy leg began to quaver.

"Say something," he said finally.

"You are quite a catch, Gus Peterson," she said with a smirk.

He started to rise from his uncomfortable kneeling position.

"Stay down," she said. "I haven't answered yet."

The jagged rocks of the ledge dug into his right knee and his surgically repaired leg throbbed like a remembered dream.

"Yes, you are quite a catch, you with your busted ankle, your badge of courage, your small-town Americana values, your hotdogs and apple-pie baseball dreams, your upstanding Lutheran parents with their contempt for little Catholic girls like me."

Gus was not sure where this was going. When was she going to say yes?

"I see you, Gus Peterson," she continued. "And I love you like no one in this crappy world will ever love you."

"Can I get up? My leg is starting to hurt."

"It should hurt," she said. "This moment is beautiful and timeless, and you should never forget it, hurt and all."

He stared up at her, transfixed. The lake surf crashed against the rocks below, the gulls squawked above. Her face was dreamy and placid, as if her mind were elsewhere.

"I know what you need. I know what you want. I am the only person who can give you those things. We are soulmates, you and me. You can't escape me; I can't escape you. Our destinies are bound together by fates and furies."

This was getting weird. Molly seemed to be quoting from literature or philosophy she'd learned in class. Gus was ready to stand up and walk away defeated.

"I love you, Gus Peterson, beyond all reason." Molly seemed to return to earth. "I've loved you ever since the first day I noticed you, in chemistry class, junior year. When you walked into the lab, I dropped a pipette and it shattered on the floor. Remember that? I've waited six years for this moment. You will make me insanely happy, and I, I hope, you. So, Gus Peterson…" She paused, and Gus shifted uncomfortably, hoping this monologue was nearing a satisfactory end. "So, Gus," she said and cupped his upturned face in her hands, "here's my answer: Yes, I say. Yes. I will. Yes."

He rose and embraced her. The squawking of the gulls crescendoed as if in sanctification. He slid the simple gold engagement ring on her finger, and it was done.

Gaslamping. That's the word. He thinks I don't know. I'm ⸱ him. Like a hawk I am. Do hawks watch? They fly so high. ⸱ m down here. Close up view. I know things. I gotta pee. Crummy little bathroom. Where's the light switch? Ahhh, there. He says I cut him. With a whatchacallit. Spoon. Spitoon. Spatula. That's it. What a joke. I know he's lying. He cut himself and blamed me. Wants them to lock me up. He and that doc. Whatsisname. They're in it together. Why is my pee orange? Supposed to be yellow. Flush it down before he sees it. He says I forget things. Maybe I do sometimes. I forgot to write Dear Molly last week. He said I did and don't remember. He showed me the paper. It was me on that page. But I don't remember writing it. I said okay. Just playing along. I'm watching him. Like a hawk. Like a hawk on the ground.

When Travis Birdsong and Julio Cervantes arrived home after an absence of thirty-six hours, it was in the backseat of a police car, Deputy Sheriff Joe Morton at the wheel. The county SUV pulled into the Birdsong's long gravel driveway and parked behind Mavis's white van. The deputy got out and left the two perps in the backseat, not cuffed but not going anywhere either, their doors locked from the outside.

Mavis witnessed the arrival with alarm from her kitchen window where she'd just finished loading the dishwasher. The sight of a young Native male in the back of a police car, as well as that of a young Latino male, suggested things could go south in a hurry if they weren't careful. Mavis called to Elvis, and they met Morton at their front door. Mavis ran past him to the black-and-white SUV and bent to peer inside, torn by relief that the boys were okay and furious at the implications of their method of return. She waved. Travis looked away. Julio smiled and waved back.

"I'll let them out. Once we have an understanding," Morton said.

"Where did you find them?" Elvis asked.

"What about Julio's parents?" Mavis interrupted. "Do they know you have him?"

"Not yet. I thought maybe you could call and have them meet us here. For a little powwow." He grinned like he'd just made a brilliant jest.

Mavis wanted to say something about the slur and glanced at Elvis for validation. He shook his head. She bit her tongue and went inside to call M'lena.

When she returned Elvis was deep in conversation with Morton, the two men leaning casually against the front fender of the SUV, as if forgetting the two eighteen-year-olds in a heap of trouble. Elvis hatless in jeans and a Newfield Track & Field t-shirt, Morton with his badge reflecting the rays of the setting sun, black sidearm protruding impudently from his black leather holster. They were saying something about Elvis's stupid militia.

"Are you going to let them stew in there all evening?" she asked Morton, still seething over his obnoxious powwow crack.

"Soon as the Cervantes arrive, let's all convene in your living room, if that's okay. Otherwise, we can head over to the county jail."

Miguel pulled into the driveway and parked his pick-up behind the sheriff's car. M'lena jumped out of the passenger seat before he'd even stopped the truck and ran to the SUV in what appeared to be tears of joy and rage. She beat her fists on the glass and shouted "*¿Que paso?* What have you done? Where have you been?"

"We can answer all your questions, if you just calm down," said Morton. "Let's go inside." He clicked a button on a key fob and opened the door and extended his hand to Travis, who ignored it and climbed out, Julio right behind him. Mavis and M'lena scurried over and embraced them, and they wriggled away, obviously chastened and embarrassed.

Inside the Birdsong living room, the seven of them sat in a

circle of straight-back chairs commandeered from the dining room and arranged around the driftwood coffee table. Mavis wished she'd known this was coming so she could have tidied up. The acrid odor of fried onions from dinner stung her nose. She hoped no one else noticed. She smiled at everyone, hoping to diffuse the tension. Despite the presence of the deputy sheriff and the circumstances of this meeting, the gathering was a familiar and comforting arrangement for her and Elvis and Miguel and Maria Elena. They had been friends for years, despite the two-decade age difference, having in common their stories of arriving in Newfield as children born elsewhere—Elvis and Mavis on the reservation and Miguel and M'Lena in Latin America—their parents drawn to this corner of southern Minnesota by the promise of employment in the brewery and corn plant, a promise that proved temporary and left their next generation relying largely on self-employment, Miguel as a handyman and Mavis and M'lena as food service entrepreneurs.

Morton explained that the two boys—men, actually, now that they were eighteen, a legal reality not lost on anyone in the room—were caught smoking marijuana and drinking beers on the old Dodd-Ford trestle bridge over the river, wearing only boxer shorts and flip flops. Apparently they had been swimming. It also appeared several others had been partying with them, judging by the number of empty Coors Light cans strewn about the bridge and on the sandy riverbank below, but the two remained mum on the subject.

"You're not really going to throw these boys in jail for drinking beer and smoking weed, are you?" said Elvis. It was more a statement than a question. "If that's your idea of policing, half the young people in this county will be behind bars eventually. Is that what you want?"

"Perhaps you are unaware, Elvis, that we have a drug abuse problem in this county. Do you expect me to do nothing?"

"I am well aware, Joe."

Morton scowled.

"Deputy Morton," Elvis corrected himself. "Mavis and I know better than anybody what drugs can do to young people. We've told Travis here of his mother's fate, to scare him away from that stuff." He looked over at Travis. "I suppose we could be doing a better job. But it's our job, not yours."

Miguel and Maria Elena nodded in agreement. Julio and Travis studied their high-top black sneakers.

"We're doing the best we can," said Mavis. "But everything in this town seems to be working against us." She stopped short of calling the county sheriff's department, along with many of their Newfield neighbors, racists. But it's what she meant.

M'lena seemed to catch her drift. "How many White kids have you picked up for drinking and smoking?" she said.

"Plenty," Morton said. "Anyway, this is not about race, it's about the law."

"Which seems to be enforced inconsistently," said Mavis.

"What is it, exactly, you expect me to do?"

"Your job, Joe. Deputy," said Elvis. "Do something about the suppliers of all the drugs and illicit alcohol. You know who I'm talking about. Everybody knows. But all you do is bust the kids, the retail customers. What about wholesalers? Why don't you bust them? Is it because they're all White guys?"

Mavis exhaled loudly. Finally, they were getting somewhere.

"I assume you're talking about Freddie and his friends," Morton said.

"The Blue Hogs motorcycle club," said Elvis, nodding.

"You know most of the Hogs don't even live in this county, right?"

"So? They're breaking the law in this county, right?" said Elvis.

The mention of the name Freddie turned Mavis's stomach.

Fat Freddie Ignatowski, owner of Fat Freddie's Body Shop in Blue Earth and founder of the Hogs motorcycle gang. Mavis considered him a virulent racist. She had long suspected that he was the source of the opiates that had started her daughter's descent into hell some twenty years ago, and that he or his gang were responsible for the repeated acts of vandalism against her vehicles. Occasionally a few of them would come into her café, acting sweet and polite while grinning at her as if to say, "Yeah, it was us, waddya gonna do about it?" They called her Pocahontas, always with a smile, an insult copied from their hero, the vile president of the United States. She'd grit her teeth and say nothing, serve them, and take their money. No one in the café ever spoke up in her defense or condemned the insults. Afraid of offending dangerous people? Or simply indifferent to the racism all around? Or oblivious, like fish unaware of the water? Native Americans had been on this land for so long that the racism they experienced from the White majority was closer to ignorance and neglect, in Mavis's opinion, than the overt hostility directed at recent immigrants. But looming over the Birdsongs and the members of their community was the distant but still raw memory of an ugly history dating to the nineteenth century. As Mavis and every member of the Dakota Nation knew, Mankato was the site of the largest mass execution in American history in 1862 when President Lincoln ordered the hanging of thirty-eight Dakotas in reprisal for an unsuccessful rebellion. Her people. The thirty-eight were hanged simultaneously from a specially constructed scaffold. A crowd of four thousand filled the streets of the city to witness the spectacle. Mavis could imagine Freddie and his Hogs eagerly joining such a throng.

"I know the Hogs can be a little wild at times," said Morton. "Not exactly fit for polite society. But that's the whole point, for them. They feel like they don't fit in."

Mavis was incredulous. It sounded like Morton was

defending them, even sympathizing.

"If you have any evidence they're dealing drugs, let me know. I will arrest them. But I need proof. So far I haven't seen any. Every time I look into it, nobody wants to cooperate."

Because you haven't looked into it hard enough, Mavis thought. Because they're your buddies.

"Which brings us back to the issue here with these boys," Morton said. "I know they weren't partying alone out there. And I know who they were with."

Travis and Julio looked up from their Chuck Taylors, suddenly interested in the conversation.

"The Hogs like to party by the river. They always leave a calling card. And there it was. A big steaming pile of shit. Right in the middle of the bridge. Still fresh, like it had been dumped just before I got there. Which one of them dropped drawers and squatted, boys?"

Travis and Julio looked at each other intently, as if playing the Prisoners Dilemma game by telepathy. Should they both clam up? Or should they both fess up? What if they were separated? Would one rat out the other? They looked back at their sneakers and said nothing.

"Look, boys," said Morton. "I didn't bust you for drinking beer and smoking weed. I brought you in because I know you were hanging out with the Hogs. I know that's where you get your beer and grass. If they are supplying alcohol and drugs to high school kids, I'm going after them. But I need your help."

Mavis felt as if she might throw up. The very idea of Travis hanging out with the Hogs filled her with rage and terror.

"Alrighty then," said Morton. "You boys think about that. I'm going to let you go today with a warning. Help me get evidence against the Hogs. Or at the very least, stay the hell away from them."

A sense of relief filled the room as much of the tension seemed to abate. Maybe Morton wasn't a complete asshole after all,

Mavis thought.

He stood up, put on his hat, and started toward the front door. He turned back to face the room and said, "You four grownups have some work to do." Then he left.

Miggy, M'lena, and Julio departed soon after, the tension in the family palpable. Travis slinked out of the living room to his bedroom.

"We will talk about this later," Elvis said as his grandson slammed his door shut.

"You're damn right we will," said Mavis. She was too angry and afraid to deal with it now.

She lost Chester Greenfield somewhere along County Road 4 when his big Ford truck passed one semi then another and she couldn't trail close enough without being noticed in her little Subaru. There weren't many other vehicles on the road at this early morning hour, and Pam Strich was already self-conscious about tailing Chester in defiance of her boss's edict and didn't want to get spotted by the bacon baron. She couldn't resist her reporter's instinct that there was something juicy going on between the mayor, the ex-mayor, and the town's biggest political fundraiser. She kept driving east on 4 with the slim hope of catching up to him, given that he could have turned off anywhere, the dirt farm roads forming a matrix of escape routes. She scanned the flat landscape, soybean fields green as a billiard table, for signs of telltale dust clouds but saw none. Pam had spent a week tailing Chester and both Whites during her off hours and the only things she was sure of were that Jack White was screwing Rosalita Greenfield and that Chester Greenfield was definitely not screwing Jill White but there was still something brewing among the four that smelled of news.

Just ahead on the highway appeared a vision that Pam almost missed and, when she roused from her thoughts, almost ran over: a lone figure, walking along the side of the road, teetering on the edge of the drainage ditch, in a simple floral house dress and slippers. Pam passed by then pulled over to the side of the road, mindful of the ditch, and put her Outback in park. She climbed out and watched the figure approach. It was an elderly woman, looking lost yet blissful at the same time. Pam recognized her immediately.

"Molly! Missus Peterson," she said, perhaps too loudly, as if to one hard of hearing.

Molly Peterson was not hard of hearing. "Who wants to know?" she said.

"It's me. Pam, from the *Clarion*. Are you okay?"

"Fuck you, Pam from the *Clarion*," she said and raised a gnarled middle finger, in case Pam from the *Clarion* didn't get the message. She turned as if to assess her distance from the dead-sunflower-lined ditch, perhaps seeking an exit route.

"Can I give you a ride somewhere?" Pam asked. "Where's your truck?"

Pam knew Molly's white antique pickup with the Mollywood logo on the doors but hadn't seen it on the road. Molly stared at her, as if confronting a wild animal and deciding whether to fight or flee. A darkness swept across her face, transforming it from a visage of defiance to one of sadness and fear. She stood motionless. She seemed to be processing the situation, examining her options. Pam considered what more calming and persuasive phrases she could employ but came up empty. She waited and watched. A big rig roared by, its unpainted steel trailer catching and reflecting the morning sun's rays, not even slowing to take in the sight of two women standing by the roadside next to a parked Subaru, suggesting car trouble and the need for help. The wind from the truck blew Molly's graying hair into a tangle. After a few moments, she rearranged her stringy locks with her fingers and walked to Pam's car without saying a word. She opened the passenger door and climbed in.

Pam took the wheel and made a U-turn, heading back toward the Peterson place. She tried to start harmless conversations. The weather. The nascent fall colors. The size of the corn crop. Molly, exuding a faintly septic odor, remained silent. When Pam pulled into the Peterson's gravel driveway, the Mollywood pickup was in front of the barn; Gus's Gran Torino was not in evidence, so the place was likely empty. She asked Molly if she should accompany her inside. Molly was stone silent. Pam hesitated, unsure if it was okay to leave a confused old lady alone in her house. Molly turned to look at her, and suddenly seemed transformed, her face brightened. "Thank you, Mary Alice," she said with a polite smile. "You are a nice young lady. So pretty. Maybe let your natural hair color grow in." She climbed out of the car and walked toward the little brick rambler.

Who the fuck is Mary Alice? Pam debated whether to follow her into the house. The woman opened the front door and disappeared inside. After several moments of deliberation, Pam decided she'd done her good deed for the day and backed out of the driveway onto County Road 4, thinking to resume her recon mission on Chester Greenfield while wondering what the hell was wrong with Molly Peterson. Senile? No way, too young.

Dear Molly,
I've had a falling out with one of my best and oldest friends (I'll call him Joe) and I'm at a loss over how to patch things up. We used to work together at the same company for over a decade until it went out of business a couple years back. We had lunch together several times a month and socialized with our wives.
Last year Joe got his real estate license and set up shop in town. Not long after, my wife and

I started thinking about downsizing now that our youngest has moved out, emptying the nest. I mentioned to Joe that we were planning to sell and of course he asked if he could handle the listing, as he was just breaking into the business and needed sales. My wife and I decided we would interview a few agents, including Joe, and list with the one we thought could get us the best price.

We decided to give the listing to a well-established agent in our area, as we thought Joe's expectations for the sale seemed unrealistic. Well, Joe went ballistic and berated me for days—in person, on the phone in emails—said I had backstabbed him and that the agent we picked was a crook and all sorts of crazy talk. I finally had to threaten to report him to the Board of Realtors and he stopped, but I haven't seen or heard from him since.

Joe and I go way back, and I hate to lose old friends. I'm trying to give him the benefit of the doubt and assume he was under stress or something. What do you think? Should I reach out to him? Or just walk away from a broken friendship?

Signed,
Perplexed

Dear Perplexed,
I'm sorry you had to go through that. It's a painful thing when friendships go astray. Especially for married adult men, who often have trouble making and keeping male friends.

But I have to say, I'm not entirely sympathetic to your plight. The reason? You broke a cardinal rule, in my book: Never do business with friends or relatives. One thing eventually will have to give: the business or the relationship.

As for "Joe," his behavior was unacceptable,

regardless of his psychological state. Such practices stain the entire local business community, or at least the real estate business. If I were you, I'd report him to the Board of Realtors, or even to state regulators. (I assume you saved copies of his abusive emails.) I wouldn't worry that it might upset him; your friendship is unsalvageable in my opinion.

I hope you learned a lesson here. Good luck with your future real estate adventures.

Hugs,
Molly

Fri. Oct. 4 at 9:51 am

James Tomlinson <jtomlinson@newfieldclarion.com>
To: Molly Peterson <dearmolly@newfieldclarion.com>
Re: Next column

Hey, Molly. Tried calling but your voicemail box is full. Just wanted to discuss next week's column. Your response seemed a bit harsh, not the usual forgiving Molly Peterson. Is that really how you want to reply? Give me a call or email me back.—Jim

Gus stared at the email from Jim, which he'd intercepted while Molly was asleep on the living room couch. He checked on her; still dozing, radio softly tuned to the baseball playoff game, in which the Twins were getting pounded. No need to disturb her, things were under control. Molly had been worrying that Jim would learn of her mental health issues and push her into retirement. Gus assured her that would not happen, and suggested she take a week or two off. He told her he would tell Jim she was under the weather and the *Clarion* could publish the "Best of Molly" from the archives, as had been done before. Meantime, he would continue to submit the column, keeping both Molly and Jim in the dark for as long as possible. He knew that someday it would all come out, but he wanted to push that someday back.

Perhaps Jim had a point about this particular column. Gus had been trying to channel Molly's voice and gentle outlook, but something seemed to be creeping into his own psyche, something that put more of an edge into his responses. He would have to watch that, and self-edit more closely if he was to continue this secret ghostwriting business.

He emailed Jim from Molly's account.

Fri. Oct. 4 at 11:12 am

Molly Peterson <dearmolly@newfieldclarion.com>
To: James Tomlinson <jtomlinson@newfieldclarion.com>
Re: Next column
Hi, Jim. Sorry about the full mailbox. I'll take care of that right away. I'm also sorry you think my advice was too harsh. Maybe so, but sometimes I run out of patience with the follies and foibles of my fellow Minnesotans. The older I get, the less I'm willing to forgive rude behavior. Is that such a bad thing? Your readers might appreciate some straight talk, some tough love, from old Molly. Let me know if you think I go too far!

Hugs,
Molly

Dear Molly,
I was at a family reunion recently where my wife and I met up with my in-laws—her parents and two brothers and their wives. Things were quite jolly at first and we made plans to go out to dinner together. As was our custom, at "happy hour" we would open a bottle of wine and have a glass before dinner. That evening I went over to the kitchen counter and poured myself a glass from an open bottle and joined everyone on the patio. My father-in-law frowned at me and asked why I took a glass from his bottle. I said I assumed it was to be shared, like all the bottles we'd

been drinking. He became indignant and said he'd been saving that bottle for himself. I thought he was joking, but he seemed quite irritated. I apologized, even though I thought he was acting like a kindergartner fighting over a toy. He continued to lecture me like I was a thief. I left the patio for a moment and when I returned my glass was empty and he had the bottle in front of him. He had poured my glassful back into the bottle!

So, Molly, what's your verdict? Was I an inconsiderate slob? Or was my father-in-law overreacting?

Signed,
Wine Thief

Dear Wine Thief,
I've never met your father-in-law most likely, but from where I sit, he seems like a real jerk. It was an honest mistake on your part; you couldn't know it was a "private" bottle not to be shared. If he wanted to keep it for himself, he shouldn't have left it opened on the counter. You apologized, which was the right thing to do, and yet he continued to lecture you? What an ass.

It's another reminder that we can choose our spouses, but we can't always choose our in-laws. It looks like you got stuck with a family that includes at least one doofus. I hope you can somehow forgive and get along. Maybe next time, switch to beer when you're around the wine hoarder.

Hugs,
Molly

James Tomlinson <jtomlinson@newfieldclarion.com>
To: Molly Peterson <dearmolly@newfieldclarion.com>
Re: Next column

Hey, Molly. I get the straight-talk and tough-love. But insulting someone's father-in-law? Calling him a jerk and an ass and a doofus? Readers might take umbrage with that. It sounds a little too much like a certain politician in Washington. The reason Dear Molly has been so popular for so long is your unique way of correcting people's social faux pas without denigrating them. Hating the sin while loving the sinner, etc. I'm going to publish this one as is, and let's see how folks react. I hope you'll be willing to dial back the tone if it doesn't play well. And BTW, I tried to call again so we could talk this over, but your mailbox is still full. Talk soon? Or drop by the office anytime. —Jim

Thurs. Oct. 10 at 1:12 pm

Molly Peterson <dearmolly@newfieldclarion.com>
To: James Tomlinson <jtomlinson@newfieldclarion.com>
Re: Next column

Hi, Jim. I'm so sorry you didn't like the column. But I hope you can trust my instinct that people need to be held accountable for bad behavior. Tough talk never hurt anybody. Sticks and stones, etc, right? Let's see how it goes. I'm willing to compromise somewhat if folks don't like it. And thanks for the invitation to phone or visit the office, but I'm feeling a little under the weather this week and don't feel up to it. I will send in next week's column, though.

Hugs,
Molly

Chester parked his truck in front of the open bay door at Fat Freddie's body shop in Blue Earth. He peered inside, looking for signs of the proprietor amid the dusty chaos, the half-painted cars, the tools and auto parts hanging on the blackened walls alongside calendars featuring color photos of nude and half-nude women. Same old Freddie. His black Harley was parked outside in the side alley. He had to be around somewhere. Chester remembered that the big hog was Freddie's everyday bike, while his real treasure, rolled out only for special occasions, was an antique Vincent Black Shadow. No sign of that. Probably kept it locked up somewhere.

A crescendo of music emanated from somewhere inside the shop. It sounded like ... opera? Chester knew a little about opera, thanks to Rosalita, and was pretty sure he was hearing strains of Puccini. Maybe *La Boheme*? *Madama Butterfly*? This was new information about Frederick J. Ignatowski. As he pondered this, the man himself waddled out of the darkness from the rear of the shop, the sound of a flushing toilet trailing behind him adding a note of discord. Greasy denim overalls and no shirt, a museum of tattoos visible on every inch of exposed skin. A bushy salt-and-pepper beard covered his neck and part of his chest, his face frozen in that perpetual arched-brow look of puzzlement. Chester surmised that Fat Freddie had gotten even fatter since the last time he saw him, over a year ago, probably near three-hundred pounds, almost as big as Chester, which elicited a brief tinge of competitive resentment. Being five inches taller, Chester consoled himself with the belief that he carried his weight much better than the fat slob before him.

Back in the day, Chester and Freddie were the bookend tackles on both the offensive and defensive lines for the Newfield Reapers, the last team to win the conference football championship, thirty long years ago. Their lives diverged after high school, Chester off to the U of M to study agribusiness and Freddie off to Stillwater prison for drug dealing followed by a second stint for fencing stolen goods. He emerged from the pen with a new skill, auto body repair, and opened his shop with a loan from his old teammate Chester. He'd paid the loan back within a few years, and the men fell out of touch for decades. Until events brought them together in common cause—events including the election of a Black man as president.

Chester stepped out of his truck. He smiled and waved. Freddie's perpetual look of puzzlement cracked briefly into a grin that perhaps unintentionally resembled a sneer. "Well shut my mouth. If it ain't ol' Seventy-Seven," said Freddie.

Chester strode toward him, and they exchanged a wrestling match of a handshake, which lasted almost ten seconds before Chester cried uncle.

"You got soft on that farm of yours," Freddie said as he released Chester's throbbing hand.

Chester flexed his fingers to check if any were broken and tried to think of something funny and manly to say to regain his dignity. "Same old Seventy-Five!" was all he could come up with.

"So, to what do I owe the pleasure, old pal?" Freddie said, breaking an awkward silence. "Thirty-year reunion's coming up. You going?"

Chester shrugged. "I got a proposition for you, old pal," he said, cutting to the chase to avoid what he knew would be a lengthy trip by Freddie down memory lane. "You got any beer?"

"Hell yeah. C'mon." Freddie led him to the dirt parking lot in back where a lonely bistro table and two white plastic chairs perched on a carpet of weeds. The chairs looked flimsy, but somehow they held up under six hundred pounds of right and left tackles when Freddie emerged with two bottles of Bud Light and the two men sat.

"What was that music coming out of your shop?" Chester asked as an ice breaker.

"'Nessun Dorma,' baby. Greatest fuckin' aria ever. You hear the ending? Where the dude sings *vincero* over and over? That means *I will win*. That's my motto. I got it on a tattoo." He turned his bare arm over to show the word *VINCERO* inked in gothic script along the underside of his forearm.

Chester had barely got through his pitch for a Bikers for Trump rally when Freddie jumped up and shouted, "I was thinkin' the same damn thing!" and slapped Chester on the back, a bit harder than Chester thought necessary. Freddie admitted his idea was limited to his Blue Hogs crew, numbering only a dozen, and a one-day ride to Minneapolis and back. "So we can disrupt one of them antifa marches or demonstrations. No violence, of course. Just a little intimidation. Flyin' the Trump flags. But I like the way you're thinking, Chester. Go big. I guess that's why you're a big-time Republican honcho."

This was easier than he expected. Chester had been wary of recruiting Freddie and the Hogs to lead his rally. At least three of the gang, including Freddie, had criminal records. Rosie had told her husband he was nuts to even consider the idea. But he couldn't think of a better way to assemble hundreds of motorcycle riders. That was Freddie's world, not Chester's.

The two men laid vague plans for a rally in the spring, after the snow melted, when the presidential election would be well underway. Chester explained that during primary season a lot of media attention would be on the Democrats trying to pick a candidate. Bernie Sanders. Joe Biden. Kamala Harris. Trump will stomp them all, he said, but it would still be a good idea to attract attention away from them with a big, showy event. "The media is like a cat chasing a laser pointer," he said. "Any shiny object will distract them."

Freddie proved a quick study when it came to political strategy and vowed to immediately start contacting other motorcycle clubs around the state. Chester decided not to mention the fund raising potential of the rally. Sharing the bounty was not part of the plan, especially given the growing urgency of his financial straits. If Freddie asked about it, he'd tell him the GOP operatives would handle that end.

Gus felt his cellphone vibrating in his hip pocket. He was in the kitchen about to fix some lunch for himself and Molly, assuming she would wake up eventually. Annoyed by the interruption, he turned down the radio, pulled out his phone, and glanced at the screen. A local area code, but not someone in his contacts. Possibly a spam call. A helpful reminder to renew his auto warranty. What the heck. He answered.

"Mister Peterson?" It was a woman, sounded young.

"Depends. Who's asking? I don't need a car warranty."

"It's Pam Strich. From the *Clarion*."

"Oh," he said. What could this be about? Nothing good, given Pam's reputation. "How did you get this number?"

"From Jim Tomlinson. I told him I wanted to interview you about Elvis Birdsong's citizen militia."

"And how is my buddy Jim?" he said, reminding her that he's good friends with her boss.

"Breaking my balls," said Pam. "Anyway, I don't care about the dumb militia. I wanted to mention something to you. About your wife, Molly."

Fuck. This can't be good. "What about my wife?"

"Maybe it would be better if we talk in person."

"What's so important that you can't tell me on the phone?"

"I just thought you'd prefer to hear this in a safe, quiet place."

Definitely not good. "The phone is safe and quiet. You think the NSA is listening in?"

Pam was silent for a moment. "Okay then. Here it is. Last week I found your wife wandering along County Road 4 in her pj's, lost and confused. I drove her home. She called me Mary Alice. What's wrong with her? Is she … you know?"

So. It's out now. A reporter knows. Who was Mary Alice? Gus felt a surge of regret that he hadn't kept Molly safe and out of the public eye, where her dignity could be destroyed. But he couldn't lock her in the house. Could he?

"Alright then," he said after a lengthy silence, Pam waiting patiently at the other end. "Let's meet somewhere. I can explain. Got a place in mind?"

"Cindy Smith's place. On West Elm."

"Cindy's? Why?"

"She's working at the bar today. Nobody home."

"Why not your place?"

"No privacy."

"Why do you have access to Cindy's place?"

"I have a key. You know about me and Cindy, right?"

Gus most definitely did not know about Pam and Cindy. "Ohhhh, right," he said.

When Gus parked in the rear of the big yellow Queen Anne, the kind of house he'd always dreamed of, Pam was already there, waiting for him at the back door. She led him into the kitchen and offered him coffee. A big black cat dashed out of the room when Gus entered, claws scratching the tile floor in a vain search for purchase. "That's just Brandi Carlile, Cindy's cat," said Pam. "She's finally stopped hissing at me, but I don't think she likes men."

The feeling's mutual, Gus almost said but didn't. "I'd rather have a beer, if there is any." He felt the need for some mellow lubrication to help him through the pending conversation.

She rummaged around in the fridge and emerged with a can of something called White Claw hard seltzer. "It's like beer," she said, "but tastier. Anyway, that's all she's got."

Gus accepted the can and popped the top. Not bad. "How about you? Got another one in there?"

"I'm, uh, abstaining for a while."

Gus figured there was a backstory there, given how often he'd seen her drinking at the VFW, but let it pass. "So. Anyway. About Molly."

"Yes, about Molly," she said.

"Molly has dementia. Possibly early onset Alzheimer's,

according to her doctor."

"Oh, jeez. I'm so sorry. She seems … too young for that."

Gus sensed pity in her voice. He hated to be pitied. He pushed past it. "It came on fast. Only a few months ago she seemed fine. A little cranky at times, a little absent-minded, but aren't we all at this age?"

Pam looked at him with sympathy but only shrugged at his question.

"You'll know someday," he said. "Anyway, she's declined rapidly since August."

"That's so sad. I read her column religiously," said Pam. "It's one of the ways I've learned about this community, what bothers people, what they value, etcetera. I wouldn't have guessed about her, um, condition, from the column. She still makes perfect sense to me."

"Well, the truth is," said Gus, unsure if he should go down this road. But he was talking to a reporter from the *Clarion* after all, and she would figure it out soon enough. "Molly hasn't written the column for several weeks. I'm writing it."

"Wow. I never would have guessed. You write just like her."

Gus ignored the compliment. "Please, keep this to yourself, Pam. 'Dear Molly' is important to the *Clarion*. To Jim. You know that. It's important to Molly, too. She thinks she's still writing it. I've always been her proofreader, checking for typos, etcetera, and she thinks that's all I'm doing. The fact is, most of the time she can't make sense of the letters she gets and can't type anything intelligible. So I'm doing it all and telling her it when it's published that she wrote it and just can't remember. She believes me, I think."

"So… you're gaslighting her then?"

"I don't know what that means."

"It means you're deceiving her, making up an alternate reality to shield her from the truth. It's from the movie *Gaslight*, where a husband uses lies and deception to convince his wife she's crazy."

"I'm not evil like that. I'm trying to protect her."

"Does Jim know about this?"

"No, he does not. I'm doing everything I can to keep up this charade. I'm emailing him from her account pretending to be Molly. I don't know how long it can last. I just want Molly to have some dignity before she…" He couldn't finish the sentence. "But please, will you keep this a secret?"

"I've always liked and admired Molly, so yeah," she said. "And now you know a secret about me. And Cindy. We're trying to keep it quiet. You know how it goes."

Gus nodded sympathetically, while imagining Cindy and Pam naked. How many piercings and tattoos on those girls?

"This is a small town," said Pam. "It's hard to keep secrets for long. How many more times will Molly wander the road in her pj's before the whole town notices?"

"I know. Just help me keep it going for a while longer."

"No problem. Anyway, I'm more interested in what the Greenfields and the Whites are up to. Any ideas about that?"

Gus and Pam kicked around a few speculations about the town's two main power couples, but Pam soon seemed bored with Gus's uninformed conjectures and ushered him out the back door. He hadn't even finished his White Claw.

Gus opened the latest edition of *The Newfield Clarion* and found the Dear Molly column in its place of honor on the top of page three. He folded the page in half to better display the column and placed it on the kitchen table in front of Molly, who was examining a piece of bacon as if it were an unidentified fried object.

"Here's the *Clarion*," he said. "You're on page three, as usual." He turned his attention back to his phone, on which he was reading the recap of the Twins disappointing season. Somehow, despite breaking the season record for most home runs, they had once again been eliminated from the playoffs by the New York Yankees. After so many years, he still daydreamed about himself on the mound in the navy blue and red, snapping his forkball past flailing big-league hitters. As it turned out, he'd had to settle for trying to hold together a high school baseball program that in his later years had dwindled to so few players that he could barely field a team, much less a varsity *and* a JV. Only an influx of Latino families had kept the program going, as most kids seemed interested only in hockey and football. His last team was one-third kids from Spanish-speaking homes.

Molly turned from the bacon and glanced down at the paper, still holding the crispy, greasy strip in her fingers. "Who's that?" she said, pointing at the artist's pencil sketch of her face done some fifteen years ago.

"That'd be you, the famous Molly Peterson."

"Doesn't look like me. Whoever drew that didn't know what they were doing." She turned back to the piece of bacon and nibbled at it.

"Anyway, you wrote a good one this week, a real zinger. It's the one about the guy who wouldn't share his wine, remember? You really scorched him."

Molly studied the page, still munching the bacon. "I guess so. What did whatshisname say?"

"Jim? He loved it."

"I haven't heard from him in a while."

"He's probably busy."

Molly slumped in her chair, her chin on her chest, as if asleep. Gus recognized it as one of her sudden spells. If he tried to bring her out of it, she might not remember who he was and react with terror or violence. Best to leave her alone but keep an eye on her from the next room. He cleared the breakfast dishes and went to the office to check Molly's email account. A few new submissions for the column. He would read those later. Nothing from Tomlinson. He hoped that no news was good news, no complaints about Molly's new astringent tone. He checked the sent mail and deleted files folders to make sure he'd got rid of any trace of his fraudulent email conversations with Tomlinson. Not that he had much to worry about from Molly. She had become so frustrated with the computer that she never logged on anymore. With her memory so befogged now it was easy to convince her she had typed the column herself.

Gaslighting. That's the word Pam Strich had used. He'd Googled it, and she was right, there was a movie called *Gaslight* with Charles Boyer and Ingrid Bergman. Gaslighting didn't have to be a bad thing, he assured himself, if it was done out of love and protection. But was it? Doubts penetrated his nebula of self-justification. He'd argued with Doc Mollenhoff over the best course of treatment for Molly, always resisting any suggestion that Molly's care be taken over by, or even shared with, others. He believed he knew what was best. Who knew Molly better than Gus? Who better understood her need for privacy and dignity? Or was he just being selfish? Deep down, when he was honest with himself, he suspected his need to keep Molly close and under his supervision was as much for his benefit as hers. What would he do with himself if she were sent away? What would provide meaning to his life? The answer was obvious: Caring for Molly would be the meaning of his life.

He reached for the small stack of the latest snail mail submissions, which he'd collected at the *Clarion* office last time he was in town for a snort at the VFW. The one on top of the pile looked familiar, addressed to Molly, care of the *Clarion*, no stamp or postal marks, probably dropped off in person. He tore open the envelope and read.

Dear Molly,
I been writing to you for months and I never see any

answer from you in your column. My parents used to read
Dear Molly out loud at the dinner table when I was a kid.
I always admired you. So it is very disappointing that you
are ignoring me just like everyone else around here. What
kind of sickness has invaded this town? Where is everybody
I grew up around? You don't know what it's like to be
invisible. To be a person one day and a ghost the next day.
I am asking you, pretty please with a cherry on top, answer
my letter and tell everyone the truth about this town and
that they better shape up.
Fed Up

Gus started to suspect this person could be dangerous. His letters were pathetic but also vaguely threatening, as if this lost soul were passing judgment on this entire community and finding it wanting. There were no specific threats. Only a slowly escalating level of grievance. *They better shape up*, it said. Or what? was the unspoken question. He set it aside on the little desk, thinking that he should start keeping a file on this character, and went back to the kitchen to check on Molly and try to solve the riddle of why she'd taken to calling him Kenny.

Whose hands are these? I think I know. So pale and wrinkled.
Blue veins. What are those dark spots? Cancer? Are these my hands?
They move when I say move. Gasagasa... gaslighting, that's it.
Trying to make me out to be crazy. I'm on to you, old whatsyername.
You say I wrote the column. That's not even my picture on it. How
can I write it? I can't even use the computer anymore. It looks like
a child's artwork when I open the lid. Something I might hang on
the fridge. If I had a kid. Where is my little boy Augie? Dead, they
say. Don't have to remind me. Dead. Supposedly. Just like Kenny

Thomas. War. Always some war. War took Kenny. And sent back ...
Gus. What happened to my breakfast? Did I finish already? That
bacon was good. Crunchy the way I like. I can still smell it. I wonder
where Mary Alice has been hiding out all these years. So lovely to
see her. Lucky for me she came along to give me a ride home. These
can't be my hands.

The next time Gus stopped by the *Clarion* to pick up Molly's mail, Jim invited him into his office. "Take off your jacket and stay awhile," he said. It was raining frogs and toads outside, and he could barely see the town square out the window through the Biblical curtain of falling water. In recent weeks, Gus had made his visits brief, grabbing the mail and leaving before Jim or anyone else in the office could engage him in conversation or send their regards to Molly.

Gus sat in his usual spot opposite Jim, the desk between them. He left his wet rain slicker on, as if planning to stay only a minute.

"You're getting my chair wet," said Jim.

Gus sighed and reluctantly hung his rainwear on the coat tree, alongside Jim's.

"How's Molly?" Jim asked, seeing no point in beating around the bush, given Gus's apparent eagerness to leave.

"Fine."

"That's not what I'm hearing."

Gus said nothing, only stared at Jim as if it were a contest to see who would blink first.

"Gus. I know what's going on. I know everything."

Gus looked up at the ceiling, as if studying the dead flies scattered across the plastic cover inside the fluorescent light fixture, their dark little bodies against the bright white like a negative image of a starry night. Jim had studied that tableau for years, but somehow never got round to cleaning out the hanging graveyard.

"Pam Strich?" Gus said finally. "She's the only one I told."

Jim nodded.

"I told her in confidence. Is that the kind of journalism ethics you teach around here?"

Jim was stung by the rebuke. He had an urge to fire back at the old man sitting in judgment of him. But then he remembered Molly and the gloom he felt since he'd learned the truth, and imagined how much worse it must be for Gus.

"I pried it out of her," he exaggerated, to protect Pam. "I am her boss after all. And what you're doing is fraud. Fraud against me, fraud against Molly's readers."

"Bullshit. Lots of advice columns aren't written by the person whose name is on the page. Abby hasn't written Dear Abby for years."

"All true, Gus. But this is different. Molly is well known and loved in this community. She's a local celebrity. People see her in town and love to talk to her. When they write in to 'Dear Molly,' they expect that they are corresponding with Molly herself."

"Well," said Gus. "Molly can't correspond with them anymore. Do you want to kill the column?"

Jim looked away. Then he looked up at the freckled light fixture. "No. I don't. 'Dear Molly' means too much to this community."

"And to the *Clarion*'s circulation," Gus added.

Again Jim took offense, this time at the suggestion that he was interested in Molly only for the circulation revenue she was worth. Well, it was partially true, if he was honest with himself, but he also loved Molly, who was like a kindly aunt to him, the kindly aunt he never had and could have used all those years growing up with his icy, indifferent mother. Divorced now for seventeen years—going into rehab and sobering up was too little too late to save his marriage—Jim Tomlinson felt essentially alone in the world, his parents slowly shrinking like raisins far away in the Florida sun, his only sibling estranged out in California, his daughter alienated from him and living somewhere in the Twin Cities suburbs, a distance of a few hours that might as well have been light years, *The Newfield Clarion* his only family, to which he clung like a man on a chunk of flotsam from the shipwreck of his life.

"What do you want to do?" Gus asked, breaking into Jim's thoughts.

"I don't know. Maybe nothing right now. Keep doing the column. This is all going to come out eventually. I need time to figure things out. Meantime, I'll make sure Pam keeps her mouth shut."

"Who else has she told?"

Jim debated with himself about answering that question. He had a notion of "who else" that might be. But that was supposed to be a secret, too, although fast becoming the worst-kept secret in Newfield. Pam was romantically involved with Cindy Smith. If she told Cindy, the Grand Central Station of all gossip trains in town, then it was all over. Their relationship was already giving him acid reflux. If Cindy made good on her threat to run for mayor again, Pam would not be allowed to cover the campaign. And he couldn't afford to hire another reporter just to cover town politics. Pam would have to choose between her job and her girlfriend.

"Nobody I can think of."

Gus stood and reached for his rain slicker on the coat rack. "Next column. Tuesday, right?"

"Right," said Jim. "Tuesday."

Elvis pulled his Browning twelve-gauge from behind the seat of his Toyota pickup, crooked it under his armpit, and turned to his assembled troops. "Let's review the safety rules, okay?" There were ten of them gathered in the parking lot behind the old boarded up Pizza Hut outside of town, the red roof still squatting like an ugly hat. A few more farmer friends of Larsen had joined the original group and brought their deer rifles. Kugelman's nephew never returned after the first day, apparently seeing no point to a militia where he couldn't brandish his assault rifle. Today's mission would be their second foray into the field after several training sessions on Birdsong's wooded land north of town. The plan was to pile into four pickup trucks and meet at the old Dodd-Ford trestle bridge over the river, two coming from the north end and two from the south. Elvis's recon sortie that morning indicated the Blue Hogs were planning a party at the bridge. Perfect opportunity to have a man-to-man talk with them about what would and would not be tolerated by the good citizens of Newfield. The guns would be there as protection for a group of old men who might provide a tempting target for biker gang threats and bullying tactics.

When they arrived, timing it perfectly at both ends, they swerved their vehicles sideways and parked bumpers to tailgates, blocking the narrow country road at each side of the bridge. Elvis's recon was correct. About a dozen motorcycles were parked on the bridge. All Harleys of various colors, festooned with glinting chrome and obscenity-laced stickers, such as: "Lock the Fucking Bitch Up." Their riders were not in sight, but when Elvis's crew gathered their guns and exited the trucks, they could hear country music blaring from down below and got a whiff of the unmistakable aroma of marijuana. Elvis strode to the bridge and looked over the side down onto the riverbed. On the wide sandy beach littered by dozens of empty Coors Light cans, several heavyset men in leather vests gathered in a circle around a bearded fat man, who was holding a can high in the air and singing along with the music emanating from a portable speaker. His impressive operatic tenor lent a patina of gravitas to the banal lyrics about trucks and dogs and beer and heartbreak.

"That would be Freddie," said Miguel as he sidled up next to Elvis.

"The one and only," said Elvis.

Now all ten of Birdsong's Brigade, so dubbed by Pam Strich in her only slightly condescending *Clarion* article, stood along the guardrail, guns propped under the arms, barrels pointing down toward the sandy beach. It must have been an alarming sight to those gathered below. One of them pointed up at the bridge. Freddie stopped singing. Somebody switched off the music. A few others pulled handguns out of the backs of their blue jeans.

"What the fuck!" hollered Freddie. He and his mates started to run toward the path leading up from the riverbed to the road.

"We're only here to talk!" Elvis yelled down to them.

Twelve Blue Hogs quickly reached the road and approached the bridge. At least four were brandishing large handguns. The two groups of men, guns drawn, faced each other on the bridge as if planning a Civil War reenactment.

"You got a funny way of talking, Elvis," said Freddie. "What's with all the guns? You old farts a hunting party? Deer season don't start till next month. You hunting pheasant?"

"We're hunting drug dealers," said Harry Kugelman.

Elvis gave him a sharp look. The last thing he wanted at this particular moment was provocative language. The tension hung in the air like summer humidity. Elvis sensed this was a crucial moment that could go very badly if someone said or did something that set just one person off.

"Well, you come to the wrong place," said Freddie. "We're smoking some weed, alright, but we ain't selling any, so I guess you'll have to keep moving along if you want to hunt drug dealers."

"Actually," said Elvis, "we've only come to talk to you fellows. We aren't the police, so we're not looking to arrest anybody. Just talk."

"So, talk," said a tall bald fellow standing behind Freddie

with the butt of a big black gun sticking out of his trousers.

"We know you've been providing alcohol to minors. We know you've been selling them marijuana and pills, too. And we want it to stop. You fellows need to find some other activities to do around here or find some other county."

"Are you telling us to get out of town or else? Or else what?" said Freddie.

"No threats. Just talk."

"Why bring a bunch of guns if you just want to talk?"

"We knew you'd be armed. And likely see us as old men you can bully. The guns are just for our own protection. So let's all just settle down."

"Good idea," said Freddie. "Why don't you all move along and let us finish our party. We ain't hurtin' nobody. And it's my birthday." A smile briefly passed through his perpetual puzzled scowl, then it was gone.

The two groups faced each other in silence as if waiting for the one of them to blink first. "That's some voice you've got there, Freddie," said John Berg. "You should sing professional." Berg's attempt at *rapprochement* did nothing to ease the tension that still hung over the old bridge.

The thick silence was suddenly broken by the metallic burp sound of a police car warning. The twenty-two men turned their attention to the road coming from the north where the county sheriff's black-and-white SUV pulled up and parked. Deputy Sheriff Joe Morton stepped out and approached the standoff on the bridge. "What the hell is going on here?" he bellowed.

"Well, howdy Deputy Morton," said Freddie. "What a coinkydink you being here, too." He looked accusingly at Elvis. Elvis shrugged.

"Start talking," said Morton.

"We was having a party at the river, and these gents here decided they wanted to join us," said Freddie. "So we was just having a little discussion about it. That's all."

"First thing, everybody put those guns away. It looks like you all are getting ready to go to war."

Elvis's crew hesitated, then he nodded to them. They carried their guns back to the trucks and placed them inside. The Blue Hogs who were armed put their handguns in compartments attached to the Harleys. The men reassembled in a circle around Morton. "Now, what's this all about?" he said.

"We were just having a conversation with these fellows about drugs and alcohol and teenagers and what sorts of things we won't tolerate in this community," said Elvis.

Morton walked over to Elvis and stood in front of him, their faces only inches apart. "I thought I warned you about citizen vigilante activities."

"Citizen vigilantes?" said Freddie. "Is that what these geezers are?" The Hogs laughed in unison as if on cue.

"Go on home, Elvis," said Morton. "All of you, get back in your trucks and go home. I will have a talk with these gentlemen about public alcohol consumption and illegal drugs."

And that was the end of the Birdsong Brigade's first battlefield action. As Elvis drove his pickup home, he hoped the Hogs had got the message loud and clear and there would be no need for future confrontations. But he doubted it.

Rosalita Greenfield sat at the kitchen table, a homemade cappuccino in front of her, while Jill White busied herself at the counter with her gleaming brass espresso machine, an Italian jukebox spinning out variations on a theme of java, filling the room with its bitter aroma. Rosie took a sip, delicious, and wiped a dot of foam from the tip of her nose. Every time she visited the Whites, she was filled with envy by Jill's magnificent kitchen, matching black imported appliances and black granite counters, white cabinetry, black-and-white checkerboard tile floor. Not that her own kitchen was so bad, it just needed an update fifteen years after the last remodel. But getting Chester to spend money on the house was like getting him to quit taking those pills, a frustrating and ultimately futile quest. She also was filled with envy by the sight of Jill White herself, an imposing figure, mayor of Newfield, with an exquisite wardrobe, and amazingly hot for a woman of near fifty. Something about that silver hair, which Jill had colored when she started to go gray at age forty, emanated an aura around her like a halo. Rosie was five years younger and taller and slimmer, but still felt intimidated by Jill's charismatic blend of power and sexiness.

"How's that cappuccino?" Jill said without turning around, breaking Rosie's reverie. She realized she had been admiring Jill's butt protruding from her tight skirt and wondering if Jill worked out and how to get curves like that.

"Delicious," she said.

"How does Cassie like Tampa?" Jill said as she steamed the milk.

"Fine, I guess. It's like pulling teeth to get information from her. It's like she couldn't get away from me fast enough." Jill said nothing, not having experienced the joys and heartaches of parenthood. Rosie remembered what it was like to be eighteen. Unlike Cassie, who could flee to college in Tampa and the warm embrace of her Aunt Juanita, Rosie had had little choice but to flee her father's violence by marrying Chester.

Jill sat across from her at the table with her own drink. "Were you staring at my ass?"

Rosie almost spit out her coffee and felt her face flush. "You have a great ass," she said after recovering her composure. "How do you do it?"

"Genetics," said Jill. "You should have seen my mother. Before the cancer. Big boobs, big butt. But also, I work out a lot,

StairMaster usually. I've got to keep up with the younger girls. I'm married to a horn dog, as you know."

Rosie knew. And Jill knew that Rosie knew. Jill had always known about Rosie's on-and-off affair with her husband and had long ago decided to accept it. She once told Rosie that she liked her, like a sister, and didn't mind Jack's cheating, as long as it was only with Rosie. A side benefit for Jill, she said, was that Jack didn't force himself on her as much when he was screwing Rosie. The man's libido was off the charts, and way beyond what Jill was comfortable with.

"Let's talk about something else, shall we?" said Rosie.

"You mean like your husband's pathetic schemes to bilk money out of everyone in town?"

"Yeah. That."

"It's not going to work."

"How bad is it?"

"You don't know?"

"I try to stay out of Chester's business dealings. Maybe that's a mistake." Rosie began to understand the vague feeling of unease that had been percolating beneath her oblivious façade of affluent farm wife.

"He's about four million dollars in debt, for starters."

Rosie wasn't sure she heard right. Four million? She took another sip of coffee to disguise her shock and embarrassment. "Wow. I didn't know."

"Now you do."

"Chester always says you need leverage to make any real money," said Rosie. "He calls it the principle of OPM—other people's money."

"He's right, but only if you use it to earn enough profit to pay it back and have some left over for yourself. Chester's investments apparently aren't earning enough. He asked for my help as mayor. Several times. Some crazy bullshit about tax swaps and land rezonings. Then he went to my husband to ask for a million-dollar cash infusion."

Rosie studied the foam pattern on the surface of her cappuccino, trying to auger some meaning from it, trying to wrap her brain around the notion that after more than twenty years of marriage she might be hitched not to the richest man in the county but to a bankrupt poser. It felt as if a gilded cage had suddenly cracked open, leaving her exposed to her worst fear, a return to the humiliation and grinding poverty of her childhood, a life of trailer parks and food stamps and alcoholism and violence, from which she had been rescued by Chester Greenfield's family fortune.

Jill gently placed her hand on Rosie's. "I'm sorry to be the one to break it to you," she said. "Maybe he can leverage his connections to the Trump campaign? The president isn't shy about doing favors for his friends."

The name Trump was enough to give Rosie heartburn. She loathed the man, with his sneering New York accent and bully-boy rich kid act. She loathed the fact that her husband was enraptured by the man. Chester had his own sneering bully streak, which she thought was cool when she was nineteen. Now it was obvious that in Trump, Chester saw who he wanted to be. The thought of that evil toad being president was enough to make her vote for Hillary Clinton, which she lied about to her husband. And she knew better than to bring it up with Jill. "I don't know about that," she said. "He's been complaining lately that he's getting the brush off. But he's got this crazy idea about organizing a big motorcycle rally, like the one in Sturgis, to raise money for the Trump campaign, as if they need more money. He's even talking to lowlifes like Freddie Ignatowski to help round up motorcycle clubs from all over the state."

"What could possibly go wrong?" Jill said with a raised eyebrow.

"I know, right? But he seems desperate to make this thing happen."

"I think I know why," said Jill. She rubbed her thumb and index finger together.

Rosie picked up the hint, as the thought had crossed her mind, too.

Dear Molly,

I've done something stupid and embarrassing, and now it seems I am paying the price. I'm a middle-aged married man and I like to play around on the internet when I'm bored, which is often. My wife doesn't seem to notice or care. She's so wrapped up in her scrapbooking she barely knows when I'm in the house. Not long ago I started chatting with someone online, and it grew into a rather intense and steamy correspondence. The catch is, I was posing as a teenage girl named Alison, just for fun, and it seems that I hooked an older man named Stanley. Long story short, he started pressing me to meet in person, as we live in the same county. I resisted at first, but curiosity got the better of me, and I wanted to see what kind of guy trolls for teenage girls online. We agreed to meet at a popular cafe. Stanley said he'd be sitting outside and wearing a yellow sweater and tan fedora. I parked a few blocks away and observed from across the street to see if this guy looked the type to beat the tar out of me when he saw how I'd fooled him. There, sitting alone at a table outside, in a yellow sweater and tan fedora, was a teenage girl. I approached her, and after we got over the shock, we had a good laugh at how we'd both been fooled. She invited me to sit. We had a nice chat, then we parted, embarrassed but amused with ourselves. Then things got weird. I

didn't realize it at the time, but she followed me home in her car. And somehow she'd got hold of my phone when I was distracted. You can guess what comes next. This girl has been stalking me for weeks. Following me in her car. Calling and texting me. Sending nude pics of herself. I think she may be crazy. So far, I've been able to keep this nightmare from my wife. Should I call the police? Then I would have to confess to my wife what I've been doing online. Should I confront this girl? What would you do Molly?
Signed,
Catfish

Dear Catfish,
First, I want to thank you for sharing your story. When I stopped laughing, I felt only pity and contempt for you. I see by your signature that you are aware of the internet scam called "catfishing," using a fake identity to lure someone into an online relationship. In this case, it seems you thought you were the cat, but it turned out you were the fish! Oh, the irony. Too good.

We get more than a few inquiries here at Mollyville World Headquarters that strain credulity and are likely made up. Your pathetic tale seems too richly ironic to be legit. But I'll give you the benefit of the doubt and assume you are telling the truth.

If so, all I can say is you deserve every bit of the discomfort and embarrassment this episode has brought you. What were you trying to do by posing as "Alison?" Make a fool of some poor soul? The fact that you ended up the fool suggests that there is cosmic justice in this world. People are fed up with all the faking and lying and scamming that, sadly, seem to be the norm these days, everywhere from the internet to the nation's capital.

My advice? Go tell your wife straight away what a putz you are. Get it over with. Next, save all those texts and call records and go to the police. The girl seems unbalanced and could be dangerous. It doesn't sound like she's made any threats or broken any laws, but a good talking to from a police officer likely will scare her away.

Meantime, Mr. Caughtfish, you might seek help for that internet addiction of yours. Find another hobby, like, I don't know, maybe scrapbooking?

Hugs,

Molly

Oct. 21, 9:55 am

James Tomlinson <jtomlinson@newfieldclarion.com>
To: Molly Peterson <dearmolly@newfieldclarion.com>
Re: This week's column

Holy crap, Gus. What's gotten into you? This doesn't sound like Molly at all. It's way too snide and mocking. How are we going to keep up this charade if you go off the rails? You sound like some snotty East Coast arts critic. Molly's fans will smell you out in a New York minute. This Catfish guy may be a putz (putz? Who says putz around here?), but jeez, show a little compassion for his predicament.

Do you seriously want me to print this? If we get complaints and demands for an explanation, I'm not going to lie. I will put an end to this farce. I know you want to protect Molly's privacy but blowing the column sky-high just to make an example out of one random putz seems an odd way to go about it.—JT

p.s. Okay to keep emailing you at Molly's address? What if she sees this? Should we use your email?

Molly Peterson <dearmolly@newfieldclarion.com>
To: James Tomlinson <jtomlinson@newfieldclarion.com>
Re: This week's column
Print it. I'm serious. This Catfish guy is disgusting. I, and the rest of what remains of civilization, have had it up to here with liars, fakes, and scammers. I guarantee that most of Molly's readers will stand up and cheer at the takedown of this phony. If anyone doubts that it's the voice of Molly, tell them she's decided after many years to stop being so damn polite and tell it like it is. Let's see what happens, okay? And don't worry about Molly's email account. She's not even using the computer anymore.
Gus

James Tomlinson <jtomlinson@newfieldclarion.com>
To: Molly Peterson <dearmolly@newfieldclarion.com>
Re: This week's column
Okay, fine. But I don't see how pulling a scam like this fake column is going to win any friends if they have "had it up to here with liars, fakes, and scammers." I will leave it to you to explain it all to our readers.—JT

James Tomlinson <jtomlinson@newfieldclarion.com>
To: Molly Peterson <dearmolly@newfieldclarion.com>
Re: This week's column
The deed is done, God help me. The column is now live on the website and will be in the paper tomorrow. Already I'm getting blowback from Mollyworld. A dozen emails already. Her fans are

upset and asking what the hell's gotten into Molly. It's a good thing we don't allow comments on her online column. What do you think we should do? Come clean right away? Or obfuscate, buy time? I want to protect Molly, too, but I don't think we can much longer.—JT

     p.s.—There were a handful of emails congratulating Molly for telling it like it is, but not many.

Oct. 22, 10:12 am

Molly Peterson <dearmolly@newfieldclarion.com>
To: James Tomlinson <jtomlinson@newfieldclarion.com>
Re: This week's column
If a few folks liked the column, that's a good sign. I bet there are a lot more readers out there who agree. Let's give the rest of them a little more time to get used to the "new Molly" before we pull the curtain up, okay?

     Gus

Cindy pulled the beer bottles out of the cooler the minute she heard the familiar rumble of the perpetually faulty exhaust pipe of Harry Kugelman's GMC pickup. If Kugelman was arriving, Berg, Larsen, and Peterson couldn't be far behind.

She was right, as usual, although Peterson was not with them. The threesome took their assigned places at the bar. John Berg gave Cindy a thumbs up when she switched the audio channel from some insipid country pop tune to Waylon Jennings and "Luckenbach, Texas." The men immediately launched into a post-game analysis of the Vikings' latest win, lifting hopes for another playoff run.

"Where's Gus?" Cindy asked as she uncapped the beers and passed them around.

"Said he had to drop by the newspaper office. Might stop in after," said Berg.

"Speak of the newspaper, did you guys read Molly's latest column?" said Kugelman, gesturing dramatically with his beer bottle as if it were a stage prop. "It's a riot. Some guy writes in and says he's been hooking up on the internet using a fake name without telling his wife, and he met up with a teenage girl who started stalking him. Molly tore him a new asshole. You gotta read it."

"Something's gotten into that Molly," said Berg. "She used to be so kind in her answers and now she's being downright rude to people."

"Gus told me she's been getting ornery," said Larsen. "She even punched him in the nose once. Bloodied him good."

"I heard about that," said Cindy, hoping to de-escalate the speculations. "Gus thinks he deserved it because he snuck up from behind and surprised her. She thought she was being assaulted."

"I don't know. There's something strange going on there," said Berg. "I haven't seen her in town in months. She's turned into Attila the Hun in her column. We should ask Gus about it when he gets here."

Cindy ached for Gus, knowing he was carrying around a painful secret, so hard to do in such a small town. She recalled fondly her life in Brooklyn, where you could disappear into the crowds so easily. Pam had told her the truth about Molly, justifying the breach by claiming it was bound to come out anyway. If Gus came into the bar today, he would be interrogated by his best friends and put in the position of either lying to them or revealing Molly's secret. How much better it would be if he was greeted not by an inquisition but by sympathetic friends ready to rally around him.

"You're right, fellas," she said. "There is something going on there."

The three men halted their beers in mid lift and turned to Cindy.

"This is supposed to be a secret, but honestly, it can't go on. It's going to come out sooner or later in this gossipy little town, probably sooner." Cindy was not unaware of the irony of her referring to Newfield as a "gossipy little town" when she in fact was the main conduit.

"You have our complete attention," said Berg.

Cindy looked around the bar to see if anyone else was within earshot. Two younger guys were playing, badly it appeared, at the electronic dartboard. She leaned into the bar to get closer. "The reason Dear Molly seems different is that she's not writing the column anymore. The truth is, she has Alzheimer's. Pretty bad. Gus has been trying to keep it secret. To protect her dignity."

"Oh, man," said Berg.

"Ouch," added Kugelman.

"Poor Gus," said Larsen.

"Poor *Molly*," Cindy corrected. "She's declined far and fast in the last couple months. Some days she doesn't even know who Gus is. She thinks her son is still alive. It's so damn sad." She sniffled and wiped a tear from one eye.

"I can't believe it. Molly. So sweet," said Larsen.

The four of them were silent for a long moment.

"So, who's writing the column?" said Berg.

"Gus."

"Gus?" the three said in unison.

As if on cue, the man himself walked through the squeaky front door. He approached his three pals at the bar and started to climb onto his stool. He stopped and looked at their faces. "What?" he said. "Who died?"

The men climbed off their stools and stood around him. Berg laid a hand on Gus's shoulder. "We know, Gus," he said. "We know about Molly."

"I'm real sorry, Gus," said Larsen.

"What can I do? Anything. You name it," said Kugelman.

Gus looked past them at Cindy, who had tears streaming down her face. "Pam told you?" he said.

"I'm sorry, Gus," she said, nodding and sniffling. "I had to tell them. These guys are your best friends. The whole town is getting suspicious. The column is so different now, and Molly is never around anymore. You can't keep this a secret. You should let your friends rally around you. You're going to need them."

"You had no right, Cindy." Gus glared at her. "This was my call. My decision where and when to break the news." The anger on his face was belied by the tremor in his voice, as if he might cry.

"You're being selfish," she said, wiping her cheek with the back of her hand. "Everyone in town loves Molly. They will want to reach out and help. But you've built this wall around you and her. Let them help."

Gus sat on his stool, and the others took to theirs. He leaned over and laid his head on his hands. Kugelman put an arm around his shoulder.

"I'm buying," said Larsen. "The usual for Gus, Cindy. On my tab."

Cindy put a cold, wet bottle of Grain Belt Premium in front of Gus. "And that column," she said, addressing the top of his head. "It's not right. You and Jim are deceiving people. Thousands of Molly's readers. They think Molly is answering their letters. You owe it to them to tell the truth."

Gus lifted his head off the bar and took a long pull on the bottle. He looked at Cindy and held her gaze for several seconds. She could almost see the gears turning. She was right, and he knew it.

To Our Readers

Many of you fans of Dear Molly have asked why the column seems to have changed its tone recently. Here's why: For the last few weeks, Molly has had to step aside temporarily to deal with some health issues. Her husband Gus Peterson has been pinch-hitting—an apt term for the longtime Newfield baseball coach. Many of you know Gus as one of the most upstanding members of our community, a decorated Vietnam War veteran and beloved high school teacher and coach. Gus has been proofreading Molly's column for years and knows her style and her philosophy better than anyone, so we at The Newfield Clarion feel the column is in good hands. If you have noticed a sterner tone in the column recently, that reflects Molly's increasing impatience with people's bad behavior and lack of common decency, a view firmly endorsed by Gus. So please keep Molly in your thoughts as we all look forward to her return as soon as possible. Meantime, buckle up and enjoy the ride!

James Tomlinson, Editor and Publisher

November

Chester knew he was in trouble the minute he walked in the front door of the house, priapic and full of amorous intent, Rosalita cold as a repo man's heart. He could feel the chill in the house even before he saw her. He'd seen this version of Rosie before, and it filled him with anxiety. She was standing in the hallway, arms folded across her chest, as if she'd been waiting for him, then turned and strode toward the kitchen without saying a word.

"Hey," he said weakly. He pulled out his vial of pills and popped two in his mouth. If Rosie was as pissed off as she seemed, he might need two more right soon. The thought of losing her, never far from mind, surged anew. Were there enough pills in the world to dampen this panic? Something was obviously bothering her. The Halloween decorations were still up, unusual for Rosie, who was always a stickler for such things. He retreated to the TV room and poured himself a bourbon, neat. The college football wrap-up show took his mind off the sword dangling over his neck. No Gophers game this week. Penn State next week.

When Rosie called him to dinner, she slammed his plate of lasagna in front of him and sat opposite at the big rustic table she'd built herself with reclaimed antique factory flooring from Red Wing.

"Are we broke?" she said without preamble.

Oh, shit. "What?" he said, stalling for time to gather his thoughts.

"Tell me the truth," she said. "How bad is it?"

"We are not broke, Rosalita. Maybe a little bit overleveraged. But we're in positive net-worth territory. Nothing to worry about." He said it but wasn't sure he believed it.

"How much leverage?" she said, putting scare quotes around the word.

"A million or so," he said. He got up from the table and returned with his whiskey glass refilled.

"I heard it's four million."

"Heard from who? Who you been talking to?"

"Doesn't matter. Is it true? Do you—do we—owe four million?"

"Fucking Jack White told you, am I right?"

Rosie shook her head, as if weary of this line of inquiry.

"Jill, then. That's it, right? That bitch told you."

"Jill White happens to be a friend of mine, one of the few friends I have in this hick town."

A friend whose husband you screwed. He thought it but didn't say it.

"Jill White will stick a knife in your ribs in a split second if it serves her interests," he said.

"You still haven't answered my question. How much 'leverage?'"

"Okay, it's somewhere around four. I don't know exactly. But it's nothing to worry about. I got everything under control. Don't I always? The value of our farm holdings and other assets are way more than four million. So, you see, we're not under water."

"So that means if you can't pay back the loans, you'd have to start selling off the farm? Is that it?"

"It's not going to come to that. Trust me, Honey." He studied her face to see if she was buying his lies. No sale, it seemed.

"This farm is not ours to sell off, is it? It's the corporation's. So you could only sell off our share. Right? And where would that leave us? And Cassie? Trusting you to handle our money was a mistake. I am such a fool."

Chester let that sentiment hang in the air like a fart, unacknowledged. Best not to agree or disagree at this juncture.

Rosie studied the congealing mozzarella on her plate, as if trying to discern some meaning from it. After a long, smoldering silence, she looked up, her face morphed from bitter anger into calculating curiosity. "What did Jack say when you asked him for money?"

Chester felt a surge of relief that Rosie seemed to have moved on. "He said he'd think about it. Which means no."

"What about Jill?"

"I figured she could help me with the property taxes and zoning. She owes me. She wouldn't be in that chair if it wasn't for my fundraisers and the help I got her from the state party. She basically threw me out of her office. The ungrateful cunt."

"Don't ever use that word around me again."

Oops. Here comes the rage machine.

"Even if it's true in her case."

Bullet dodged. This was interesting. Rosie and Jill had always seemed close, despite the infidelities. "I thought you two were friends."

"Frenemies, maybe. She gets on my nerves. Always looking down on me, like her little sidekick, her little servant girl."

"Seems like she forgave you for screwing her husband. More than I did, for sure." That one hit home, he could tell by the look on her face. It was a topic rarely raised in their house, but it always landed like a slap.

"She holds it over me. Like she's morally superior." Rosie's defense was to turn the conversation back on Jill.

Chester raised an eyebrow at her and almost said something unkind but thought better of it.

"Is there some other way we can get some money out of them?" she said.

Now we're getting somewhere.

Through the clear glass bottom of the Miller High Life bottle as he raised it to his lips to drain the last foamy drops, Travis Birdsong could make out a bright orange glow moving toward him. He dropped the empty bottle in the sand, and there was Julio Cervantes holding a burning joint out for him. He shook his head and Julio shrugged and passed the joint back to Jimmy Oster.

They were deep in the woods, alongside the river far from the usual party spots. Fat bald men in leather vests bellowed to country music blaring from a motorcycle's amped up stereo speakers. Travis asked if he could have another beer. "One more," said Freddie. Travis opened the Yeti cooler and pulled out another, twisted off the cap and took a long swig, nearly chugging the whole bottle. "Slow down there, Kemosabe. Don't get shitfaced, I ain't givin' you a ride home," said Freddie. Travis ignored the insulting nickname. He'd heard such slurs, intentional and unintentional, so often that they blended into the background noise of life in rural Minnesota along with country music and Twins and Vikings games on the radio. "Anyways, you got to get yourself back in shape and get your ass back out on the football field. The Reapers need you bad. You know, we haven't won the league since—"

"Yeah, I know. Since 1989. And you were the star of the team."

"I did my part," said Freddie with false humility. Any second now would come the story of how Freddie sacked the Blue Earth quarterback on the final play to clinch the title game. Someone turned up the music and a cluster of Blue Hogs farther down the river beach started drunkenly singing along with Luke Combs to "Beer Never Broke My Heart."

"Liquor ain't good for you Indians," said Oster, changing the subject, much to Travis's relief. "You should stick to weed. The Indians taught the White man how to smoke, after all."

"Can't smoke no more," said Travis. "Got to pass a drug test before I can get reinstated."

"How about you, Quixote?" said Oster. Travis knew Julio hated the nickname, just as he hated being asked if his father Miguel was the guy who wrote that novel. "How come you're smokin' weed? Ain't you on the soccer team?"

"Shhh," said Julio and put his finger to his lips.

"He ain't been caught yet," said Freddie. "Unlike shit-for-brains here." Travis chose to ignore the dig. His own grandfather had called him the same thing when he got busted and suspended from school.

"So, when can we join up with you guys, for real?" asked Julio.

"When you going to have your own motorcycles?" said Freddie.

Over my grandparents' dead bodies, thought Travis. He glanced over at Julio. His mother would never allow it, either, but Miguel might. There wasn't much Miguel would deny his only boy. Just as there wasn't much Maria Elena would deny his sisters Mirabel and Dulcinea.

"You mean you would let us join if we had our own bikes?" said Julio.

"I didn't say that," said Freddie. "That's the minimum requirement. It takes a whole lot more if you want to be a Hog."

"Can you even ride one of them things?" said Oster, gesturing at his own silver Harley with the black saddlebags and high handlebars.

"Sure…," said Travis, unconvincingly.

"Bullshit," said Freddie. "Maybe it's time you learned."

"Anytime," said Travis, not sure he meant it.

"I mean right now."

All the Hogs were staring at him. He couldn't back down now. They'd never accept him if he looked chicken.

Freddie led him over to his big black Harley parked on the side of the road. It looked enormous, like a low-slung spaceship. "You can ride a bicycle, right?"

"Of course," said Travis, trying not to let his voice tremble.

"Same thing, mostly." Freddie coached him through some basics, had him sit in the extra-large saddle with both feet on the ground, kick stand up, and showed him where the controls are. "It's the opposite of driving a car," he said. "You shift gears with your foot, you work the clutch and gas with your hands, and you brake with foot or hands, depending."

With one foot on the ground, Travis started the engine. It was much louder than he expected, and the vibration rumbled upward from his seat to the top of his head. He let out the clutch, pulled back on the accelerator grip, and the bike took off so fast he almost fell off the back. At thirty yards down the road he was already rocketing along. He panicked and hit the brakes, both front and back, and the bike shuddered and skidded out of control. It came to a screeching stop, the tires blackening the gray asphalt, and fell over, pinning Travis underneath. The engine had killed, and he could hear uproarious laughter behind him. He tried to pull himself out from under the bike, but his leg was stuck. Freddie ran alongside and pulled the Harley off him like it was a mere bicycle. "You okay? Anything feel like it's busted?" he asked calmly. "We don't want no broken bones on our star running back."

Travis pulled himself up and took a few steps. His jeans were shredded on one side, but he didn't feel any serious pain. "I'm alright," he said. "Embarrassed maybe."

Julio sidled up and regarded him with hands on hips. "You a crazy mo-fo," he said. He wasn't smiling, and Travis couldn't tell how he meant it.

"S'okay, buddy. You passed the first test," said Freddie. "Having the balls to get on a Harley with everyone watching." The laughter had died down and the rest of the Hogs gathered around and slapped him on the back and offered him beers. "That's enough riding my bike," said Freddie. "You done scratched the paint job. Lucky for me I own a body shop. You best get your own bike and practice in a parking lot. You, too, Quixote. Then maybe we'll see about makin' you Hogs someday."

"I thought the Blue Hogs was only for White people," said Travis.

"We're lookin' to diversify. Expand our base. A big tent and all that." Freddie sounded as if he'd been listening to politicians like Jill White.

"Then why do you all come into my grandma's café and call her Pocahontas?" said Travis as they walked back to the river.

"We don't mean nothin' by it," said Oster, passing the joint back to Julio.

"My grandma doesn't think so."

"We're just having a little fun. You know we like Mavis. Best eggs and bacon in the county."

"She says you mean it as an insult, and you copied it from Trump."

"He don't mean nothing by it, either. He's just teasing that lady senator. She's so damn serious, like a schoolteacher. He's just sayin,' 'Lighten up, Lizzie.'"

Freddie walked over to the nearest cottonwood tree, unzipped, and painted a dark, bell-shaped stain on its trunk. He zipped up and turned toward the gathering. "No, young Travis here is right. We got to stop calling her that. If she thinks it's disrespectful, then it's disrespectful. Anyway, none of us wants to piss off ol' Elvis."

Oster raised his beer bottle and said, "Baddest mother in town."

"How many confirmed kills did he have in Nam?" Freddie asked Travis. "Ten? A hundred?"

"I don't know. He doesn't like to talk about that."

"Must have been a lot. It's only the fakers and liars who like to talk about it." Freddie saluted with his bottle then drained it in one swig.

Travis regarded this scruffy mountain of a man, nearly as wide as he was tall, huge gut overhanging the big Harley belt buckle barely holding up his greasy jeans. He's not such a bad guy, Travis thought. Maybe grandma's got him all wrong.

The music switched to Blake Shelton's "God's Country" and the Hogs joined in again, slurring the words even more this time.

Travis looked to Julio and said, "We should get going. You coming with?" He pantomimed manipulating an Xbox controller. "Call of Duty, or Halo?"

Julio exhaled smoke, shook his head, and passed the joint back to Oster. Travis stared at him for a moment, but Julio wouldn't make eye contact, so he strolled over to his rusty trusty Honda Civic parked by the roadside and drove away.

Dear Molly,

My father is turning 87 and still lives in the same house he has owned for 60 years. The same house I and my siblings grew up in. He's a widower and we've given up trying to talk him into assisted living. He won't budge, and we're all tired of the discussion. He's still semi-sharp, but needs help with shopping and meals and appointments, etc, as he doesn't drive anymore. One of my siblings, my youngest brother, has taken it upon himself to move in with Dad and take care of him. Good for him, right? In exchange he gets free room and board and the use of Dad's car (he doesn't have one of his own), which he relies on to get to his favorite tavern in town to slam down Jägermeister shots every afternoon from 2:00 to 5:00, after which he usually returns in time to make supper, three sheets to the wind as the sailors say. Sometimes the leftovers get put away and the dishes done. Sometimes not. Every time one of us siblings makes a critical remark about the neglected condition of the household, he dares any one of us to take his place. None of us are in a position to do so and he knows it. Anyway, his dare is a bluff. He has nowhere else to go. All this by itself would be bad but tolerable. However, there is the matter of his children, Dad's grandchildren, which my brother begat from his many girlfriends. I would call them trailer trash, but that would be unfair to the denizens of America's manufactured housing. Parasites. Tattooed drug addicts. Criminals. They have formed a steady parade of couch surfers and freeloaders streaming through my Dad's home, stealing from him, turning his basement into a drug den. The last straw was the bedbug infestation brought in by these lowlifes. We had to throw out most of the furniture and fumigate the whole house.

We're at a loss what to do. Call the cops? Evict my brother from the house? Force Dad to move into assisted living?

Signed,

Rope's End

Dear Rope's End,

Yes. Yes. And yes.

Any more dumb questions?

Hugs,

Molly

"We should have called first," said Maria Elena. She was balancing on the crook of her arm a cardboard box full of homemade lemon tarts, cherry danishes, and a cinnamon apple pie. They were still warm and smelled sweet.

Her husband Miguel stood beside her and pressed the doorbell a third time. "He would have said don't come. You know how proud and stubborn Gus is."

"Maybe they're not home," she said, shifting the box to her other arm. She almost hoped it was true, even though she'd spent hours preparing the pastries. She could always sell them to Mavis.

"His car is right there, by the barn. Molly's truck, too," said Miguel.

"I feel awkward, just showing up like this. What if Molly is…you know… not at her best?"

"You had the right idea, M'lena," Miguel reassured her. "When people are having hard times, it's better to just show up with food or support. Don't make them ask for things. They're having a hard enough time." He reached for the bell again, and the door opened before he could press the button. Gus peeked out from a six-inch crack of an opening. He had a tired and worried look on his face, and M'lena immediately regretted coming. Then he smiled, albeit weakly, and opened the door wide.

"Miggy. M'lena. How nice. What have you got there?"

"Just some fresh pastries. For you and Molly."

"Okay if we come in?" said Miggy.

"Is this a bad time? Sorry if we're intruding," said M'lena.

"No. No. Come in, come in," Gus said and stepped aside. He led them through the front entryway into the kitchen. M'lena glanced sideways into the living room but didn't see Molly. Asleep maybe? Dishes were piled in the sink and an odor of undone laundry hung in the air. She placed the box on the kitchen counter. "These are still warm. Fresh from the oven. You can reheat them if you want them later."

Gus opened the box. "Thank you, M'lena. These look wonderful."

There followed a brief silence in which Gus seemed to be struggling with what to say next. He closed the lid on the box. "Should I put these in the fridge?" he said.

"Yes, of course. Let me help."

"So," said Miguel. "How is she?" The question made her wince. So direct, so soon. She again hoped they weren't intruding.

"Oh, she has good days and bad days. Come into the living room and sit down."

Once seated on the couch with Gus in his leather chair, M'lena sensed that the moment for small talk had passed. "Can we see her? Or would we be disturbing her?"

"Last I looked, she was asleep in the barn. She likes it out there."

M'lena and Miguel traded looks of alarm and embarrassment.

"She's perfectly fine out there. At least until it starts getting cold. There is a heater, but I'd rather not use it. Don't want her burning down the barn."

"Maybe later," said Miguel, unconvincingly.

"Maybe. So," said Gus. "How's Julio? Staying out of trouble?"

M'lena glanced at Miguel, silently asking how honest they could be. She decided there was no point in being coy with Gus. They were prying into his life with Molly. Why hide the truth about Julio? He and Molly were among the few Anglos in town who treated her and her family with genuine warmth and respect, not just grudging tolerance. "We're worried about—"

"So far, so good," Miguel interrupted his wife. "You know how it is with teenagers. All kinds of temptations." By the look on Gus's face, M'lena could tell he didn't buy it, but was too polite to press the issue.

"Hello," said a soft voice. Standing in the doorway, having

apparently come in through the kitchen, was Molly. She wore an odd smile, forced, as if trying but failing to get a joke. Her gray hair was disheveled with stray bits of straw sticking out. Her flannel nightshirt bore a few drying splashes of mud. Her bare feet were grimy.

"Hey, Sugar," said Gus. "Look who's here."

"Oh," she said, and smiled broadly. She sat in her Shaker rocker and gently rocked.

"We were just talking about Julio," said Gus. "You remember Julio."

"Of course," Molly said. "Julio." She giggled, as when solving a particularly knotty crossword puzzle clue. Miguel and M'lena laughed along with her. M'lena tried to keep smiling as she recalled happier times with Molly, good-natured haggling over beans and squash at Mollywood, running into each other in town and going for ice cream.

Molly continued rocking and stared at them with that same odd smile frozen on her face. M'lena gazed into her eyes for a few moments. It was obvious and crushingly sad. Molly had no idea who they were.

Gus climbed into bed, fully clothed, hoping to drop off to sleep as soon as possible, with no nighttime preambles. He stared at the ceiling and tried to banish the events of the day from his mind. It didn't work. Molly was asleep in her rocking chair in the living room. He could hear her snoring from the bedroom. Lately she had taken to sleeping in odd locations around the house, and sometimes outside of the house, anywhere but with her husband. It was just as well, as the few times she'd shared their bed recently she woke not knowing who he was and started screaming and thrashing. Eventually, she would calm down and call him Kenny.

Molly had good days and bad days, just as Doc Mollenhoff predicted. Bad days and worse days, it now seemed to Gus. Today was one of the worse days. She didn't physically attack him this time. In any case, he'd learned how to better defend himself. He was almost seventy and scrawny, but still, Molly was no match for him. Yet he had no defense for her cruel accusations. Claims that he'd had lovers. Allegations of attempts to poison her, to collect non-existent insurance policies on her. Worst of all, charges that he was responsible for Augie's death. This from the woman who some days thought her son was still alive and prepared breakfasts and lunches for him. The placements she'd set on the kitchen table tore Gus apart every time.

In the morning, Gus rose and made coffee. Molly was still snoring in her rocker. He would make bacon and eggs when she woke up, which could be any minute, or at one in the afternoon. Best to leave sleeping logs lie. He took his mug of steaming black Folger's into the office to tackle next week's column. Now that word was out, in Jim Tomlinson's public disclosure, Gus felt liberated, free from the obligation to mimic Molly's voice and sensibility. The column was his now his platform for setting the world straight. There was much setting to be done. There were only a few new submissions to Dear Molly's email account, none of them interesting. He wandered over to the closet in search of old snail-mail letters that Molly had stashed in her archive to be combed through later. Later was now. The pile he retrieved from a shoebox was about six inches high, some of the letters going back months. These must have been the rejects. But why would she save them? He flipped through them and saw why so many had been set aside. Mostly recipes and household hints, from people clearly not getting the point of 'Dear Molly:' problem to solve, quandaries to untangle, dilemmas to unravel, moral crises to clarify. Toward the bottom of the stack he came across another inchoate hand-written rant, obviously from the same nutjob who had written before.

Dear Molly,

I've always read and respected your advice in the newspaper. You are the voice of wisdom in this unwise land. Which makes it all the more painful that you have decided to ignore me, just like everybody else in this cold, cruel town. I have been writing to you for months, and yet you refuse to even acknowledge my existence. Am I some kind of insect you can casually squash under your shoe? That's how it feels to be me. An insect squashed under the shoes of my fellow man. Can you understand what that's like? Am I asking so much? Only that you acknowledge me and address my concerns about the lack of common courtesy in this community. Please recognize me. I can't be responsible for my actions if this humiliation continues much longer.
Signed
Fed Up

Below that one was another one. Below that, still another. Then more. Five altogether. This dickwad had been harassing Molly for months. The same unspecified grievances against all of Newfield, apparently, although it was impossible to determine exactly where he—she?—was writing from. Here in town? Or Winnebago? Blue Earth? Amboy? The threats were vague, nothing actionable. No one named as targets. No specific actions promised. Just the same sense of resentment. And escalating frustration aimed at Molly for not responding.

Gus was filled with a disturbing mix of pity and contempt for this loser. And not a small amount of fear. Was this person serious? *"I can't be responsible for my actions?"* That sounded like someone with no sense of personal responsibility, no sense of social responsibility. This was exactly the kind of dysfunction that typified the current state of society. Screw it, he decided. It was time to respond. Maybe flush the bastard out. This called for the special handling that Molly had long ago established for sensitive letters: a blind response. He would submit his answer to the signee, but not the text of their letter. He placed his fingers on the computer keyboard and let it rip.

```
Dear Fed Up,
I understand your frustration with the lack of
civility and recognition of our fellow citizens'
contributions. A point for all of us to reflect
on.
But I have to be honest, your numerous letters
to 'Dear Molly' over the last several months
seem a bit unhinged. You have not specified any
particular affronts to your dignity or personhood,
just a general resentment that people don't
prostrate themselves at your feet in thanks.
Thanks for what? You don't say.
I have three simple words for you: Get. Over.
Yourself.
Life on this rock spinning around this star
doesn't owe you anything. You have to make your
own happiness, earn your own respect. Earn our
respect. Your whining sense of entitlement is
exactly what's wrong with American society
today. All rights, and no responsibilities.
Please seek help for your pathetic condition.
And stop writing to me.
Hugs,
Molly
```

Gus walked into the Bird Song Café and all conversation stopped. The only sound was Tammy Wynette on the jukebox twanging "Stand by Your Man" and the clatter of coffee cups replaced on the tabletops and flatware on dishes. Mavis Birdsong rushed out from behind the counter and hugged him. Nearly everyone in the café stood and applauded.

"What'd I do?" said Gus as Mavis released him.

"I'm so sorry about Molly," said Mavis. "It breaks my heart."

"Mine, too," he said, almost inaudibly.

"I think it's wonderful that you've taken over the column for her."

A short, bow-legged man Gus didn't recognize, a farmer by the look of his dusty boots, seed cap, and jeans, walked over and stuck out his hand. "Tell like it is, Mr. Peterson. Tough love, that's what people around here need."

A woman at a corner table shouted, "Tell Molly we love her and we're praying for her. And you keep up the good work!" He remembered her as Phyllis something, the beautician, from his history class maybe twenty years ago.

Mavis led him to his usual table. "Breakfast is on the house today, Gus. You're money's no good here." Before he could protest, she turned toward the grill. "Travis! Get this man a fresh pot of coffee!" The house special breakfast was huge: a platter of huevos rancheros with chorizo, potatoes, toast, tomato juice, and a mug of coffee that Travis kept refilling. Gus couldn't clear his plate, as the food had grown cold during the many interruptions from well-wishers who stopped by his table to give their regards to him and Molly.

He left the café feeling good about his life for the first time in months. Good enough, he felt on a beautiful fall day, that he could walk all the way across the town square to drop in on Jim Tomlinson at the *Clarion*. The maple trees that ringed the park perimeter and lined the diagonal pathways were past their peak fall colors, but they still bathed the square in soft amber and pale rose hues filtering the low-angled sun. A fresh layer of fallen leaves painted the grass like dabs of watercolor on a green canvas. They crunched under his feet as he wandered off the path and cut across the lawn to save steps. It was one of those perfect autumn days in Minnesota, blue sky, nearly sixty degrees, that made the looming months of ice seem far off, near enough to start thinking about winterizing but far enough not to fret about.

The *Clarion* office was lively with all six news employees in evidence, phones chirping, conversations in full swing. He was greeted warmly by Lexie the receptionist who waved him straight through to the editor's office. The other staffers smiled and called out to him. Tony Trecanelli the sportswriter stood up and snapped off a military salute. Pam smiled at him, too, but with a questioning look in her eyes as if seeking confirmation that he'd forgiven her. He had, and smiled back. Gus wasn't sure he liked all this attention. He'd got used to hiding behind a wall of secrecy designed to stave off the wagging tongues.

Tomlinson stood when Gus entered his office. He was beaming, not the usual sour look of the dour newsman. After both men sat, Tomlinson said, "Nobody likes to admit they're wrong, Gus, but I'm a big enough man to say I was wrong and you were right."

"How so?"

"Your Crabby Appleton version of 'Dear Molly' seems to have struck a chord around here. The complaints we were getting those first few weeks have fallen off, and now we're getting mostly positive reviews. Some people apparently missed my editor's note, and they think it's still Molly, but they are all in for the new Queen of Mean, as somebody dubbed her. The ones who know it's you are saying congratulations and good for you. Your taking over for Molly has really impressed some folks. Really, heartfelt good wishes. To both of you."

"Wow," said Gus. It warmed him to know he could share this cornucopia of affection with Molly this afternoon. It might raise her spirits, too. That is, if she remembers that she has an advice column and thousands of fans. He truly did not know which Molly would be waiting for him when he got home. He hoped Helen Larsen had stopped by to look in on Molly as promised.

"There's more," said Tomlinson. "Web traffic to 'Dear Molly' has gone up twenty-five percent this month over last. I'm getting inquiries from advertisers who want to buy sponsorship positions on the page. And believe it or not, in this digital dystopia of 2019, we're actually getting new print subscriptions. First time since … I can't remember."

"You think it's because of the column?"

"I know it is."

"Does that mean I get a raise?"

The smile fell from Tomlinson's face. Then he chuckled and nodded. "You don't miss a trick, do ya? Yeah, I think we can work something out."

Gus felt a momentary surge of guilt that he was negotiating for more money now that he was writing the column, while he had never pushed Molly to do the same. But, he reminded himself, the extra money would benefit Molly, too. Right? "You bet we can," he said. "You've been underpaying Molly for years. She was too nice to call you on it. I'm calling you on it."

"Okay, okay." Tomlinson held his hands up as if in surrender. "How about a ten percent bump?"

"That's a start," said Gus.

When Elvis wandered into the living room after clearing the breakfast dishes, Mavis took note of the page number and closed her book. She would bookmark it later, as soon as she found her missing strip of paper. Maybe under the couch. Things had been going missing for weeks, it seemed, like she was losing her grip on the household, on life itself.

"What's that you're reading?" he said.

"Louise Erdrich." She held up the book so he could see the cover. "*La Rose*. You should read it."

"Her books are kind of depressing, aren't they? All those poor drunk Indians freezing their asses off in North Dakota."

"You're just being ignorant. Nobody writes about Native people like Louise Erdrich."

"How about Sherman Alexie?"

"Not even close."

"Stephen Graham Jones?"

"If you like that sort of thing."

"Tommy Orange?"

"He wrote one book."

"I liked that one. I hope he writes another," he said. "Erdrich. She's Anishinaabe, right? Ojibwe."

"Yeah, Turtle Mountain Band. So?"

"Just sayin'."

"Just sayin' what? She's not one of us?"

Elvis said nothing, apparently finding himself lured into a rhetorical dark alley again, where Mavis awaited with a verbal blackjack. She enjoyed the mental image.

"Anyway," she said. "You should read this one. There's a good lesson in it for you."

"Yeah? What's that?"

"Right there on the first page. Some dumbass goes deer hunting near his own house and ends up shooting a neighbor's kid dead. That's what happens when dumbasses go wandering around town with guns." She tilted her head and stared at him, as she always did when driving home a point. He got it, she could tell by the way he shifted his feet and changed the subject.

"Are you happy for Travis?" he said.

"Of course. He's back in school. Back on the team. Let's hope it sticks this time."

"Coach says he's going to hold Travis out of the next game. Make him earn his way back into the starting lineup with a week or two of practice."

"He's their best player."

"Not at the moment he isn't. Coach Phillips knows what he's doing."

"If you say so."

"If you say so" was Mavis's way of saying, "You're wrong but I'm not going to argue you out of it, I'm going to let you stay wrong." Elvis was well trained to not to press the issue.

"What about his idea of getting another job during the school year?" said Elvis. He crossed the room and plopped down into his tan leather La-Z-Boy and cranked his feet up.

"I told him he can have more hours at the café," she said. "But he doesn't seem interested. I don't know what he wants."

"Maybe more than minimum wage is what he wants."

"It's all I can pay, for what he does."

"I have a pretty good idea what he wants money for."

"Don't say it."

"A motorcycle."

"I said don't say it."

"It's what he wants. He's eighteen. We can't stop him if he has the money. How much does he have saved?"

"About eight hundred," she guessed.

"Sounds like we won't have to worry for a while."

Whether Travis had enough money to buy a motorcycle was the least of their worries, Mavis thought. A feeling of dread descended on her like a raincloud, threatening to douse her in sorrow and regret. "I don't like this whole motorcycle thing," she said. "Do you think Freddie Ignatowski is grooming him?"

"That'll be the day, when the Hogs accept Brown boys."

"What if they're recruiting Travis—and Julio—not for their gang but for something else?"

"What something else?"

"I'm thinking what they did to Jeannie."

A heartbreaking image entered Mavis's mind, of her beautiful teenaged daughter, so full of life and possibilities. Jeannie could be a little wild at times—boys, beer, and weed—but not out of the ordinary for Newfield High School teens. She had her sights set on college, in Mankato where her father had gone. She loved avant-garde theater and art. Until she didn't. At first slowly, then suddenly, she changed, from a loving daughter to a surly, secretive, combative nightmare of a teenager. Mavis suspected her daughter was stealing from her. Then it became obvious that Jeanne was on meth or pills. Mavis and Elvis were never sure where she got them, but it was well known, even then, that the Blue Hogs were involved in distributing crystal methamphetamine and opiates. Jeanne didn't finish high school. She ran away with some lowlife named Oscar and returned a year later, age nineteen, with a newborn baby. Mavis was horrified by the condition her daughter was in. Emaciated, her beautiful hair shorn to a stubble, a few teeth missing. She was almost incoherent. Mavis tried to talk her into moving back in with her parents. Jeanne agreed but stayed only one night, gone in the morning, the baby boy left behind. Elvis searched for months, until they located her in Minneapolis. For years they tried to coax her home without success. They looked into having her committed, but a lawyer advised them Jeanne likely would not be declared mentally incompetent. She was a defiant drug addict, an adult who had to agree to seek help.

"We don't know for sure it was them," said Elvis.

"I know it was. I dreamt it."

"You and your dreams."

"What if they try to hook Travis on drugs?"

Elvis considered that for a moment. "I will kill them myself."

"You'll do no such thing. You'll go to the police."

"Lot of good that would do."

"What do you think *you* could do?"

"There are things."

"What things?"

"Do you remember that book, *The Love Hunter*? Another Minnesota writer. Hassler, I think his name was."

"Yeah, what of it?"

"A guy's best friend is dying of a terrible disease, and he doesn't want to see him suffer. So he plans to take him duck hunting in the wilderness and mercy kill him, make it look like an accident."

"What's your point?" she said.

"These things can be done. Hunting season is here."

"Don't even think about it."

From the look he gave her, Mavis knew her husband had little faith in local law enforcement and very probably would do something awful. He'd killed in Vietnam, still had nightmares about it, and Mavis had no doubt he could do it again. Much as she distrusted the sheriff's department, she pondered the distasteful prospect of asking them to intervene before Elvis did something stupid.

Jim Tomlinson entered the *Clarion* office through the back door, thinking he would kill an hour or so answering emails before heading home to his lonely bed. He'd taken himself out to the movies in Mankato. *The Irishman*. His kind of movie. Scorsese. DeNiro. Pacino. It reminded him of his days as a young reporter, toiling away in the newsrooms of small-town Minnesota (he hadn't come so far, had he?), dreaming that someday he would be the one to find the body of Jimmy Hoffa, instead having to content himself with finding AWOL politicians and judges in sordid motel trysts.

He looked forward to these quiet nights in the office with no phones ringing and no one bothering him with trivial questions. It was also a time to engage in his private, recently rediscovered pastime, which took the form of a fifth of Glenfiddich single-malt and a *Newfield Clarion*-branded shot glass, a relic from a subscription giveaway in less sober times. He could almost taste it, the exquisite burn as the first shot slid down his gullet on its way to stoke the fires of his belly. As he emerged from the back hallway, he was surprised to find the lights on in the newsroom. It was nearly ten o'clock. There was one person in the room, tapping away on a laptop. Pam Strich.

Pam Strich. The proximate cause of his reacquaintance with his old friend and nemesis John Barleycorn. It had taken him months to come to terms with it, but now he could not get her out of his mind. It was absurd. He was her boss and nearly twenty years her senior. And she was a lesbian, romantically involved with Cindy Smith. It made no sense. But still. He had thought maybe alcohol would drown his incipient lust and ease his crushing loneliness. Not so, apparently. Perhaps he needed to drink more.

He guessed she hadn't seen him yet when she got up and headed to the stairs down to the basement, no doubt visiting the tiny bathroom. He quietly slipped into his office, turned on the lights, and poured himself a double. Slammed it back. Ah. Sweet burn of youth. He put the bottle and shot glass back in his desk drawer. He told himself drinking in the office was more dignified than alone in his dreary apartment, which was what alcoholics do. Drinking in a newsroom was a proud tradition. But is there a sadder journalism cliché than the old newspaperman with a bottle in his desk drawer? Not that he could think of.

When Pam emerged, her eyes immediately caught the overhead fluorescents in the boss's office. "What are you doing here so late?" she said as she appeared in his doorway.

"I was going to ask the same of you," he dodged. "Although I must say I'm mighty impressed by the dedication. Just a reminder, though, we don't pay overtime here at the *Clarion*."

"Duh," she said, rolling her eyes in an adolescent way that

was both annoying and adorable.

"Whatcha workin' on?" he said.

"Just transcribing my notes from the board of ed meeting. That's b-o-r-e-d of ed."

"Heard that one before. Gimme another."

She snickered and went back to her desk. They ignored each other for another half hour, tapping away at their screens. Pam got up to visit the rest room two more times. Strange. Young people usually don't have to pee that often, not like us old dudes. What if she's shooting up down there, he wondered as he poured himself another nip of the 'fiddich before she came back.

It was almost eleven when Pam closed her computer, grabbed her bag, and headed for the back door. Tomlinson stood, threw on his jacket, and turned out his lights, not even bothering to shut down his PC so he could walk out with her.

"Going my way?" he said. Lame. Do better.

"Home to bed. Early meeting tomorrow. Town council committee."

"Hold on, Pam," he said, and touched her forearm, stopping them both in the darkened hallway. "I just want to say … I know I've been hard on you … but … you're doing a great job. I'm proud of you."

"Thanks." She beamed charmingly, the faint light glinting in her studs and rings.

In psychology and brain science, there is a concept known as epiphenomenalism, the idea that our sense of free will is an illusion, that our bodies do what is predetermined for them to do and our minds catch up with that action a split second later and take credit for it, as if we'd willed it. This was the only explanation Tomlinson could muster for what happened next. He found himself pinning Pam against the wall, his hands gripping her shoulders, and pressing his lips against hers, tasting her Burt's Bees coconut lip balm with his probing tongue. He had no recollection of deciding to kiss her.

It seemed to him that she allowed it for several seconds, but in truth she pushed him away immediately.

"What the fuck?"

"Oh, Jesus. I am so sorry."

"What is the matter with you? You're my boss." She wiped her mouth with her sleeve as if her lips were contaminated by a toxin.

"I don't know. I don't know. I'm so sorry," he said. "I shouldn't have. It just happened. Like someone else was doing it."

"Bullshit. I could get you in a lot of trouble for doing that. Ever heard of sexual harassment?"

His knees gave out in shame and he slid down the wall into a crouch. He looked up at her. In the dim light he could see her face twisted in outrage. "I'm such a loser," he said.

Pam crouched before him and looked him in the eye. He turned away. After a moment she started to laugh. "Oh, the irony," she said. "Thick enough to cut with a machete."

"What's so funny?"

"We are. Does it occur to you this scene has happened before?"

"I never..." he started to say.

"Not you. Me. In a dark deserted hallway, in a newsroom late at night. Me and a luscious little intern named Sarah. I kissed her. Unfortunately for me, she kissed back. And there started my downfall at the *Pioneer Press*."

He remembered that story. She had told him about it right up front, during her job interview. He hired her anyway. Purely a gut feeling. His instincts were pretty good, in retrospect. Not perfect. But pretty good. She was a damn good reporter, if something of a loose cannon at times. Based on her gruff exterior, he'd assumed she'd endured a rough, blue-collar upbringing but later learned she was raised in affluence in the toney suburb of White Bear Lake. He often wondered what sorts of demons followed her out of such privilege, but the few times he'd probed, she'd shut him down. He now wondered if he subconsciously believed he had permission to kiss her because of her own history of being inappropriate. He shook his head. "What a pair we are."

"So, you see, I can't really justify acting all offended and outraged. I'm no hypocrite. Anyway, it's nice you think I'm hot. Even though I don't go for boys. But we forget this ever happened, right?"

"Right. You must think I'm pretty pathetic. Forty-five years old and single, a loser."

"No. I think you're lonely. It's not a crime. You just need to find someone more, um, appropriate." She stood and held out her hand. He took it, and she hauled him up to a standing position with surprising strength for such a small woman. "Also," she added. "I could taste whisky on you. How long has that been going on?"

This was going from bad to worse. "Just a sip, now and then, for old times' sake. You know. Like an ex-smoker wanting just a whiff."

"C'mon. Remember who you're talking to. I know all the cons. All the lies. Just like you told me once not long ago."

"How are you doing, by the way? How's it going?"

"Good," she said. "Sober now for fifty-four days. Don't change the subject."

"I can handle it."

"That's what we all say."

Tomlinson had enough of this conversation. Busted, and lectured to, by his own protégé. How suddenly the power dynamic between them had shifted. In one ill-timed moment, she had something on him now. Two things: He had a crush on her and was secretly hitting the bottle again. "Well, it's late. We should go." He started toward the door.

Pam didn't follow. She said to his retreating back, "If you want to start dating, like, straight women closer to your own age, I think I might know someone."

"Who?" He stopped and turned.

"Well, this might seem weird. But my therapist. Marie."

Great. Now she feels so sorry for me she wants to fix me up with…

"Your therapist?"

"Mmmhmm. I get the sense she's lonely, too. Sometimes she gets this faraway look in her eyes, and I have to bring her back into the room. She's pretty, too. Pretty hot. Close to forty, I'd guess."

"Thanks, but I don't know. That *would* be weird. And unethical maybe?"

"It wouldn't bother me. I'd be the one in the middle, but neither of you would be allowed to talk about me. Employee confidentiality and client confidentiality. If you broke that I could sue your asses."

"So romantic. You're some matchmaker, you are."

"I could talk to her. Feel her out."

She was serious. For a fleeting moment, he warmed to the idea. Someone to go to the movies with at least, instead of buying a solo ticket like a sad loser. Wait. That's crazy. Get a grip. And there was another thing. His no-longer-secret drinking. Marie Thibodaux was an addiction counselor and no doubt would nail him like a butterfly to a corkboard.

"Thanks, but I don't think so."

"Suit yourself," she said and slipped past him out the door.

Dear Molly,
I am engaged to the girl of my dreams. We've been dating since high school and have set a wedding date for next spring. Recently, her parents threw us an engagement party at their

country club, and something happened there that has troubled me for weeks. I wandered away from the party to find the men's room, and when I emerged, my future mother-in-law was standing outside the door in a strapless little number with two martinis in her hands. She told me to drink mine down all at once because, as she said, you'll need it. She was obviously well into her second or third or fourth cocktail. I know your column appears in a family newspaper, so I will be vague and say only that she was inappropriate with me. Best as I can recall, all clothing remained in place. But she made it clear that her daughter's happiness was paramount and that she would be "putting me through my paces"—those words I remember clearly—to ensure that I was "up to the task." Then she licked my face like an overfriendly German Shepherd and walked away. I am obviously creeped out by this whole thing. Should I mention it to my fiancée? She and her mother are very close, and I would hate to come between them or alienate the love of my life. Should I say something, or pretend it never happened, write it off as a drunken faux pas?
Signed,
Facelicked

Dear Facelicked,
Run.
That is my advice to you.
Run as fast as you can, as far away as you can, while there is still time.
You know what they say about mothers-in-law, right? They are a glimpse into the future of who your blushing bride will become. Based on this particular mother-in-law, I would say your future with Ms. Right is a minefield. Alcoholism? Check. No sense of boundaries? Check. Sexual predation, with a side of kink? Check.

If you go through with this wedding, best case
scenario is you'll find yourself married to a
Xerox of this harridan thirty years hence,
drowning your regrets in a bottle. Worst case?
She cheats like a carney, breaks your heart, you
kill both her and her lover OJ-style, and end up
hanging yourself in a prison cell.
Or not. Your choice.
But don't let me tell you what to do.
Hugs,
Molly

Ohhhh. Where am I? Whose truck is this? What happened to my little VW Rabbit? It's yellow. I love that car. Somebody stole it. And whose brick box of a shitty little house is that? This is not my beautiful house. This is not my beautiful car. Is that from a song? The B-52s? No, wait, The Pretenders? Save big money at Menard. Is that how it goes? I always liked that jingle. Where are the keys to this thing? I keep losing things. Maybe he took them. Old whatshisname. Or that doctor. Evil, evil man. Better go inside. Whose house is this? That fridge is junk. Kitchen needs paint. My house is tall and white with a big porch in front. With a swing. Is this Augie's house? No. Can't be. I know about Augie. Don't have to tell me. Kenny's house? Maybe. No, his was a trailer. I see a garden out there. I know about gardens. Let's see what they got. Nothing. There should be tomato plants here. All gone, pulled up. What a mess. Needs a good weeding and raking. Where's a rake? In that old white barn? Looks like it's about to fall down. Dark in here. Light switch? There's the rake. Need gloves. Get to work. What a mess. Whose house is this?

Pam arrived early for the game. Friday night, under the lights, the American fall ritual. She wasn't so interested in football and cared not whether Newfield could beat the visitors from Waseca. The crowd in the grandstands was her game. These autumn gatherings were among the biggest social events in town, and she had availed herself of the opportunity to observe the locals in their native habitat ever since joining the *Clarion* the previous year. These were her sources and subjects for news articles, and it never failed to break the ice in interviews with an observation on the latest Reapers football game.

She climbed the stands to the top row from where she could see everyone as they entered the stadium. She wished she'd brought a seat cushion, as the metal benches were cold on her butt. She took off her wool scarf, folded it, and sat on it. A pair of Nikon binoculars dangled around her neck, ostensibly to better see the action on the field but even more useful for people-watching, as if she were a bird fancier in the woods. On this day the species she was stalking was *Newfieldas Juntas*, the small circle of power brokers who held sway over the town: the Greenfields and the Whites. Also, perhaps, *Bluehogus Crassus*, aka Freddie Ignatowski, the Reapers' number-one fan and rumored co-conspirator with Chester Greenfield in some nascent Trumpian clusterfuck that Pam was sniffing out. They were all regulars at the Newfield football games, Chester and Freddie obviously trying to relive their halcyon days on the field. She would watch them all evening for signs of tacit conspiracy, convenient momentary disappearances.

It was still a half hour till kickoff. The marching band was filing onto the field for a pre-game set, an orderly line of red-and-gold uniforms and shining brass. The Reapers mascot, a senior dressed like a farmer in overalls carrying a big old scythe, jogged to the fifty-yard line and twirled his blade overhead like a weapon. A few early birds were scattered around the stands. No one of immediate interest to Pam. Until she spotted a lone figure sitting in the top row at the far end, no one else anywhere near. She had an idea who it was but glanced through the Nikons to confirm. Yup. Marie Thibodaux, bundled up in a plaid blanket, a red hoodie pulled low over her face. It wasn't that cold, somewhere in the low fifties, but it likely would dip into the forties before the game ended.

In two months of meetings, Pam had been unable to crack open the hard shell that protected Marie Thibodaux from … something. Something awful, maybe. She could sense it in Marie's world-weariness and sad eyes. Then again, a lot of the Indians she'd seen in Minneapolis looked that way. Her journalist's curiosity wouldn't let it go. But every time Pam tried to use her reporter tricks to pry open the carapace, Marie deftly deflected and reminded her that Pam was the patient and she was the therapist and would be asking the questions. Meanwhile, Marie had made an unquestionable impression on her. Pam had stopped drinking, sober for fifty-nine days now. The truth was, she was afraid of her. Afraid not only of her wrath, but also afraid of her disappointment and disapproval. The initial lust she had felt toward Marie had morphed into something akin to hero worship.

Pam wondered if she should go talk to her. It might be awkward to be seen in public with your shrink, and possibly unethical to be seen in public with your patient. Fuck it. If anyone sees us together, it's just the nosy reporter chatting up the pre-game crowd, right? She stood and walked along the empty benches, her clogs clanging embarrassingly on the metal planks. She hated to be so conspicuous; better to be the stealthy observer. Marie turned toward the clanging and recognized Pam with a broad smile. Pam sat next to her.

"Coffee?" Marie said, as if this were a normal everyday meetup. She produced a plaid-clad Thermos that matched her blanket.

"Thanks, no. Keeps me up."

"I didn't know you were a football fan," Marie said as she put the Thermos away.

"I'm not. Not really. I'm just here to observe the town folk, maybe catch up with some sources who have been avoiding me."

"Clever girl."

"First time I've seen you outside your office. You don't get around much, do you?"

"Oh, I get out. I do most of my shopping and errands in Mankato and Blue Earth. I'd rather not be recognized around town by my clients."

"Like this, you mean? I can go away if you want."

"No, 'sokay."

"Are you here alone? Or meeting someone?"

"No. Just me."

"No boyfriend? Or girlfriend?"

"Aren't you the nosy one."

"Come on, Marie. We're not in therapy right now. Loosen up. Let me get to know you."

Marie took a sip from her coffee cup. "What do you want to know?"

"Tell me about your love life. You already know all about mine."

"Nothing to tell. I like to keep to myself."

That was an understatement. Pam's attempts at investigative reporting had turned up nothing, as if Marie Thibodaux had arrived via spaceship.

"What if I told you I know a single guy in town who's interested in meeting you?"

Marie eyed her with suspicion. "Who?"

"Before I tell you, are you even interested in meeting anyone? I don't want to waste anybody's time."

"Maybe. Depends who it is."

"My boss. Jim Tomlinson. He's a good guy. Divorced. Lives alone."

"You want to set me up with your boss?" Marie scrunched

her nose as if smelling something rancid.

"I know. Kinda weird. But it wouldn't bother me. You two wouldn't be allowed to discuss my personal business, right? Confidentiality and all that."

"How do you know he wants to meet me? Did he tell you?"

"Yes," she lied.

"He doesn't even know what I look like."

"I pointed you out to him," she lied some more. "At Mills Fleet Farm. He said you looked hot." She hoped Marie wouldn't press for more details. This lie was already getting out of hand. But for a good cause, she told herself.

"Did he ask you to ask me?"

"No. But I thought maybe I could smooth the way. What should I tell him?"

"Tell him if he wants to meet me he should call me himself. You can give him my cell."

That mission accomplished, Pam moved back to her seat and scanned the growing crowd through her binocs. The band wrapped up the school song and filed into the stands. The players charged out of their respective locker rooms and jumped around *en masse* as if on pogo sticks, the Reapers' metallic gold helmets reflecting the overhead lights. Pam located the Greenfields first, in the front row at midfield. They were not sitting with the Whites, whom she spotted chatting with the school principal Mrs. Lavransdottir in back of the end zone. And there was Freddie, in his vintage Reapers jersey, gold with a faded red number seventy-five stretched across his ample girth, standing with the cheerleaders as if he were one of them.

The rest of the game was a blur. Pam spent most of the time eavesdropping on conversations, chatting up a few local officials, steering clear of Jill White, and keeping her eyes on Chester Greenfield. Her targets of interest all seemed to be avoiding each other, which she thought strange. The only part of the game she remembered, should anyone ask, was when Travis Birdsong took the ball late in the fourth quarter and broke through the middle of the line for a fifty-yard touchdown run, giving the Reapers only their second victory of the season. As she scanned the crowd through the Nikons to watch the fans cheer, she noticed Marie Thibodaux, still alone in the top corner, smiling broadly with a tear visible on her cheek.

When Gus got home from the grocery store, the first sight to greet him as he climbed out of the car was Molly, buck naked, no Emmylou t-shirt, on her hands in knees in the garden, apparently pulling weeds. It was mid-November and a chill had draped across the land as the sun sank behind a western cloud bank. Molly seemed oblivious. He left the bags in the car and quietly approached, stepping between the crunchy fallen maple leaves to hide his steps in the soft grass. Gus could tell she was muttering to herself. "Whose house is this?" she seemed to be saying over and over. He stopped about ten yards away, still behind her line of vision, and considered how to approach her. He didn't need another bloody nose, or a gashing with a garden tool. Should he get a blanket to cover her first? Or try to talk her out of whatever fugue state she was in? "Molly," he said as gently as he could. Too gently, as she apparently didn't hear him and continued muttering. "Molly. Sugar," he said louder.

She stopped what she was doing and glanced at him over her shoulder. She stood and faced him, her nakedness smeared with mud as if she'd been wallowing not just weeding, clumps of dandelions in each hand, their dirt-clotted roots dangling like soiled gray hairs. "Kenny," she said and smiled.

"No, Molly. It's me."

Her smile tightened. "Harry?" she said. The smile broadened again. "I've missed you, Harry. Where have you been?"

"It's Gus, Molly. Your husband."

She put a finger to her lips and giggled. "We mustn't tell old Gus." She walked toward him, dropping the weeds and reaching toward him. "Give us a kiss," she said.

"Jesus Christ, Molly. I'm your husband Gus. Who the hell is Harry?" A thought occurred to him, but it was too terrible to consider, and he swept it out of his mind like a piece of litter.

She stopped and lost the smile again, looked down and seemed to notice for the first time she was naked. "Go away!" she screamed and ran toward the house.

"Molly!" He chased her, afraid she might hurt herself in this state. As he entered the kitchen, he heard the bedroom door slam shut. Should he follow? Did the door-slam signal still hold, given that Molly rarely slept in there anymore? He stopped outside the door and listened; Molly was sobbing. "Molly?" he said.

"Go away," she yelled.

"Do you need help getting cleaned up?" He grabbed the door handle and considered going in. Then he heard the shower turned on in the master bath and took it as a sign that Molly was coming out of her fugue and taking care of herself. It had been a constant struggle for him between allowing Molly a semblance of dignity and the urge to nurse her like a child. He opted for dignity.

Gus retrieved the bags from the car and put the groceries away, then retreated to the living room and plopped on the couch, staring into space, trying to imagine what lay ahead. Maybe Doc Mollenhoff was right. This might be too much for him. Would he ever muster the courage to put her in a home? And who was Harry? Did she mean Kugelman? The only Harry he knew. He didn't want to think about it. Not any of it. Including the increasingly bizarre and unhinged correspondences from Mr. Fed Up, who had continued to write despite Gus's demand that he stop, not even acknowledging that Gus had responded in the column, as if he hadn't seen it. Gus began to suspect he was dealing with a possible psychopath who might prove to be dangerous. There had been no overt, specific threats, but the poor tortured soul had recently descended to a very dark place, full of conspiracy theories in which the whole world was against him.

Jim Tomlinson strolled into the Newfield High School stadium just as the sun was setting and the lights had come on, bathing the scene in the harsh glow of nighttime football. He rarely missed a Reapers game, not as a journalist—Tony Trecanelli would write up the summary for the *Clarion*—but as a proud Newfield partisan, class of 1991. He never played sports, too scrawny and bookish. One of the nerds, in other words. These crisp Friday nights, redolent of the aroma of grilled hot dogs and roasted peanuts and the blare of marching bands, were pure nostalgia, although he never cared for the game itself, especially the bullying jocks he'd spent his four years avoiding. His fondest memories of high school were his English classes with Ms. Janssen, rest in peace, and AP history class with Gus Peterson. After Newfield he'd attended Carlton College in Northfield, close enough to come home on weekends. Even when he'd gone on to work in New Ulm, Red Wing, and Rochester, he managed to come back on many fall Friday nights. Now, as editor of the *Clarion*, he saw the Reaper games as the place to see and be seen, the ideal venue for schmoozing with community leaders—and advertisers.

On this night, however, he had another agenda. He scanned the seats and found Marie Thibodaux sitting alone in the top row at the far end, wrapped in a plaid blanket, just where she said she'd be. She smiled and waved at him. It was their second meeting and first real "date." They'd met for coffee three days earlier at the Caribou a few miles up Highway 169. He had been as nervous as a teenager on prom night. Marie picked up on that and teased him gently, which put him quickly at ease. She had a calm, self-possessed manner about her. He was embarrassed after twenty minutes to realize he had done almost all the talking, Marie simply keeping the conversation percolating with probing questions. Oh, right, he'd thought, she's a therapist. It's what they do. Jim got past worrying about Marie smoking out his drinking habit and decided maybe she was just the sort of person he needed in his life right now. He was immediately infatuated. She was not only mesmerizing but strangely beautiful, in a weathered, chiseled way, just as Pam had described her. When they parted, it was she who suggested they meet again and proposed the Reapers football game on the following Friday night. Jim was taken aback by the thought of so public a venue. He was thinking more like a quiet dinner at a nice place in Mankato. Was he ready to be seen with a woman in public? It had been so long. In a small town like Newfield, they'd be the next hot topic of gossip, no doubt. Part of him thought it might not be so bad, to be the object of gossip instead of the collector. Truthfully, it would feed his ego to be connected to such a mysterious beauty, whom no one in town seemed to know.

He climbed the grandstand and sat next to her. She offered him a steaming hot cup of coffee from a Thermos, for which he was grateful. The temperature was already down in the forties and likely would hit the thirties before the night was over. A whiff of November snow was in the air. Marie picked up their conversation where it had left off at Caribou Coffee, as if no time had passed. He again found himself talking about himself, answering her questions, and tried to turn it around and draw her out. She was stingy with personal information, offering little more than her sketchy biography, her recent life in South Dakota, changing the subject when he asked about her birthplace and family life. Their conversation soon drifted to other subjects, especially politics, in which Marie confessed her increasing radicalization since the 2016 election and her growing interest in Native American culture and causes, as if she'd rediscovered a lost home. Jim became so absorbed in talking with Marie that the two hours flew by with barely any attention paid to the action on the field. He glanced at the scoreboard during one pause and saw there was only a minute left, and the score was tied. For the second week in a row, the game was decided in the final seconds, with a trick play that started with Travis Birdsong taking the ball toward the sideline in a classic power sweep, hoping to skirt the New Ulm line with a wall of his blockers leading the way, then he pulled back and heaved the ball across the field into the far corner of the end zone, where the Newfield quarterback had snuck by the opposition unnoticed and gathered in the pass for a touchdown. The place went wild.

Jim and Marie stood and applauded along with the hundreds of other Newfield loyalists astonished by the stunning speed and clever deception of the play that ended the game in victory for the Reapers. Jim spotted Elvis and Mavis jumping up and down on the grass behind the endzone pumping their fists with joy and he pointed them out to Marie.

"Those are his grandparents," he shouted to be heard above the din.

"I know," she said. She was crying.

"You know them?" he said.

"Long time ago."

A lightbulb blinked on in his head, and he started to connect the disjointed dots of her backstory. Marie was Indian, the Birdsongs were Indian. How did they know each other? Was she from Newfield?

"Can you wait for me?" she said. "There's something I have to do."

Bathroom, he assumed. "Meet you by the exit gate," he said, needing a restroom stop himself.

She clambered down the steps of the grandstand and walked directly toward Elvis and Mavis out on the field, who had just finished hugging Travis and let him go to the locker room to celebrate with his teammates. Jim decided to follow her, curious what she was up to. Obviously not going to the bathroom. His bladder could wait. Marie tapped Mavis on the shoulder. The woman turned toward her. Jim reached the bottom tier of the stands and started across the field. He could make out a few words spoken between them. Elvis turned to see what his wife was doing. There was a shriek. Jim couldn't tell if it was from Mavis or Marie, but it was definitely a woman's cry, piercing, heart rending. Departing fans stopped to see what the commotion was. Mavis threw her arms around Marie, and by the time Jim sidled up to the scene, both Mavis and Marie were howling with sobs. Elvis looked stunned, as if he couldn't process what was happening. Then he pulled Marie from Mavis's shoulder and hugged her as if else he might drown. Then Elvis, Mavis, and Marie were locked in a three-way hug, emitting an eerie combination of tears and laughter.

"Hi," said Jim. He felt small and irrelevant, like a busboy at someone else's wedding.

"Oh, Jeannie, Jeannie," cried Mavis.

Marie stepped away and turned toward Jim. "My mom and dad," she said.

Elvis and Mavis smiled at him. Marie—aka Jeannie, apparently—wiped the tears from her eyes and gathered herself. Professional again. She introduced Jim as "a friend." The Birdsongs grinned and nodded. "We know Jim," said Elvis. He offered his hand for a shake, which Jim was happy to accept, as he had no idea what else to do with himself.

"Hi, Jim," said Mavis. "Are you two…?" she started to ask Jeanne/Marie.

"We're friends, Mom."

Elvis said, "Where…? How long…? Why…?"

"Later," said Jeanne/Marie. "I got lots to tell you. But now, when can I see my baby?"

Elvis and Mavis had no answer for that. Their smiles disappeared and they went stone silent for several beats.

"Do you mean…" said Jim, with an inkling finally of what all this was about. The look they gave him cut him off in mid-sentence. Sore subject, obviously.

"Yes, Travis is my son," said Jeanne/Marie, breaking an awkward pause.

"He doesn't know you," said Elvis. "He knows about you, he's seen pictures, but he stopped asking years ago. He's moved on."

"This will be a shock to him," said Mavis. "We need to think about this."

"Let's not do this tonight," said Elvis. "Why don't you come over to the house tomorrow."

The three reunited Birdsongs exchanged another group hug, then Elvis and Mavis moved toward the locker room doors to await Travis. Jeanne/Marie watched them recede from view and was quiet for a long moment.

"Do you want me to leave?" said Jim.

"No, stay with me. Let's get a bite somewhere."

The only place open after nine on Friday night was the China Palace at the east end of town on County Road 4. It was the only "ethnic" restaurant in the area that wasn't a taco joint and had been in the same location, a former International House of Pancakes with the steep blue roof still there, for thirty years but under several owners, first a family from Taiwan, now a Vietnamese couple named Nguyen. Jim prided himself that he was one of the few people in town, along with Gus and Elvis, who knew to pronounce it "win" rather than "nagooyen." The menu was Asian fusion, with dishes from all over the east, from Hunan to Thailand to Vietnam. They ordered extra spicy beef pho and hot black tea.

"I don't even know what to call you now. Marie? Jeanne?"

"They're both my names. Jeanne Marie Birdsong. Then I married a tragic character named Leroi Thibodaux and took his name. When I moved back to Newfield, I went by my married and middle names. I wasn't sure how I'd be received. My life here was not a pretty picture. A hot mess, actually."

"So, what should I call you?"

"I guess I'm Jeanne to my friends and family and Marie to my clients. So, Jeanne."

"What happened to Leroi?"

She seemed to think about it for a moment, as if deciding how much of her story to tell. "He OD'd," she said. "In a cheap motel outside Mitchell, South Dakota. It was called the Sioux-Z-Q. Had a big fake tepee on the roof, visible for miles around."

"I'm sorry." For all of it, he meant.

"I was waitressing at a truck stop on I-90. Found him when I got home. You can probably fill in the rest. His death was a wake-up call, the final bell on my wild youth at age twenty-nine. Scared the life out of me. Went into rehab. Got clean. Then GED, then community college, then South Dakota State, degree in social work, internship on the rez, then here, a year ago, once I felt strong enough to face my past."

"What about Travis?"

"I gave him up when he was a baby. I was an addict, living on the streets, nobody to turn to. So I dumped him on my parents and ran away. Eighteen years ago. I've been trying to find my way back ever since."

"What are you going to tell him?"

"What can you say? I just hope he doesn't kill me on the spot. Actually, that might be better than him hating me for the rest of my life."

Their waiter, the Nguyens' teenage daughter Mae, brought their check and hovered, as if to rush them along. Jim glanced around the empty restaurant and saw the closing time routines were well underway. He reached into his wallet and gave Mae a twenty.

"That's a lot to deal with," he said after a few moments of silence.

"Sorry. I should have told you sooner."

"No, I meant for you."

"I may be a therapist, but I'm as big a mess as any of my clients. I've got more baggage than a 747. Maybe that's why I understand them."

"For what it's worth, Pam thinks you're the bomb."

"We're not supposed to talk about her."

"Right."

Something about this night seemed odd. "Did you plan this family reunion for tonight, on our date?" he asked.

"No." She shook her head vigorously and looked into her lap. "But I got caught up in all the excitement over Travis and seeing them so happy. It seemed like a good moment." She paused for a moment, then looked up at him. "Plus, I felt safe with you there. In case, you know, it didn't go well. I wouldn't be alone."

It pleased him to hear that. But still, there were things that didn't quite add up. "Why did you wait so long to show yourself to them?" he asked her. "You came back to Newfield, what, a year ago?"

"I don't know. Shame, I guess. Cowardice. I was afraid they'd reject me. I really hurt them, you know. Back then. I said awful things. So I watched from afar, screwing up my courage." She paused and looked like she might cry. "With all my training, you'd think I'd know how to deal with shame. But it's not so easy when it's your own."

"Have you been coming to all of Travis's football games?"

"No, just the last couple. It took me a while to get over my fear of being noticed. But nobody recognized me. In so many years on the street, I learned how to make myself invisible."

Jim dropped her off at her place and didn't ask to come inside. She leaned across the passenger seat of his Prius and kissed him on the cheek. As he watched her walk to her apartment stairs he tried to process everything he'd learned in the last hour. A persistent and annoying voice in his head told him to stay well clear of this rebuilt car wreck of a woman, while an electrical pulse in his bloodstream drew him toward her like iron filings to a magnet.

Dear Molly,

I've been happily married to a wonderful woman for 37 years. I've been a loyal and loving husband, never once cheating on her. As far as I know, she's never cheated on me. Anyway. I'm writing to you because something extraordinary has happened. I've fallen in love. With another woman. I didn't mean for it to happen. But I believe God has a reason for everything, so I feel I must explore this to understand what God is telling me through this woman.

And what a woman! Her name is Angelique. We've never met because she lives in Lagos, Nigeria, but we've been emailing and texting for six months now. She sent me her picture, and she is the most beautiful woman I've ever seen. In fact, she bears a striking resemblance to Phylicia Rashad. (Remember her from The Cosby Show?) I believe Angelique is an actual princess, from a noble family. She also might be a witch doctor or sorceress because of the uncanny way she can see into my very soul from thousands of miles away. I think about her day and night. I believe a grave injustice is being perpetrated on her by the corrupt regime in Nigeria. She needs me, and I am actually in a position to help. She said if I can wire her $100,000, she will be able to bribe her way out of trouble and escape to America where we can finally be together. That amount is all our life savings, but what's money compared to the bliss of union with your one true love?

My question for you, Molly, is: Should I wire her the money and hope for the best? Or should

I go to Lagos to find her and rescue her myself? She's being protected by her three brothers, who she says are in an Afro-pop boy band called Boko Haram, but I think it best to get her out of the country soon as possible. What should I do?
Signed,
Over the Moon

Dear Mr. Moon,
Here at Mollyville World Headquarters, we have a special place for missives such as yours which we call the round file. I assume your story is a joke, because no one is stupid enough in this Year of Our Lord 2019 to fall for the Nigerian email scam, which has been rattling around the interwebs for nigh on twenty years.
But you know what? As a service to the remaining gullible and clueless out there, I am going to answer your plaint as if it were legit. Perhaps I can put it to rest once and for all, for all future marks and suckers, that there are no Nigerian princes or princesses who need you to wire them money so they can later shower you with untold riches. Or, you know, other things. It. Is. A. Scam.
I am sorry to be the one to burst your bubble. The world can be a harsh place. But all is not lost. I have a solution for your dilemma. All you need to do to achieve the happiness you seek is to withdraw your life savings in small bills, tape it up in a secure package, preferably a used Amazon Prime box, and mail it to Dear Molly, c/o The Newfield Clarion, 33 East Elm St., Newfield (our fair city), Minnesota, 64576. I guarantee happiness will ensue.
Hugs,
Molly

Jeanne Marie Birdsong Thibodaux, still unsure who she was or what to call herself, pulled into the driveway and parked behind her father's truck. She sat in her rust-pocked Corolla for a long while, staring at the brick rambler in which she'd grown up and had abandoned nearly two decades ago. The windows and door trim looked newly painted sky blue, not the same color she knew growing up. She couldn't remember what that was. The shrubs around the foundation and the maple trees in the yard had grown taller. Eighteen years taller. Somewhere inside was the son she never knew, never held and loved, never saw grow into a strapping football star, just like his grandfather. They were finally about to meet, a boy's lifetime later. The thought of it gave her the shakes. Her training as a social worker did not equip her for moments such as these. She'd guided others through trauma, recovery, and redemption, but still she had no idea how to navigate this herself. She felt glued to her seat, unable to move, unable even to grasp the door handle.

Her mother emerged from the house and smiled and waved at her from the stoop. Jeanne burst into sobs. Mavis climbed into the passenger seat and reached her arm toward her. Jeanne leaned over and buried her face in her mother's shoulder, quaking. "It's okay, baby. You're home now," Mavis whispered. She gently rocked her daughter. "Why did you wait so long?" The pain and longing she heard in her mother's voice brought forth another round of wracking sobs.

"I was … afraid … everyone hated me."

"Never, my prairie flower."

They remained in a silent clinch for several minutes.

"I don't know if I can do this." Jeanne sniffled and sat up.

"He knows you're here. We've prepared him. He's waiting inside."

"What did he say?"

"He's confused. Conflicted. As you can imagine."

"Why did you name him Travis?"

"If you recall, you left us a baby with no name. Baby got

to have a name. Your father had an uncle in North Dakota named Travis." Mavis looked her in the eyes and said, "It's time, baby. Let's go."

Elvis was waiting for them at the front door. He embraced his daughter. "Welcome home, Jeannie. You stay this time, okay? We still got three bedrooms. One's yours."

Her parents led her into the living room. "We're going to give you some space now," Mavis said as she followed Elvis out to the back patio. "We'll catch up. After."

Jeanne stood alone in the living room, taking in the familiar-strange surroundings. Same beige walls. Same glass coffee table. New couch. New easy chair. An aroma wafted in from the kitchen—roast chicken?—triggering childhood memories she couldn't quite identify but filled her with joy and sorrow. She started to cry again.

A bedroom door opened. Travis walked into the living room tentatively, as if trying to make no sound, taking in the sight of the mother he never knew. He stopped ten feet from her. Tall, with long black hair. He was beautiful. But his was not the facial expression she had hoped for. So many times over so many years she had imagined this moment. She wiped a tear from her cheek and held out her arms. "Can I hug you?"

"How do I know you're really my mom?"

"Ask your grandpa and grandma. They know."

"You got some 'splainin' to do."

"Oh, Travis. I'm so sorry." She was, more than he could know, but it sounded weak. She felt inarticulate, so disappointing for someone trained to talk people through rough moments like this.

"Why'd you do it? Why'd you run away?"

"You know why. I was a drug addict. No way was I fit to raise a child. I saved you from a horrible homeless life by bringing you here. And now look at you. I'm so proud and happy." She approached him stealthily as she spoke, as if trying not to spook a nervous animal. "Let me hold you. Please."

Travis stood impassively, neither giving permission nor

forbidding it. She wrapped her arms around him and buried her face in his chest and sobbed. He remained stiff, motionless, as if carved from marble. Then he pulled her arms off him and stepped away.

"Who's my father?"

Jeanne looked away, then down at her feet, unable to make eye contact. How to tell him? It could have been any of dozens. When she was selling herself on the streets of Minneapolis to fund her addiction. White men. Black men. Indian men. Latin men. Asian men. A veritable United Nations of scum. All their faces blurred into one taunting sneer. She raised her eyes to Travis and examined his features. Definitely not one of the Black men. Probably Indian or Latin.

"Doesn't matter," she said. "I didn't stay with him long." It was the truth, technically. Whoever it was, she hadn't stayed with him for more than thirty minutes.

"Did he have a name?"

"Oscar," she improvised, recalling an actual name from her shameful past.

"Tell me about him."

"Please, not now. It's still painful. He abandoned me. Us." Again, technically true, after paying his twenty bucks.

Travis seemed to accept that, for now. "Why did you come back?"

"Because I'm ready now. I got my life back. I've been clean for seven years. I went to college. I have a job. I'm ready to be forgiven. Please. Forgive me. Let me back into your life." She sat on the couch and patted the cushion next to her. "Come sit. I'll tell you everything you want to know."

When Elvis and Mavis came back into the house, Jeanne and Travis were still on the couch. Travis sat stiffly, unsmiling, but had allowed her to hold his hand.

Molly emerged from the bedroom after what Gus assumed was another of her long naps following a bath or shower. She stood in the archway to the living room in her pink chenille robe, her hair bundled in a twisted towel. A promising harbinger, he thought, of a possible moment of lucidity.

"I know what you did. With that girl." She was scowling.

What fresh hell is this? "What are you talking about, Molly? What girl?"

"Don't play dumb. You know. And I know."

She seemed lucid, alright, but not in a way Gus was ready for. What exactly did she know, or think she knew?

"I don't know what you're talking about."

"I … I can't remember. Her name. Long time ago."

"You're imagining things, Molly. You know how that goes. It's part of your … illness."

Gaslighting. He was doing it again. He knew it but believed it was the only way to keep her calm and himself sane. Maybe change the subject. Divert her attention. "Molly, why have you been calling me Kenny? And Harry? Who are they?" He had an idea who they were, but hoped to draw her out, perhaps uncover some secrets he wasn't sure he wanted to know. There was a Kenny a couple years ahead of them in high school. Kenny Thomas. Killed in Nam. He'd heard gossip that he had been Molly's boyfriend once, which she denied and refused to discuss. He didn't press it; after all, the guy was dead. And Harry? There was only one Harry, as far as he could remember, and the very thought of it made him nauseated.

A shadow fell across her face. Her eyes looked unfocused, and she stared across the room, as if seeking answers on the opposite wall. He was losing her. "Molly?" No response. She was shutting down again. After an awkward moment of silence, she said "Pfft," and walked through the kitchen out the back door. He followed and watched from the window as she got down on hands and knees, in her bathrobe, and started weeding the empty tomato patch with her bare hands. Another shower would be needed soon enough. He went into the home office and fired up the computer to check on more letters to Dear Molly. Not much he could respond to for publication. A few hate mails from people offended by his snarky persona, but mostly "attaboys" for being such a fearless truthteller. He went to the kitchen window again to check on Molly, make sure she didn't wander off. Then returned to the computer and came to an email from an anonymous Hotmail account. The subject line chilled him: "You will not ignore me," it said.

Fri. Nov. 18 at 1:12 am

Fedup <fedup@hotmail.com>
To: Molly Peterson <dearmolly@newfieldclarion.com>
You will not ignore me
Dear Molly,

I know you're not Molly. I know who you are. No matter. I have run out of paper so I am emailing you. Don't bother trying to trace me, I'm using a fake account on a public computer. You should appreciate that, being a fake yourself. Ha ha. I guess I should thank you for finally answering my letters. Better late than never. But no I will not be thanking you. I did not like your rude reply. Who do you think you are, Gus Peterson, so high and mighty. I know Molly would never be so rude. Her ignoring me was better than you disrespecting me. You have made a big mistake. You had a chance to make a friend. I very much need a friend. Instead you have made an enemy. You do not want me as an enemy. Unless you apologize, in the newspaper where everyone can see it, I cannot be responsible for my actions. If there is blood, it will be on your hands. That is a promise.

Signed,
Fed up
p.s. Don't go to the police. If you do, I'll know. And you will regret it.

There it is. A direct threat. And what did he mean, "I'll know" if I go to the police? Is this guy a cop? Someone who works in the sheriff's office? "Shit's gettin' real," Gus muttered to himself. His first instinct, as the anger bubbled up, was to delete the email, but he didn't, thinking he might want to save it with the rest of the letters as evidence, should he need it later.

No way was he going to apologize to this piece of shit, especially not in the column. Responding as he did was obviously a mistake, an act of hubris on his part that was now coming back to bite him. Should have kept ignoring the creep. Eventually he would have gone away. Maybe. Time to go back to plan A, silence. Don't give him oxygen. Wait, is it a him? Or a her? Definitely a him. He closed the laptop, then he checked on Molly again. Still weeding. Go out and get her? Coax her inside? No, just keep an eye on her. He retreated to the bedroom and sat on the bed, contemplating the turn his life had taken: slowly losing the love of his life to dementia, while picking up a new "friend," a possibly insane stalker. He'd never felt so alone, at least not since that night he was lost in the jungle, cut off from his platoon, napalm fires burning all around. It dawned on him suddenly. He knew what he had to do: He would track down his anonymous correspondent himself and find out what was eating this guy before something awful happened.

I know what he did with that girl. He thinks I don't know. I know. Invited her into our house. My house. The brazen little thing. Let her sleep in Augie's room. When he was away at the U. Six months was it? Seemed like a year. I ran her off, I did. What was her name? Can't remember names anymore. Except mine. Molly. Molly. Molly. And Augie. Augustus junior. When is he coming home? They say he's dead. I know better. He's coming through that door one day. One fine day. I know it. Got to keep food in the house for him.

His favorites. Cap'n Crunch. English muffins. The ones with raisins. Lurtsema! That was his name. What happened to that Prairie Home fellow? I liked him. Is this my living room? Who painted the walls white? Did I? Maybe. Don't remember. I will never forgive him. Old Whatshisname. He sent my boy away. He let him go. I said no. Don't go. It's not a real war, it's a fake war. Started by those evil old men. Dead bodies were real. War was faked. If my boy's dead I know whose fault it is. What? Who's there? "Who are you?" *People come through my house like it's a bus station.* "Gus? Oh, it's you. What do you want?" *Always wanting something.* "I will never ever forgive you. I know what you did. You can't gas me." *Liar.* "No, not her. My boy. You killed my boy."*

"Patience, youngsters, patience," said Freddie. "All in due time. Meanwhile, help yourselves to the cooler. Beer's on me."

He regarded the two boys with envy and contempt as they eagerly pried open the lid of the Yeti and pulled out ice cold bottles of The Champagne of Beers. And maybe with a dollop of pity, which was about as much sympathy as Freddie Ignatowski could muster for anyone. Envy for their youthful energy and enthusiasm and the fact that their glory days on the fields of honor were not yet long past. Contempt for how gullible they seemed, chickens ripe for plucking. And pity for the journey on which he was about to launch them.

The Hogs were back at the river under the old Dodd-Ford Bridge, their favored party spot, to which they'd returned after Deputy Morton had promised to leave them alone as long as they stopped providing drugs and alcohol to minors. Oops, thought Freddie. Well, he rationalized, they didn't exactly seek out these young customers. Travis and Julio had come to him, asking to score some Oxy. That was on them. Might as well be hospitable and offer a beer or three while they were here.

He led them to a sandy stretch under the bridge, away from the raucous biker bash and the blaring country-pop, all frantic fiddling and screeching pedal steels.

"Now listen up, young Travis," he said. "You too, Pancho Sanza." Julio rolled his eyes at the malapropism and looked away. "If I sell you these pills, you gotta make me a promise. Promise you won't take any until after football season's over. You got one more game, and we ain't beat Blue Earth in seven years. After that, knock yourself out."

"I'm not on the football team. I got to wait, too?" said Julio.

"Oh, yeah. I don't give a shit about soccer. Pussy sport. You do what you want."

Travis and Julio exchanged glances, as if silently negotiating. Freddie cared not what they worked out between them, long as the Reapers beat the pants off the Buccaneers. He had a big fat dime riding on the outcome, getting seven points.

Time to cut to the chase, as it were. "Did you bring cash?" he said.

Travis nodded.

"How much?"

"Hundred."

"How much they cost?" said Julio.

"A buck per milligram. You want tens? Ten bucks a piece. You want eighties? Eighty bucks."

"That seems high," said Julio.

"You can pay less elsewhere. But not for an unlimited supply, like I got. And no questions asked." It was Freddie's oft-repeated mantra, his automatic sales patter. High-volume deliveries with no red tape had built him a local drug empire over the years.

"We'll take ten of the tens," said Travis. He reached for his wallet, extracting five twenties.

"Hold on to that and wait here," Freddie said. He walked a few yards down the river then around a bend behind a grove of trees hanging over the water. He returned a minute later with a metal canister inside a dripping wet plastic Ziploc bag, from which he excavated a small vial. The two boys seemed to be in a heated discussion in hushed voices that might have involved Travis's mother Jeanne, based on what he'd overheard. The less said about Jeanne Birdsong, thought Freddie, the better. "Here ya go," he said. "Ten tens."

The vial and the cash traded places and Travis and Julio walked away and started to climb the riverbank toward Travis's Civic parked on the road.

"Ain't you gonna finish your beers?" Freddie shouted after them.

The rest of the Hogs, having turned away from their party, laughed as Freddie gave them a thumbs up sign.

Gus stood in the living room, stunned into silence. He faced Molly, who was seated on the couch. She was picking that old scab, one that used to bleed all over him and that he hoped had finally healed. Scabs like that never heal. He couldn't tell straightaway if she was in a lucid moment or not. She didn't seem to recognize him when he walked into the room, then snapped out of it when he said his name. Now she was speaking calmly, rationally, spewing hateful poison into the room. How many times had they had this conversation over the last sixteen years? How long must he bear the guilt over their lost son? Wasn't the pain of loss enough?

Augie wasn't a boy. He was a man, twenty-four years old, who knew his own mind. After September 11, he'd forged a path from which he would not be dissuaded. Not that Gus didn't try. He invoked his own experience in Vietnam, another adventure built on lies in which he'd found himself on the side of war criminals, and advised Augie that Iraq was a mistake, a disaster waiting to happen, in which there would be no honor. Augie had signed up hoping to hunt down Al Qaeda in Afghanistan, but was diverted to Iraq, where he was told he could save the world from a madman with weapons of mass destruction. He had swallowed the bait hook, line, and sinker. His father had answered the call, he said, as had his grandfather. Why shouldn't he? In the end Gus had no argument for that. Molly cried when Augie shipped out.

"Please, Molly. Let's not do this. Not again. Let it go."

"Cindy. That's her name. I remember now," Molly said. A look of triumph lit up her face from its usual confused scowl.

Gus stammered, thrown off by her sudden turn. Molly Whiplash, he called it, after her disconcerting tendency to shift the topic on a dime. "I … I thought we were talking about Augie."

"Don't change the subject. You always do that."

No, Molly, that's you, he thought. "You know Cindy. She works at the VFW."

"I mean the Cindy who lived with us twenty-some years ago. It was 1997. You think I forget things, but I don't forget things. I didn't forget what you two got up to behind my back."

"It's the same Cindy. You know that, Molly. She moved back to Newfield two years ago."

"I know. I know why you go to that bar all the time. You're still getting in her pants, aren't you?" It was more a statement than a question.

"God no, Molly. Stop. She's an old friend, that's all. Remember? We took her in after her parents died in that awful car crash. So long ago. I know you didn't like the idea, but she was one of my students and had no family in town. It was the charitable thing to do. Everyone said so."

"Why did you let Augie go off to war?"

Gus sighed and his shoulders drooped. There was no

winning these interrogations, and no escaping them. He wondered if her verbal U-turns were deliberate, a mind game to keep him off balance, or if it was just the way her addled brain worked. "I tried to talk him out of it," he said. "You know that. But he was determined. He was a grown man, not our little boy. We had to let him go, Molly. How many times do I have to say it? We had to let him go."

Molly started to cry. Gus moved toward her, to offer comfort. She got up from the couch with startling agility and strode into the bedroom and slammed the door. Well, at least she can sleep on the bed for a change. He listened at the door. The bed springs squeaked under her weight. Satisfied that this episode was at an end, Gus retreated to the office to finish the latest Dear Molly. He didn't even bother gaslighting her about it anymore. She never brought up the subject of the column. He wondered if she even remembered it. He checked the email inbox, and there it was. Another missive from Fed Up.

Thurs. Nov. 21 at 12:12 am

Fedup <fedup@hotmail.com>
To: Molly Peterson <dearmolly@newfieldclarion.com>
RE: You will not ignore me
Dear Molly,
Or should I say Dear Gus. Yes, it's me again. I'm still here. You think if you ignore me I will go away. I will not go away. Until I get what's coming to me. First you will apologize for your rudeness. Then if I am satisfied that you mean it I will tell you my story. And you will print my story in your column. Is that asking so much?

I believe if you meet me in person you will see I'm not a bad guy. I'm not the freak people seem to think I am. Then maybe you will understand me. And if you apologize in person I will accept your apology and then we can be friends instead of enemies. Wouldn't that be nice? I am willing to give you that opportunity. Meet me under the Green Giant at 10:00 on Monday morning, November

25. You know where I mean. Come alone. If you ignore me and do not show up I will take it as a vile insult. At least have the courtesy to RSVP to this email if you can't make it.

I look forward to meeting you.

Fed up

Gus was annoyed yet intrigued. The jerk would not go away. But here was a chance to confront him in person. Finally find out who this nutjob is. But what if he really is nuts and shows up with a gun? Bent Torkelson, the county sheriff. That's it. Time to go to the police, despite the crank's threat. He gathered up the saved letters and printed out the emails. He would visit the sheriff in the morning.

Jeanne Birdsong, as she'd decided to call herself—she would erase the Thibodaux name via official channels later—pulled into the parking lot and killed the engine. The place looked pretty much the same as it had the last time she'd seen it, twenty-some years ago. Same ramshackle, flat-roof, brick hulk of a building with a big sliding steel door for a front wall, which was now rolled open, as business was in session at Fat Freddie's Body Shop. The sight of the place gave her chills, from memories both ugly and pleasurable. Furtive trips down to Blue Earth as a teenager, body wracked with aches and nausea, followed by surging, woozy relief that eased her trip home.

She gave the horn a tap to announce her arrival, got out of the car, and walked hesitantly toward the dark interior of the shop and its attendant odors of paint, chemicals, and oil. The smells brought the memories back more vividly and she momentarily felt lightheaded.

Out from behind a 1940s low rider with its windows taped over emerged Freddie Ignatowski, holding a paint sprayer in one hand and lifting a mask off his furry face with the other. "Well, well, well," he said. "The prodigal daughter returns. I heard you was back in town, but I didn't believe it. And here you are. You look good, Jeannie."

Freddie probably thought he was smiling in a friendly way, but to Jeanne it was a familiar and ugly sneer that immediately raised her anxiety level.

"You ruined my life, asshole."

"Now, Jeannie, don't go blaming me. I didn't make you an addict. You made yourself one."

"You knew how addictive those drugs were, but you sold them anyway. To teenagers."

"That's a lie. Those pills were prescribed by doctors. Totally legit. Not like that homemade shit like meth and smack. Legal pharmaceuticals. Not my problem if you took too many."

"You sold meth, too."

"Not anymore. I quit that game. Too much competition … from very bad people."

Jeanne looked around the premises to see if anyone was watching or listening. "Are you alone here?" she asked.

"Just you and me, baby," he said with a leer. "I sent Donnie out to get us some lunch. I can call him if you want and bring something for you, too."

"Anyway," said Jeanne, ignoring the offer. "This ain't about me." Thirty seconds into her first conversation with Freddie Ignatowski in nearly twenty years and already she was sliding down to his level of ignorant, vulgar speech. She caught herself. "Not about me. You hear?"

He said nothing, only scowled at her with his usual look of impatient puzzlement. He dropped the paint sprayer gun to the concrete floor with a loud clatter, pulled the mask off his head, and approached her. He stopped a few steps away, his bulging beer belly invading her space, and glowered at her.

She refused to be intimidated. She pulled a plastic vial of pills from her purse and held it up like a prosecutor presenting evidence at trial. "I found this in Travis's car. There are two left. How many did you sell him?"

His eyes widened for a second, then his face returned to its default sneer. "How do you know what's in there? And how do you know if I sold 'em?"

"Don't be cute, Freddie. I'm not stupid. I am a former addict. I am a licensed drug and alcohol addiction counselor. So don't try your bullshit on me."

"Well, look at you. A real do-gooder. Still don't prove I had anything to do with anything."

The sneer again. So brazen. She stuffed her clenched fists and the vial in her jacket pocket. "Everybody in town knows where these drugs come from."

"What does Travis say about that? Did you ask him?"

Hearing her son's name tumbling from that scornful mouth nearly made her swoon with rage. She calmed herself. "If you want to know if he ratted you out, the answer is no, he didn't. He refused to give me any information. Said he didn't know what they were or where they came from."

"Yeah, well, I don't blame him. I wouldn't trust my mom either, if she abandoned me as a baby and disappeared."

A verbal gut punch. "Fuck you, Freddie." She turned and walked back toward her car, glancing over her shoulder to see if the brute was following her. There was no one else around; Freddie's shop was on a dead-end street, more of an alley than a road. What if he attacked her? He outweighed her by almost two hundred pounds. She'd learned a few things in her years on the streets, a woman alone. How to kick a man in the balls and shins, stab him in the eyes with keys or utensils. She reached into her purse and grabbed her car keys. She opened the door and turned to look at him. He hadn't followed her but stood there with a smug grin on his grimy, bearded face.

"I'm on to you, Freddie. This is not going to end well for you. That's a promise." She climbed in and drove off back to Newfield, not with that woozy pleasurable feeling of old, but with barely suppressed rage and fear.

"I thought this place was off limits for you." Cindy was stacking beer mugs on the counter behind the bar, Merle Haggard serenading her on the sound system about a bottle letting him down, when Pam walked in shortly after the VFW opened for business. Cindy spoke the line coolly, careful not to betray any emotional state.

"I'll just have a Diet Coke," said Pam. She sat on the barstool directly in front of Cindy.

"Good for you." Cindy avoided eye contact. Seeing Pam put her in a confused state. She hated being in a confused state, it made her feel vulnerable. She opened a can and poured the soda into a glass of ice.

"I came," Pam started to say, then swallowed and took a sip. "I came to say I'm sorry."

It had been more than a week since the blowup, a screamer of an argument in which Pam accused Cindy of first enabling her drinking and then resenting her sobriety, after Cindy scolded her for being a "drag" and a "busybody." Cindy began to replay the scene in her mind. "You won't even get high with me anymore," Cindy had said. The words she had spoken so cruelly in a beery haze now made her cringe. "You're so boring. Working all hours, spying on people like a stalker."

"It's my job!" Pam had said, sounding so indignant, so wounded. "That's what reporters do."

Cindy knew she was being unfair, but the words had tumbled out of her mouth like shit rolling downhill. "And fixing up your boss with your therapist? How fucked up is that? Do you need them to be your mommy and daddy? Is that what that's about?"

"No! What is wrong with you?" Pam's voice had risen a full octave. "They happen to like each other. They were both lonely. Why do you have to make it something creepy?"

"It's just weird is all. Marie, or Jeanne, or whatever her name is, came back home to reconcile with her family, her kid, which is brave as shit, and you have to go and meddle in her personal life? Don't you understand boundaries? Oh, right. You don't. You're a reporter."

Unforgivably cruel. Pam had been close to tears.

"I think I get it. You want me drunk and messed up and helpless so I'm dependent on you. I'm easier to control when I'm fucked up, right? What did I expect, from somebody who gets people drunk for a living and pries their secrets out of them when they're most vulnerable? I see you, Cindy Smith."

"That is so unfair. Hey, where are you going? We're not done here. That's right, walk out on me. Bitch. And don't slam the—fuck!—door."

The row had upset Brandi Carlile so much that the cat disappeared for two days and then urinated on the bed upon returning. The women hadn't spoken since.

Cindy looked at Pam and saw that she was tearing up. Her stomach did a flip and she knocked over a bottle of gin, then caught it clumsily before it crashed to the floor. "Me, too," she said after taking a moment to collect herself. "I was out of line. I never should have said what I said. You've got yourself clean and sober, and I'm damn proud of you."

"I know I haven't been all that present for you," Pam said. "This is so hard. Staying sober, trying to hold on to my job, my life. Jim is watching me like a vulture, like he expects me to fail. I'm overcompensating, working all the time, trying to expose the corruption in this town."

"In that you have my complete support."

"I worry that being with you is going to get me partying again. Whenever I see you, I want a cold beer and a joint and to dance with you like no one's watching."

Cindy reached across the bar and put her hand on Pam's. They gazed at each other, pain and longing in both sets of eyes. Cindy reflected on the fact that she'd been complicit in Pam's drinking problems and was ashamed that she'd criticized her for going straight. She was probably complicit in any number of drinking problems in Newfield. It did not fill her with pride. She knew she had to break the cycle. Starting with Pam.

"So," Cindy said. She paused to let the silence sink in, signaling a shift in the conversation. How to say it? "I've been thinking. I've decided I'm definitely running for mayor next year."

"Cool," said Pam with a big, encouraging smile. "You would kick ass as mayor of this town. Sweep out the Jack and Jill mafia once and for all." She stared down at her drink and the cheeriness leaked from her face.

"You know what that means, right?" said Cindy.

"Yeah. I know what it means." She withdrew her hand from Cindy's.

"We can't be together. Starting now—"

"I said I know what it means."

"Don't be mad. Please. We've always known this was a possibility. That we were a temporary thing, right?"

"Yeah," Pam sniffed and wiped a tear from one eye.

"I mean, really. A reporter dating a politician? We both knew that could never work. Unless one of us quits their job, which neither of us is willing to do, right?"

"Right."

"And you may be right about me. Maybe I'm not good for you. If all you think about when you see me is partying."

"It's not like that."

"What is it like?"

Pam seemed to consider the question. Then to dismiss it. "Can I come over tonight? One more time?"

Cindy hesitated. Was Pam trying to cling, hoping to rekindle the flame? She was tempted, imagining the coconut taste of Pam's mouth, the way her taut little body felt when she wrapped her own limbs around her. "We'd better not."

Pam slurped the last of her Coke and started to leave.

"Wait," said Cindy. "We're still going to be friends, right? Allies. Together we can make this town a better place. For people like you and me. For everyone."

"Now you sound like a politician."

"I'm serious. Just because we stop sleeping together doesn't mean we can't do things for each other. I'll help you take down the Whites and Greenfields, the big story you've dreamt of, and you can help me become mayor. We can own this town."

"You've thought of everything, haven't you?"

Not everything, Cindy thought.

Gus stepped outside of the sheriff's office and stared across the open fields surrounding the building. He could see the Jolly Green Giant statue to the south, looming over the trees, and hear the faint roar from Interstate 90 coming from the north. The meeting with Sheriff Bent Torkelson had not gone as Gus had hoped. He went into the meeting with expectations high, having met Torkelson a few times in the past and had voted for him twice. He knew him well enough to know that Bent was not a nickname, it was his given name. The sheriff had been pleasant and welcoming. He agreed to talk to Gus himself instead of pawning him off onto a deputy or office clerk. When Gus handed him the stack of letters and emails from his anonymous correspondent, Mr. Fed Up, Torkelson had read them all carefully. He listened politely to Gus's concerns, then said,

"The guy is obviously disturbed—about something. But who knows what. Can you think of anyone who might have a grudge against you? Anybody you might have wronged in the past?"

Gus had said no, not that he could remember. Then he asked if the emails could be traced. Torkelson said their cyber expert likely could locate which public computers Fed Up had used, but added that probably wouldn't be necessary unless things escalated. He said he'd seen many examples of vague threats like this, and they never amounted to anything. He reminded Gus that freedom of speech in America gives citizens a lot of leeway in the things they can say, even ugly, hurtful things, unless they include specific threats against an individual. Torkelson concluded that Mr. Fed Up was most likely a harmless crank and there were no specific threats that law enforcement could act on. He did say, however, that if Gus wanted to take the proposed meeting at the Green Giant statue, which was only a few blocks from the sheriff's office, he would be willing to send a deputy to provide surveillance. Gus thanked him and said he'd think about it.

On the drive home via Highway 169, Gus turned it over in his mind again and again what he'd just done. Was it a mistake? Mr. Fed Up had specifically said not to go to the police and that he would know if he did. What did that mean? Gus had gone to the police anyway. There was still a chance the law would stay out of it and let Gus handle it himself. Could he? He felt like he was hurtling toward a confrontation whether he wanted one or not. By the time he got home, he had decided he would drive back down to Blue Earth on Monday as scheduled and meet this creep face to face.

Monday morning, he made sure Molly was safely set in her preferred routine, after breakfast, ensconced in her rocking chair with The Today Show on the TV, her cellphone on the table beside her, phone numbers for Gus, Helen Larsen, and Theresa Berg programmed on speed dial. He figured he would be gone no more than an hour or two and would check in with her from the road. He hoped she would remember who he was.

He parked in the lot outside the Green Giant Museum. It had been years since he'd been inside. Once was enough to peruse the shelves of vintage cans of corn niblets and peas, the retired canning machines, and the corny gift shop tchotchkes. As he climbed out of the Gran Torino, he glanced across the way at the parking lot of a Dollar Store. A county sheriff SUV was discreetly parked under a tree, as Torkelson had promised. Gus walked toward the towering Green Giant statue, which stood arms akimbo fifty-five feet tall, visible for miles around, including by startled cross-country drivers passing through on I-90. He approached the platform elevated ten feet off the ground between the giant's legs, a popular spot for portrait taking, and climbed the stairs. He scanned the grounds of the museum and surrounding fields searching for anyone approaching. A couple of families pulled in and took photos, then went inside the museum. He waited five minutes. Then ten. At ten-thirty he gave up, figuring he was the victim of a prank, or perhaps a mind game played by a twisted soul. He returned to his car and headed back to Highway 169.

When he arrived home, he was relieved to see that Molly's truck was where it was supposed to be. He'd hidden her keys some time ago but worried she would find them or had a spare key he didn't know about and would drive off somewhere into who knows what kind of catastrophe. He made a mental note to himself to disable the truck mechanically somehow. Maybe flatten the tires. He entered the kitchen and called Molly's name. Nothing. He walked into the living room and found her rocking chair empty. The TV was still on. A commercial for adult diapers. How fitting. He called her name once more. Checked the bedroom. The office. He was about to go out to the barn when he passed the door of the bathroom. There she was, splayed on the floor in her pink robe, face down on the shag rug. He felt a jolt as if shocked by a live wire.

"Molly?" he said softly.

No response.

"Molly!" Louder.

He knelt over her. Touched her back, gently shook her to wake her up.

"Molly," he said again. "Molly."

To Our Readers,

By now many of you have heard the terrible news. Word travels fast in a small, tightknit community like ours, especially when that word is sad news about one of our most beloved citizens. We lost Molly Peterson on Monday and I can barely type those words. I won't dwell on the details. Can't. All I can say is, a stroke took her from us many, many years too soon. There is a fine obituary elsewhere today in the Clarion. This isn't it. This is my inadequate attempt to share some of my personal thoughts about Molly.

My first recollection of Molly was when I was a kid, maybe 9 or 10, hanging around my Dad's newspaper office. Mrs. Peterson, as we all called her, was the face of the newsroom, the first person you saw when you entered the front door. She sat at that big oak desk—it's still here—greeting visitors, answering the phones, typing, and generally mothering the entire staff. Somehow, she learned of my weakness for Dr. Pepper, which my parents would not allow me to have, and would sneak a can to me whenever I came into the office, establishing a secret bond between us that never frayed.

A dozen years later, when I came home after graduating from college, my Dad took me on as an unpaid intern until I found a paying job elsewhere. (He was adamantly opposed to nepotism.) By then Molly had started writing the advice column that eventually became known as "Dear Molly." It was a logical step for her, as my Dad explained. She was always the most mature and level-headed person in the room, "a wise old soul" he called her. (She was 41.) She'd been dispensing sound advice to friends and colleagues for years, so why not share her wisdom with the wider public?

I soon left for gainful employment in New Ulm, then Red Wing, then Rochester. I followed the news from Newfield online and always had a printed copy of the Clarion mailed to me each week. I witnessed from afar as Molly grew into a local institution, a small-town sage not just for Newfield but for much of southern Minnesota, as her column was reprinted in several other newspapers.

Eight years ago, my parents retired to Florida, and I came home to take over the family business. The first person to greet me on my first day as editor and publisher was Molly. She presented me with a beautifully wrapped box tied with ribbon. I tore it open and found a six-pack of Dr. Pepper in cans. We had a good laugh. By then I'd sworn off soda pop, but I kept the six-pack as a talisman. It's still there on my desk.

Molly's thousands of fans and admirers, and I proudly count myself among them, have benefitted for years from her gentle, sensible, Midwestern common sense. Whenever Molly untangled a familial or social dilemma, her advice always seemed to leave folks feeling like, "Of course, why didn't I think of that?"

We are all better for having known you, Molly. And we will be worse for losing you. God speed. Here at the Clarion, we plan to continue the "Dear Molly" column for as long as Gus Peterson is willing to write it. I know Gus will keep Molly's good common sense alive for us, filtered

through his own unique voice.
James Tomlinson, Editor and Publisher

"I never should have left her. She would still be alive if not for me."

"You stop that right now, Gus Peterson." Helen Larsen crossed the living room where a dozen mourners sat with him after the funeral and burial and she put her hand on his shoulder. "The Lord had his time for Molly, and there is nothing any of us could have done about it."

"Truth," said her husband Carl. He took another swig of beer and gazed loopy-eyed at the ceiling.

"Amen," said Harry Kugelman.

Gus gave Harry a side eye. Fuck you, Harry, he wanted to say but didn't. When he had confronted Kugelman about Molly's invocations of his name, he'd first played dumb, then after a few more beers confessed that he did go out with Molly a few times many years ago, when Gus had gone off to college in Minneapolis. He figured she was available, he said, but swore they never slept together. Gus wasn't sure he believed him.

The funeral had been a lovely, stark, and dismal affair as the cold winds of November swept across the northern prairie. Snow threatened in the dark gray clouds but withheld its payload as if awaiting a more opportune moment. Molly descended into a grave carved from rich black loam as hundreds of admirers dressed in somber hues huddled against the ill winds. Gus's long-estranged brother Marcus had flown in from California for the service, a possible thaw in their relationship that for Gus took some of the edge off the bitter weather. Father Frank Sheehan, Molly's pastor at St. Stephen's Catholic Church, spoke lovely words, which Gus appreciated, although he could detect more than a few infuriating eyerolls and smirks from the mostly Lutheran attendees.

At home for the wake, Gus had imbibed a few too many Grain Belts and began to ramble. "How the hell is it justice that Molly is dead and fucking Donald Trump lives?" An awkward silence ensued. Gus cared not if the visitors were discomfited.

"Maybe this isn't the time for politics?" said Kugelman. It was more a statement than a question.

"There is never not a time for politics," said Gus. "After every damn school shooting, motherfuckers say it's too soon to politicize. They just want to sweep their evil shit under the rug. I say: Fuck. Them." He took another swig from his beer bottle.

"Preach, brother," said Marcus.

Gus left the crowded living room, which was beginning to oppress him, and went to the bathroom to take a piss. The same room where he'd found Molly's lifeless body. He closed the door, knelt over the toilet bowl, and vomited.

When he emerged, Cindy Smith was waiting outside the bathroom door. "Gus, don't do this to yourself," she said. "Let's send everyone home so you can go to bed."

He laid his hands on her shoulder, as if steadying himself. "Stay with me, Cindy. Don't leave me alone here."

"You know I can't do that. But I will kick everyone out and help you into bed."

"What will the neighbors think?" he said with a silly giggle.

"Shut up," she said.

In the morning, Gus woke with a killer hangover and a hole in his heart. He managed to pull himself out of bed and stumble into the kitchen. The first thing he saw was the breakfast placement Molly had left for Augie four days before, still there, untouched, which he hadn't noticed amid the chaos and grief. He hurried back to the bathroom and vomited again.

After cleaning himself up, he realized he needed to talk to someone. The previous day he was sick of everyone's sorrow and pity and wanted them to go away. Now he felt the crush of loneliness surrounding him as he comprehended a life without Molly. Which was what brought him, most unexpectedly, to the tall arched doors of St. Stephen's, just east of town, the stone edifice where Molly and several generations of her family had been baptized, worshipped, and buried. He came to see Father Sheehan, a man he scarcely knew but whom Molly had sought for solace for almost as long as they'd been married. Molly had insisted that they marry in the church and that Gus convert. He went along with it but never became an active member of the congregation.

Father Sheehan greeted him warmly and showed him into his book-lined office in the rectory next to the church. The room hinted at a faint aroma of cigar smoke. He asked Gus to send his regards to his friend the Reverend Tom Benson, pastor of Holy Redeemer Lutheran Church, the congregation of Gus's parents in which he had not set foot for fifty years. Gus sensed the priest was messing with him, teasing him for being neither fish nor fowl. Sheehan quickly turned effusive in his condolences for Gus's loss, as if it were his loss as well, which in a sense it was. So sincere was his expression that it made Gus uncomfortable. The priest seemed to sense this. "I'm a terrible host," he said. "Let me get us something to drink."

He left Gus alone in the office. Gus studied the shelves of books that covered nearly all the walls and examined the titles and authors' names on the spines. Interesting juxtapositions. Thomas Merton, but also Richard Dawkins. Soren Kierkegaard, but also Friedrich Nietzsche. Karl Barth, but also Sigmund Freud. Gus had never read any of them, but he knew who they were. On the desk were a pair of hardback novels. *Gilead* by Marilynne Robinson and *Elmer Gantry* by Sinclair Lewis.

Sheehan returned with a fifth of Jameson's Irish whiskey and two glasses. "Interesting library," Gus said. "Famous theologians and famous atheists, side by side."

"Put them together, and you get the middle ground: doubt," Sheehan said. "The human condition, in other words." He uncapped the bottle and poured an inch into each glass. "There's a lot more overlap than most folks think. Take Kierkegaard and Nietzsche. They were proto-existentialists. They both said you are responsible for own your beliefs, or non-beliefs. No one else. You have to choose. Then you have to own your choice. Live it. To the max. Good advice, in my book."

Gus took a swallow. As he had already stopped by the VFW to be fortified by Cindy prior to this visitation, the first shot put him in a mood to mince no words. "I know you've been a good friend and confidant to Molly," he said after draining his glass. Sheehan refilled it. "I appreciate that. But what I want to know is, what good did it do? What the hell good is your God who takes people who are loved and needed and rips them away, rips out the hearts of those of us left behind?"

Sheehan stared at him for a long moment. This was clearly a question he'd been asked a hundred times, maybe a thousand, and still he carefully seemed to be measuring his words. "I can't answer that, Gus. We can't know what God is thinking or why He does what He does."

Gus felt an urge to lash out again, but held his tongue, as Sheehan seemed to be genuinely pondering his question. The priest took a long pull on his whiskey glass before he continued speaking.

"But we *can* know how we should respond to the pain and suffering that is visited upon us. We can't always control it or prevent it, but we can control what we do next. Do you see what I mean?"

Gus tried to see, but all he could imagine was rage against the machine of the cosmos and the need for compensation for his loss. And then he recognized the sentiment. He understood that he was feeling something akin to the *cri du coeur* he'd been reading in the missives from Mr. Fed Up. He knew exactly the cause of his own anguish, while the source of Mr. Fed Up's suffering remained a mystery. A mystery to be solved, before something awful happened.

❖

Chester turned on the heat in his tractor cabin as the temperature had dipped into the mid-thirties overnight. Winter was taking its sweet old time arriving this year but now was beginning to make its presence known. He tuned the satellite radio to his favorite station, in the mood for some Blake Shelton or Garth Brooks.

Wally Johnson picked up on the first ring, which Chester took as a sign that he was rising in importance in Minnesota GOP circles. Money talks, he thought to himself with a bitter smile. When he'd first pitched his Bikers for Trump idea to Wally, he half expected to be dismissed out of hand, like the small-town rube he was in the eyes of the big city boys. But much to his surprise and delight, Wally had endorsed the idea, likely seduced by the big dollar figures Chester tossed about like candy, and instructed Chester to start making the arrangements for a springtime ride.

"Chester, my man! What's the good word?"

"Hey, Wally. The word is all good." He switched off the radio. "Bikers for Trump is coming along beautifully. We've got a route mapped out and are reaching out to law enforcement around the state to smooth the way. They are being very cooperative. I expect more than a few of 'em will be joining us."

"That's what I like to hear. Nice work, buddy. How many you think we're gonna have?"

"So far, I'd say at least a thousand. Maybe two if we expand into other states."

"Got a date pinned down?"

"We're telling folks sometime in mid or late May."

"Well, I got some good news for you. The White House is close to confirming a campaign stop in Minnesota in May, maybe even Memorial Day weekend. And they love, love, love the bikers things, so there's a good chance we can make it happen. Maybe have the biker caravan meet up at a Trump rally, meet the man himself."

"Fantastic!" Chester felt lightheaded. His far-fetched dream seemed like it might really happen. "So, as for the fundraising, I was thinking—"

"Hold on, buddy. Don't get ahead of yourself. There's a new wrinkle here we need to talk about." Wally paused, as if checking his notes. Chester didn't like the sound of 'new wrinkle.' What could that mean? "After consulting with the White House," Wally continued, "we've agreed that it would be best to leave the money end to the state party. That way you can focus on the logistics of the event. You've done a helluva good job getting this thing off the ground. We need you freed up to bring it home."

Chester recognized the rhetorical ploy. He'd used it himself: Butter them up first before hitting them with the bad news, apply the Vaseline so the screwing goes down easier. He let his silence carry his reaction across the connection.

"Anyway, we've asked Jack White to handle the fundraising part down there on the ground, reporting up to me. I know you and Jack will make a great team."

Chester could barely contain his rage. Fucked over again. By Jack White, again. He gathered himself, calmed down, not a good idea to blow up at Wally. "What makes you think Jack White can handle it?"

Now it was Wally's turn to go silent, as if digesting Chester's implication. After a pause, he said, "Jack and I go way back, you know that, Chester. He and Jill are among our top party reps in southern Minnesota. We appreciate your fundraising prowess, but we think it's in the best interest of the Trump campaign to spread responsibilities around. The more the merrier, right? I mean, we're all on the same team."

Chester had no reply for that. His bitterness at being outmaneuvered by the Whites, cut out of the money, was partly leavened by Wally calling him part of the "team." If he handled this right, like a good team player, maybe he could win himself a seat aboard the Trump Train. As for his money problems, he would have to come up with a new plan.

"You bet, Wally," he said with forced enthusiasm. "Happy to do my part. You know that." He nearly choked on the words.

"Good man. Gotta go."

Click.

Chester stared at his phone screen to confirm that Wally had indeed hung up on him. Again. The prick. He turned off the tractor's diesel and climbed down from the cab. Time for a visit with the Whites.

The receptionist at Jack White Chevrolet reported that the boss was away for the day, not sure how to reach him. Maybe call back tomorrow. Chester got into his truck and drove to town hall.

The mayor was in her office and did not seem surprised to see Chester when he barged in unannounced past the receptionist. "It's okay, Lois," she called out to her assistant. "I was expecting him."

"You've screwed me for the last time." His normally pink face had turned crimson.

"Close the door," she said. "Sit down."

He remained standing. "You and Jack. I swear."

"Calm down, Chester. I know what you're mad about. I want you to know that it was Wally's idea to put Jack in charge of the fundraising."

"You think I'm stupid?"

"Hold on. Let me get Jack on the line. He can explain everything." She turned on the speakerphone and punched in a number.

"He's not in the office. I checked."

"I'm calling his cell."

Jack White's voice crackled over the speaker, sounding winded as if he were running or doing something else strenuous. "Is this important? Kind of busy right now."

"Chester's here with me," Jill said. Chester thought he saw the beginnings of a smirk cross her lips.

"Fuck. Hold on," said Jack. They could hear a muffled conversation come across the speaker, as if someone's hand was covering a phone mic. "Howdy, Chester," Jack said when he came back on. "I have an idea why you're in Jill's office."

"How about you tell me what the fuck is going on?"

"I assume you've talked to Wally."

"I assume *you've* talked to Wally," Chester answered.

"You can see his point of view, right?" said Jack. "He's got to answer to the national campaign, the White House. They don't know you, Chester. They know Wally. And they want Wally to oversee the money angle. It's nothing personal. Just business."

"This whole event was my idea."

"Believe me, Chester, everybody knows that. If it comes off as brilliantly as I know it will, you will get the credit. Anyway, it's not just about raising money, it's a powerful symbol of Minnesota's support for the president. And I'm pretty sure Wally can get you a meeting with the man himself."

"He damn well better."

Chester opened the door and stalked out of the office, slamming it behind him. He thought he heard laughter coming from inside. Fuck them. He reached into his pocket and realized he'd forgotten his pills again. He could really use them right now. He needed something to calm himself down, as the old rage beast within was awaking from its slumber.

As soon as Gus opened the door, Cindy could tell he was plastered. She was used to seeing him with a few beers under his belt, sometimes more than a few, and recognized the glassy-eyed look. "Can I come in?" she asked. She held up a shopping bag full of groceries. "I brought dinner." He said nothing and limped back into the house, leaving the door open. She followed him into the kitchen.

"How does roast chicken from the Co-op sound?" She lay the bag on the counter and started to unpack.

"You didn't have to do that, Cindy," Gus said.

"I know. But I did and here I am." She studied him for a moment. "You're drunk, aren't you?"

"So what."

He stood by the refrigerator. Cindy wondered what was inside there. Food? Or just beer. She would check later. He looked and sounded so defeated. She approached him with her arms stretched out, offering a hug. He lowered his head and studied the floor. It hadn't been swept or mopped in a while. She interpreted his body language as resignation, permission, and wrapped him in her arms and gently pushed his head onto her shoulder. He was trying not to cry, she could tell, and he was failing. "Oh, Gus. I'm so sorry." He stood upright and stepped back. Her shirt was damp where he'd rested his head. She grabbed both his hands in hers.

"It's been a long time since we hugged like that," he said.

She reached up and wiped a tear from his cheek with the back of her hand. Indeed, she thought. More than twenty years. "I remember," she said.

They sat opposite each other at the kitchen table. "It never should have happened," he said. "I'm sorry. It was wrong."

"No it wasn't. I wanted it to happen. And I never regretted it."

"I was your teacher. You were my student."

"I was eighteen. An adult."

That was the rationale Cindy had fallen back on over the decades whenever guilt feelings reemerged. As if being legally an adult could erase the sordid shame of committing adultery with your high school teacher. Had she seduced him? Or had he seduced her? She couldn't remember. She remembered wanting it to happen, after months of living in close quarters under Gus and Molly's roof. That was back when Molly still worked in the *Clarion* office and

Gus and Cindy occasionally found themselves alone in the house in the mid-afternoon on days when Gus didn't have baseball practice. The sexual tension was palpable, apparently so thick in the air it triggered Molly's radar and she started popping in unexpectedly during the day. Not that she ever caught them *in flagrante delicto*. Gus seemed to think they'd got away with it when Cindy took flight to Minneapolis to enroll in community college summer courses to prepare for admission to the U.

"If it makes you feel any better, you were the last man I ever slept with," she said. "You retired the trophy." She meant it as a joke, but Gus wasn't laughing.

"Did I… Did it … make you turn gay?"

Cindy almost burst out laughing but caught herself. It was funny, in a sad, weird way, but now was not the time for levity. "Of course not," she said. "It doesn't work that way, Gus. I'd suspected I was gay since I was about fourteen, even though I dated guys in high school. I didn't fully accept it till later. I met a girl at the U who showed me the truth about myself. It had nothing to do with you."

Gus was silent for a long while, apparently absorbing this. Then he said, "I always believed that Molly never knew. I often thought of confessing but couldn't bring myself to it. Now she's gone. No chance for me to make it right. She never once mentioned it in all those years. Not then. Not ever. Until recently. In her last days, she accused me. Out of the blue. I couldn't believe it. I denied it. Gaslighted her again."

"Oh, she knew, Gus. She always knew."

"How …?"

"Why do you think I left so abruptly? I never even said goodbye, remember?"

"Molly?"

Cindy nodded. "She said, and I quote, 'Get out of my house. Today. Before I hurt you.' She was holding a meat cleaver." Gus went wide-eyed, a look of alarm lighting his visage. Cindy guessed he was remembering what Molly had done to him with a spatula. "I was gone before you even got home that day."

"I always thought you just wanted to get away from here," he said. "Away from me."

"That's what I wanted you to think. And it was true, the part about wanting to get away from Newfield."

"You never told me any of this."

"In the time since I've been back, when have we ever talked about any of it? We act like it never happened."

"I wish it never happened. I've lived with the guilt all these years. I could have fessed up and Molly probably would have forgiven me. But I was a coward. Afraid of losing her respect for me. I thought I'd got away with it. And Molly never let on that she knew. Maybe that was her way of punishing me, making me live with the guilt and shame rather than clearing the air. It's strange that she never said anything after you came back to town. She must have forgiven me. She stayed with me and was a wonderful wife all those years. But she kept her forgiveness to herself, I guess, and let me twist in the wind."

Gus seemed more depressed than ever. The crushing loss of Molly was enough by itself, but now added to that was a lifetime of regret. Cindy put a hand on his shoulder. "You're so alone now, Gus. No Augie. No Molly. You don't even have a dog. And it breaks my heart. I want you to know—listen to me now—I want you to know that I am here for you. Not like before. Like now. As your friend. You looked out for me once. And again when I came back. Now it's my turn to look out for you."

Jim Tomlinson stared at the coffee maker on his kitchen counter, waiting for the hissing and steaming to commence. The machine looked so tired, so dated, its white plastic housing stained with a decade of spilt coffee residue. He glanced around the kitchen and realized how dreary it was, the Formica counters chipped, the cabinets in need of paint, how dreary his whole apartment had become without him noticing. He noticed it now. For so many years he had worried that he would end up a disappointment to his father, without noticing until now that he had become a disappointment to himself.

The glass pot finally filled, and he poured two mugs. One black, one milk no sugar. He hoped he remembered correctly. He carried the mugs into the bedroom. "Get it while it's hot," he said cheerily. Lame. Why couldn't he ever think of anything witty and urbane to say? He was supposed to be a writer after all.

Jeanne Birdsong sat up in the bed and covered her bare torso with the comforter. "Mmmm. Smells good," she said. "Almost as good as my mom's coffee."

He handed her a mug and sat on the edge of the bed. "I could never compete with Mavis," he said, then took a sip. "Nobody can."

After their last date, when Jeanne had kissed him goodnight but left him behind in his car, he wondered if she would ever see him the way he saw her. He thought about her all the time, mooning like a schoolboy. The vibe he was picking up from her seemed to place him firmly in the friend zone. Until last night. They'd gone up to Mankato to hear some country music in a downtown bar. They both drank Cokes. Nothing in her behavior suggested a change of heart, a warming toward him. But afterwards, when he neared the turn toward her place, she suggested they go to his place instead. He happily agreed, although wishing he'd anticipated this turn of events and tidied up his dismal bachelor pad. Once inside, skipping the prologue, she grabbed his hand and led him into the bedroom. She asked him to leave the room dark, which he did. He'd daydreamed of the day he would see her naked, but that was soon forgotten when Jeanne enveloped him in her arms and legs and affixed her mouth to his like a Moray eel. Afterwards, he asked her about the need for darkness. She said she was ashamed of her body, marred by long-regretted tattoos and scars from beatings and knife wounds. In the morning light, she relented and allowed him to explore her skin, head to toe. Slash marks on her wrist from a failed suicide attempt. A long scar on her belly where she'd had her spleen removed after a brutal kicking and beating of which she had no memory. A knife wound on her buttocks, courtesy of a meth-addled prostitute. A half-dozen tattoos, a few of which she couldn't account for. In spite of all the physical damage, she showed no psychological scars, only a proud determination and self-confidence. He was already falling in love with her. Was he good enough for her? There was the matter of his alcoholism, the subject of which had not arisen. Yet. He knew it was a matter of time. Better to tell her before she sniffs it out and forces a confrontation. Or an intervention; isn't that what they call it?

He noticed that she'd set the coffee mug on the nightstand and stared at the opposite wall, her face fallen from afterglow to worry lines.

"Everything okay?" he asked.

"I'm thinking about Travis. Worried."

"He's a good kid—"

"I found drugs in his car. A vial of pills, probably Oxycontin."

"Oh, no. Are you sure?"

"He denied it, said he didn't know where it came from. He's a lousy liar. Just like his mother. I have a good idea where it came from. Freddie fucking Ignatowski and his so-called biker gang."

Jim knew all about Freddie. He'd heard the suspicions voiced by Jeanne, Mavis, and others, but there were no recent arrests or convictions, so nothing ever appeared in the *Clarion*. He wondered if that would be a more fruitful line of inquiry for Pam Strich than chasing the chimera of the Whites and Greenfields. "How do you know it was Freddie?"

"Please." She looked at him like he was a moron. "Everybody knows where the drugs in this town come from. I would expect the editor of the newspaper to know that."

"I've heard the rumors. The police have turned up nothing on him. There's nothing I could put in the paper."

"It was Freddie who got me hooked on meth and pills. When I was eighteen. That's how long it's been going on. I lost twelve years of my life because of him. That's twelve years I'll never get back."

Jim felt suddenly weak and ineffectual, having done nothing to uncover and root out the drug problem in the community that had ravaged the lives of people like Jeanne. He was filled with loathing toward Freddie and the whole Blue Hogs crew and vowed to correct that oversight.

"You know he did time for drug dealing, right?" she said.

"Yes. I know." He thought he detected an accusatory tone on her voice, as if she were saying, 'How could you not investigate if you knew that?' "It was a long time ago."

"Anyway, I went to see him," she said. "At his shop."

"Alone?"

"Yes, alone. I'm not afraid of anybody. He denied everything, of course, but with a sneer. I could see it in his eyes. Lying his ass off and thinking it funny."

"What are you going to do?"

"It's not what I'm going to do that concerns me. It's what my father might do. I showed him the pills and told him about confronting Freddie. And I told him who hooked me on drugs all those years ago. 'Stay away from him,' he said. 'I'll handle it.' My Mom thinks he might do something awful, maybe even kill him. She's gone to that cop, Morton. Asked him to keep a close eye on Elvis and Freddie … before something bad happens."

Dear Molly,
Recently I was shopping at the mall where I saw a gang of loitering teenagers being loud and acting unruly. Nothing unusual about that, I was once a "mall rat" myself. But what upset me was their language: a loud and steady stream of f-words, as if it were the only vocabulary they knew. In that same mall I heard music blasting out of a boutique and it, too, was filled with obscenities. When I was young, we acted up and did crazy things, but there were limits, taboos we respected. One of those taboos was yelling the f-word in public. Apparently that awful word has lost its ability to shock. Well, not to me it hasn't. Please, Molly, tell me why young people have to be so crude and offensive, and what we mature adults can do about it.
Signed,
Disgusted

Dear Disgusted,
Fuck if I know.
Hugs,
Molly

Nov. 24, 2019

James Tomlinson <jtomlinson@newfieldclarion.com>
To: Molly Peterson <dearmolly@newfieldclarion.com>
WTF?

I am not printing that, Gus. What's wrong with you? I know you are suffering, in pain. We all are, okay? That's no excuse to flip the bird at our readers. Please send me another column by tomorrow. Don't make me have to print another "Molly is on vacation" notice.—Jim

Dear Molly,

I make it a habit whenever I see someone in military uniform to thank them for their service. I have been doing that for many years, as I am truly grateful to them for defending our freedoms.

Recently my daughter-in-law criticized me for doing just that. She said I was perpetuating America's "imperialism" and "military-industrial complex." She's been to college so I guess I shouldn't be surprised by her attitude.

It seems to me that her view is a common one among the younger generations. Where is their patriotism? Where is their gratitude? Where is their respect? They seem to think only of themselves and their "woke" mindset.

Please, Molly, tell your readers how important it is to show respect and gratitude to our armed services men and women.

Signed,
Grateful

Dear Grateful,

You're absolutely right. Thanking military personnel for their service is decent and always welcome. I recommend we also thank police and firefighters and schoolteachers and mail carriers for their service. All public servants, in fact. Even those hard-working folks with TSA who annoy you with delays at the airport. And those most reviled figures of all: IRS agents. Thank them all.

But you know what? Your daughter-in-law is right, too. America's military history has much to answer for. Just ask the innocent civilians of Vietnam, Afghanistan, and Iraq. That's not the fault of individual service men and women, but it is naïve and wrong-headed to believe they are "defending our freedoms." It's that kind of thinking that justifies American overseas military adventures, with often disastrous results.

The truth is, no one is coming to take away our freedoms. Our greatest adversaries in modern times, Nazi Germany and Imperial Japan, the Soviet Union (now Russia) and Communist China, are separated from us by enormous oceans. None of them has the capacity or will to cross oceans and conquer the United States and take away our freedoms. As for our northern and southern borders? Two friendly and non-militaristic neighbors: Canada and Mexico.

The only real threats to our freedoms have always come from within. From our fellow citizens, the overzealous reformers and the intolerant bigots. The risks of insurrection or infiltration, real or imagined, are not the purview of the U.S. military, but of domestic law enforcement. So hug an FBI agent sometime.

Next time you see a member of the U.S. military, go ahead and thank them for their service. Just be clear what you are also thanking them for: making the world safe for the profits of America's multinational corporations.

Hugs,
Molly

Nov. 25, 2019

James Tomlinson <jtomlinson@newfieldclarion.com>
To: Molly Peterson <dearmolly@newfieldclarion.com>
RE: WTF?

Jesus H. Christ, Gus. Maybe I should print your "Fuck if I know" column instead of this one. We'd get less blowback. This is like poking a sharp stick in the eye of our largely conservative, patriotic readership. But I can't disagree with your point. After all you've been through, you're one of the few people I know who has the moral authority to write something like this. So I'm going to print it. Just remember, after a subscription and advertising boycott puts the *Clarion* out of business, I'll be down in Florida with Mom and Dad sipping piña coladas on the beach and wondering why the hell I ever let you take over "Dear Molly."

Have a nice weekend.—Jim

Gus had to smile. Say what you want about Jim Tomlinson, the man has balls. He was probably right about the blowback. Gus was beyond caring at this point. Bring it on. These were things he needed to get off his chest. Damn the consequences. What could anyone do to him? Force Jim to replace him? Cancel the column? There was nothing anyone could do that would be worse than what he's already been through.

Gus was having one of those days. The house he and Molly had shared for forty years seemed larger and gloomier than he ever imagined. The emptiness, the silence, made him want to escape to the friendly murmurings of the VFW. Maybe later. First there was the matter of the latest missive from Fed Up.

Nov. 26, 2019

Fed Up <fedup@hotmail.com>
To: Molly Peterson <dearmolly@newfieldclarion.com>
Thank you!

Well, you followed my instructions. That wasn't so hard, was it? I'm sorry it was a wasted trip for you. But it was not wasted for me. I was observing you from a distance. You waited thirty minutes before leaving, not unreasonable. You see, I can be very reasonable. No one to fear or sneer at. Now that I know I can trust you to follow directions, it's time we meet in person, for real this time. I promise I will show up and I promise this meeting will be worth your time. I have a story to tell and you will want to hear it.

I will be in contact with you about the time and place of our meeting. I am very much looking forward to this and I hope you are too.

Your friend,

Fed Up

p.s. I am sorry about your wife. She was a good person. She was nice to me once.

```
To the editor,
I've long been a fan of your "Dear Molly" column.
I was saddened to hear of Molly's passing. I
admire her husband Gus for taking up the column
and using it to speak the truth, as inconvenient
and uncomfortable as it may be. He has the
backbone to say what needs to be said, what many
of us think but are afraid to say in this age
of political correctness. I like to think he is
inspired in his truth-telling by our president.
However, I was shocked and disappointed to read
the latest column in which he attacked the United
States military in a most unpatriotic way. Who
is he, a retired high school teacher, to pass
judgment on the greatest country in the history
of the world? American military might has been
deployed in the service of freedom not only for
its own citizens but all over the world.
I sincerely hope that in the future you will
discourage your columnist from such negativity
and focus on what makes America great.
Barney Johansson
USMC retired
Good Thunder, Minn.
```

Dear Mr. Johansson,

It's rare that we at the Clarion respond to our letter writers. We welcome a wide diversity of opinion on our pages, and we thank you for yours.

In this case, however, we feel we must set the record straight about our columnist and his recent remarks about military service. Gus Peterson is indeed a retired high school teacher (and baseball coach). He is also a wounded and decorated veteran of the Vietnam War who gave up a promising baseball career to answer the call of duty. Gus and Molly lost their only child, Augustus, Jr.—Augie to his friends and family—in the Iraq War. Whatever your thoughts about the justifications for those two overseas military adventures, there is little doubt they were ultimately unsuccessful debacles and highly questionable sacrifices of American youth.

In the "Dear Molly" column, Gus Peterson speaks for himself and does not represent the views of the Clarion. Yet we wholeheartedly support his right to speak his mind. And your right as well. Thank you for your service.

The Editor

Freddie Ignatowski opened the mini fridge in the back of his garage and extracted a can of Bud Light. Time to close up shop and call it a day. The to-go box on the top shelf reminded him to take home his Thanksgiving leftovers from Perkins for tonight's dinner. His sole employee Donnie had gone home early, so he had the place to himself. And what a good day it was. Donnie, bless his little heart, had given him a toe-curling hummer to put him in a good mood for the weekend, just like he'd been doing since their long-ago days and nights at Stillwater. He often questioned whether the secret pleasure was worth the risk of what would happen if his Blue Hogs crew ever found out. Anyway, there was also the two repair-and-paint jobs finished, worth a couple grand. Best of all, the news that his latest shipment of Oxy was on its way from Mexico. All he had to do was come up with the fifty K, take delivery, sell into his usual channels, and he'd get his investment back tenfold, at least a half mil. He was about ten grand short but felt sure he could come up with that in no time.

He sat at the old metal desk next to the bathroom door, cracked open the beer can tab, and took a gulp. He was about to follow it up with another guzzle—he could drain a twelve-ounce can in two or three slugs—when he heard tires crunching on the gravel parking lot out front. Should have pulled down the garage door so people know we're closed, he thought. Irritated, he sucked out the remaining beer and crushed the can in his hand, pulled on his leather Hogs jacket, and went outside to tell the potential customer to come back in the morning.

It was no customer, it was Chester Greenfield, just emerging from his big black truck.

"Just closin' up, Seventy-Seven," Freddie said. "But c'mon in and have a beer."

"Don't mind if I do, Seventy-Five," he said.

Freddie thought he detected a worried look on the man's usually cocky face. Two beers in hand, they exited the back door and took up their usual happy hour spot at the flimsy table and chairs in the rear lot. The sun was going down and a chill settled in, but it was not too cold yet for some patio drinking. They had been meeting once a week to go over details and progress on the biker rally. Freddie had proved to be quite good at selling the idea to motorcycle clubs around the state and now was reaching out to those in South Dakota, Iowa, and Wisconsin.

"How goes the Bikers for Trump deal? We gonna get to meet the big man?" Freddie said. Chester had dangled that possibility, which Freddie repeated numerous times as an incentive for commitments.

"Can't promise yet, but it looks like there will be a campaign stop in Minnesota in May, so we might be able to coordinate schedules. Wally Johnson said if we can pull it off successfully he thinks we can get a meeting."

"That would be awesome. How about the money? How much you think we can raise?" Freddie had long suspected the cash cow potential was what was really driving Chester and he'd managed to wheedle the details out of him. Never one to let a good opportunity pass, Freddie had cut himself in for a share of the take.

"Well," said Chester. He took a long drink, belched, and gazed at the darkening sky. Freddie sensed Chester was weighing his words carefully and reminded himself to be alert for bullshit and doubletalk. "There's been a bit of a snag there."

"A snag? What kind of a snag?"

"Wally has put Jack and Jill White in charge of collecting the checks. They're supposed to deliver everything directly to Wally. So we're screwed."

"Fuck, man! Whose idea was that?"

"The Whites say it was Wally, but I think they smelled the money and inserted themselves into the picture. That's how they operate."

"What can we do about it?"

"I'm not sure, at this point."

"I can send some of my boys, put a scare into them."

"Don't be stupid. Jill's the mayor, remember? She's pals with the sheriff."

"Then what's the goddamn point of all this? Fuck the rally." This is what you get when you trust the suits. They're all the same.

"We can't back out now, Freddie. You've already promised so many people. The Trump campaign has endorsed it. We'll just have to figure out another plan. Maybe we can build on the rally, come up with something even better. Anyway, this is a big setback for me. I'm over a barrel, financially. I was counting on the rally to bail me out."

Freddie sensed a shift in the direction of the conversation. Time to recalibrate. Play the concerned friend. "How bad is it?"

"I got to come up with a million in six months. And at least a hundred K in three months, to keep the wolves away."

A hundred K? thought Freddie. There's a big ol' fish nibbling at my line. Time to set the hook. And I owe him one. He did me a solid so many years ago. "I might be able to help you there, Seventy-Seven. Can you get your hands on ten grand, like pretty quick, next few days?"

"Yeah, no problem, why?"

"I'm workin' on a deal that will pay back tenfold. Sure thing. Put in ten, get back a hundred. How's that sound?"

"Tell me more," said Chester.

By The Associated Press

MINNEAPOLIS—In the classic 1976 film "Network," a television news anchor on the verge of a nervous breakdown rants into the camera, exhorting his audience to turn off their TVs and rebel against the system. "I'm mad as hell and I'm not going to take it anymore," chants the anchorman, Howard Beale, a fictional character played memorably by the actor Peter Finch.

Now comes a real-life Howard Beale in the person of Gus Peterson, a small-town newspaper columnist in southern Minnesota who has won a loyal following with his weekly infective-filled diatribes against the follies of modern society.

The column is called "Dear Molly," named for the originator of the feature, Molly Peterson, Gus Peterson's late wife who died from a stroke in November after several months of declining health. In September, Peterson began ghostwriting his wife's column, which appears once a week in The Newfield Clarion and several other southern Minnesota newspapers, after she was unable to continue. At first no one was aware of the ruse, not even James Tomlinson, editor and publisher of the Clarion and longtime family friend of the Petersons.

"Gus had been proofreading Molly's column for so long that he knew how to exactly mimic her style and her philosophy," said Tomlinson. "I had no idea he was writing it, at least not until I began to notice a gradual shift toward a more confrontational, even angry, tone that was not at all like Molly Peterson."

Newfield being a small, close-knit town of about 2,000 residents, it was not long before the Petersons' secret leaked out. The response from the newspaper's readers was "overwhelmingly positive," said Tomlinson. "People around here have a genuine love for Molly, and they were touched by Gus's effort to keep her wisdom alive when she could not continue."

The Clarion's readers embraced not only the pathos of the Peterson family drama, but also the bracing, astringent voice that Gus Peterson brought to the column, which had long been beloved for its folksy Midwestern common sense. In this deeply conservative rural community of farmers, which President Trump carried by more than 20 points in 2016, Peterson has been regarded as a refreshing truth-teller, much like the president, although his politics don't exactly align with Republican doctrine.

A sample of recent salvos from 'Dear Molly' includes this response to a letter writer who complained of being stalked by an internet troll who he'd thought he'd been scamming:

Dear Catfish,

First, I want to thank you for sharing your story. When I stopped laughing, I felt only pity and contempt for you. I see by your signature that you are aware of the internet scam called "catfishing," using a fake identity to lure someone into an online relationship. In this case, it seems you thought you were the cat, but it turned out you were the fish! Oh, the irony. … The fact that you ended up the fool suggests there is cosmic justice in this world. People are fed up with all the faking and lying and scamming that, sadly, seem to be the norm these days, everywhere from the internet to the nation's capital.

To a woman who said she wanted to divorce her farmer husband because he had fallen into financial difficulty:

Dear Farmer's Wife,
I was going to respond with a comment about rats and sinking ships, but that cliché doesn't do justice to the contempt I have for you. Whatever happened to honoring our commitments? Do the words "for richer or poorer, in sickness and in health, till death do us part" mean nothing anymore? … There is far too much of this sort of "me-first" mentality in our society today. … People need to return to some basic principles of honor, loyalty, and decency. Else we are doomed.

To an unfortunate correspondent, signed as "Over the Moon," who claimed to have fallen in love with a "Nigerian princess" on the internet:

Dear Mr. Moon,
Here at Mollyville World Headquarters, we have a special place for missives such as yours which we call the round file. I assume your story is a joke, because no one is stupid enough in this Year of Our Lord 2019 to fall for the Nigerian email scam, which has been rattling around the interwebs for nigh on twenty years.

Peterson's no-holds-barred attitude caused a minor stir when he wrote that U.S. military personnel should be thanked for their service, but not for "defending our freedoms," rather for "making the world safe for the profits of American multinational corporations." That drew a firestorm of protest from the Clarion's readers, which Tomlinson felt necessary to defend as Peterson's right of free speech.

For his part, Peterson was reluctant to comment for this article, given that he is still mourning the death of his wife of 45 years. He said he has turned down several requests for television interviews, as he is a private person with no desire to become a celebrity.

"In all her years writing 'Dear Molly,' my wife never drew this much attention," he said. "I don't deserve it. She did."

December

Rather than wait for Mr. Fed Up's instructions for their meeting, Gus decided to try to track him down first, better to meet on his terms rather than those of this stalker who had apparently decided that they were friends now. Fat chance, thought Gus. Some of Fed Up's most recent missives had contained alarming signals. For instance, the references to guns and ammo, which suggested he might be armed to the teeth, or at least fantasizing about it. And some of his lingo strongly suggested a military background. Gus recognized the tenor of it all, having seen too many cases of post-traumatic stress disorder during his visits to VA hospitals for ankle surgeries. He'd had touches of it himself, not that it ever induced thoughts of violence. The possibility that his anonymous correspondent was a heavily armed veteran with psychological problems chilled him to the marrow. In the epidemic of mass shootings over the last two decades, he knew most perpetrators were not veterans with PTSD. But some were. These were gut feelings, he realized, nothing definitive that he could take to the sheriff's office. Torkelson had already blown him off once, and Gus didn't think another visit would bring a different result. Maybe he was being a touch paranoid, but he also didn't think he should pursue this on his own. He needed to confide in someone he could trust, someone who would have his back while not scaring everyone in town with loose talk. Which is the line of thinking that brought him to Elvis Birdsong's house.

When he parked the Ford on the Birdsongs' driveway, he didn't see Elvis's truck, only Mavis's white van. It was late afternoon; she likely had already closed the café and come home. He rang the doorbell. Mavis greeted him and invited him in, but Gus demurred, explaining that he only needed to chat with Elvis for a moment. Mavis said her husband had gone deer hunting and likely wouldn't be back until late or possibly tomorrow if he decided to camp for the night. Gus thanked her and started to leave. She said to his back, "I'm worried about Elvis, Gus." He stopped and he turned to her, assuming she would say more. "Come inside, please," she said.

She offered him coffee, which he declined, and they sat in the living room. Elvis's La-Z-Boy looked inviting, but he thought better of it and sat in a straight-back chair.

"I'm afraid Elvis is going to do something crazy, something awful," Mavis said. She had his full attention. Her voice had a pleading tone, on the verge of tears, as if she were lobbying Gus to intervene. He listened patiently as Mavis unpacked her suspicion that Elvis was not really deer hunting but searching for Freddie Ignatowski with the intent to shoot him. She told him the whole saga of Jeanne and drugs and Freddie and Travis and Elvis's avowal to deal with the situation. Gus knew Freddie was a disreputable character with a prison record, but he was unaware of the direct link to the Birdsong family. Elvis's zeal in organizing the militia, which Gus had thought was a bit over the top, now made more sense. As he left, he promised Mavis the next time he came across Elvis he would talk him out of doing anything violent. She asked him to call Elvis's cellphone and try to talk to him right away. His call went straight to voicemail. He left a message warning Elvis not to do anything rash and to call him back soonest.

He climbed into his car and sat for a moment. Should he

search for Fed Up by himself? Or try to find Elvis first? He knew Elvis had a hunting camp on some wooded land he owned north of town where they held militia drills, but he worried that showing up there during hunting season was a good way to get himself shot by mistake. He didn't own any blaze orange attire. In any case, it seemed Elvis had other priorities right now and perhaps would not be available to help Gus flush out Mr. Fed Up. He settled on Plan B and drove off to the VFW.

Cindy greeted him with a smile when he walked through the squeaky door and she reached for a bottle of Grain Belt in the cooler. Gus stopped her and said he needed to talk. Now. The bar was crowded with afternoon drinkers, the music loud and the boozy chatter louder, nearly drowning out Willie Nelson. Cindy motioned him to follow her into the small office behind the bar, where she closed the door behind them. There were no chairs; they sat on cases of Schell's. "What's up?" she said. "I can only leave the bar untended for a minute."

Rather than give her the whole story of Mr. Fed Up, Gus said only that he was being stalked by someone who might be dangerous and that he could use some advice and assistance. But it had to be kept quiet.

Cindy was visibly alarmed. "How long has this been going on? Why didn't you tell me?"

"I can explain it all later. Will you help me?"

"I get off in an hour. Go home and I'll meet you there."

When Cindy arrived, she didn't bother to knock or ring the bell. She barged right in as if she owned the place, which was fine with Gus, given how often she'd been coming around to look in on him after the funeral. They stood in the kitchen with cold beers in hand. Gus laid out the story of his anonymous correspondent and showed her the handwritten letters and printouts of the emails. She agreed that the tone had turned ominous. She asked about involving law enforcement, and he related his disappointing reaction from the sheriff and Fed Up's cryptic warning to not go to the police.

"Are you going to meet with him?" she said.

"I think I have to. Soon as he tells me where and when. I need to find out who he is and what he wants. If I blow him off, he might do something crazy."

"You think he's a shooter?"

"I think he has all the warning signs. Don't you?"

Cindy looked out the kitchen window and was silent for a long moment. Then she turned back to Gus. "I think you better let me come along."

Gus had toyed with the idea of having Elvis follow him at a distance as backup. But no way was he going to ask that of Cindy. "He warned me to come alone." Gus shook his head emphatically. "And I'm not putting you in danger."

"But it's okay to put yourself in danger?"

"I may be an old guy with a limp, but I can still handle myself. I learned a few things in the Army, how to hurt somebody quickly."

"That was fifty years ago, Gus." Cindy reached into her leather bag and produced a shiny black handgun, the .357 magnum she kept behind the bar. "You're not going without this."

She laid it on the kitchen counter with a loud clang of metal on Formica and left before he could protest. He picked it up. He'd forgotten how heavy the things were. He ejected the clip. It was full.

Dec. 6, 2019

Fed Up <fedup@hotmail.com>
To: Molly Peterson <dearmolly@newfieldclarion.com>
Your move

Hello, Gus. It's time we met. I hope you are as eager to meet me as I am to meet you. I promise you will be glad you came.

Remember what I said. Do not bring anyone else. Do not go to the police. Just you and me. Mano a mano, as they say. Meet me down by the river at 8:00 am on Monday. Take Mill St. to the river crossing and park your car off the road. There's a good spot under the trees. Follow the river north about a half mile then turn right at the bend and walk maybe a hundred yards into the woods until you see a hunting cabin in a small clearing. I'll be waiting for you there. Don't disappoint me.

      Your friend,

      Fed Up

Gus rose early on Monday morning and saw from the kitchen window that it had started to snow overnight. Winter was late in coming, with only a few flurries during November and early December when nothing stuck. This looked like the first major accumulation, small flakes falling hard. Already the barren garden plots and the lawn were coated with a dusting of white. The sagging roof of the old barn was turning white to match the cracked and faded paint on the sides. The effect reminded Gus of how beautiful winter in Minnesota could be and how it could transform the dreariest landscape into something sublime, as long as the wind wasn't howling or the mercury sinking below zero.

      After draining the last of his mug of coffee and polishing off two pieces of toast, he turned his attention to the black hunk of metal on the counter, exactly where he'd left it after Cindy had gone. He hadn't wanted to touch it after he reinserted the clip, as if picking it up again would commit him to using it. It looked wildly out of place in his kitchen, like a malignant appliance with conscious, evil intent. He thought about what Cindy had said. She was right, of course. Who was he kidding? A sixty-eight-year-old man with a balky leg walking unarmed into a remote location to meet a possibly deranged stalker. He picked up the pistol and tucked it into the back of his pants, like he'd seen done in countless crime shows and heist movies. And most recently by members of the Blue Hogs at the Dodd-Ford bridge. The gun felt strange and cold against his underwear and heavy enough to pull his pants down. He tightened his belt a notch and pulled on his down parka as he walked out the front door.

He drove toward town in the old Ford, wondering if it was a mistake not to have put on the snow tires. Rear-wheel drive American cars didn't handle well in snow, as he knew too well. He could have taken Molly's truck, but he hadn't been able to bring himself to drive it. As he drove cautiously past the neighbors' farms, the snow was beginning to blanket the fields. Stubble of pale corn stalks in sections not yet plowed under poked up through the white like defiant middle fingers flipping the bird to Old Man Winter. It would be a futile gesture. Soon they would disappear for good.

He arrived at the narrow crossing over the river on Mill Street, officially now labeled by the county as 287th Avenue. He pulled onto the shoulder and slowly coasted down the gentle incline toward the riverbank. There was plenty of room to park under the bare cottonwood trees, just as Fed Up instructed. No other vehicles in sight. Gus wondered if his mysterious "friend" hadn't arrived yet, or if he'd simply walked to the meeting spot. He pulled out his phone to check the time. Ten minutes to eight, perfect timing. He noticed his cell signal showed no bars. So not only was he alone, he was cut off from communication. Undaunted, he set out on foot along the riverbank, grateful that the water level was low due to the persistent drought that had extended well into fall, making it easy to follow the sandy shore. He counted his steps as he pushed branches out of the way and tiptoed around wet spots. The counting was tedious but kept his mind occupied and not obsessing over the danger he might be wandering into. When he reached a thousand, he guessed he'd gone half a mile. He turned right and walked away from the river through thick underbrush and within a few minutes came to a snow-covered clearing. There, smack in the middle, as Fed Up had promised, was a weather-beaten old shack, its battered roof turning white. In his instructions, Fed Up had referred to it as a hunting cabin, but it looked more like an abandoned tool shed. The one small window Gus could see was covered from the inside with yellowed newspaper. There was a faint glow behind it, suggesting an interior light. Gus reached back to assure himself that the gun was still tucked away, and he approached the cabin.

Elvis Birdsong was pleasantly surprised by how many members of his loose and undisciplined militia had agreed to meet him at the Dodd-Ford bridge for another showdown with the drug-dealing scourge known as the Blue Hogs. Nearly all of Birdsong's Brigade, as they now called themselves semi-ironically, signed on for the Monday morning confrontation. Most of them were retired so there was little concern over missing work. Gus Peterson had not responded, not answering his phone, texts, or emails.

Only Elvis knew that the gathering was a ruse, an opportunity for him to isolate Freddie Ignatowksi in the woods in order to, if the conditions were right, arrange a hunting accident. When he arrived at the bridge most of his crew was there, bundled in blaze orange against the driving snow as they gathered around their vehicles, trying hard to look like a deer hunting party. Elvis was satisfied they formed a quorum that could testify later, if necessary, as to his whereabouts on this morning. He gathered his troops around the hood of his truck and explained that he would be going off on a recon mission and return in about an hour. The rest of them were to hold the bridge and call his cell if and when the Hogs showed up. He climbed into his truck and drove away toward the first of several spots where he expected to find Freddie doing his usual drug deals. He checked his Browning A5: four deer-slug shells.

Gus approached the door of the shack and rapped twice.

"It's open," came a male voice from inside.

Gus entered. The cramped little room was nearly dark, lit only by a battery-powered camping light on a small table under the newspaper-covered window. Outdoor light streamed in through the open door to reveal one side of the shack. Gus saw something hanging on the wall that stopped him cold.

"Close the door," the voice said.

When the door clicked shut, the room darkened again. Another light flicked on. A flashlight aimed at his face, almost blinding him. Gus turned aside and stared at the wall. Even in the dim light he could see several rifles mounted on racks. Some had scopes. There was also a military-style assault rifle on the floor propped up against the wall.

"You came. Good." The flashlight clicked off. As his eyes adjusted, Gus could make out the figure of an adult male seated on a stool. The face was in shadow, partially obscured by a hoodie. In one hand he held a chrome-plated handgun, which he raised and pointed at Gus.

This is where it ends, Gus thought. Coming to join you now, Molly. A warm trickle of urine ran down the inside of his leg.

Unless, he thought. Could he reach for his pistol before getting shot? He contemplated this, weighing the risks against the rewards, when the man spoke again. "Turn around." He stood and pressed the barrel of his gun into Gus's chest. "Now." Gus turned. The man reached under Gus's jacket and pulled the magnum out of his pants. He shoved him hard into the back of the door. Gus crumpled to the floor, his face clawed by the rough wood.

"Nice try, old man. You come to kill me?"

Gus stood and turned to face him. He could feel blood streaming down his face from his nose. Maybe his mouth. "No, no. Just to protect myself," he said, holding his hands up in supplication. The man still had the chrome pistol pointed at his chest. "I ... I didn't know what I was walking into. Or who."

Outside the wind picked up and a few wisps of snow leaked in through cracks in the roof. The door rattled.

"Sit down." The man gestured with his gun toward another stool in a corner next to the door. He flipped a switch on the camp light, which brightened the room so Gus could get the full picture. It contained a small arsenal. Handguns. Shotguns. Hunting rifles. Assault rifles. Boxes of ammunition. Vests. Camo gear. Gus's worst fears confirmed. A mass shooting waiting to happen.

Gus sat. The man sat across from him and pulled the hood back from his head. He was youngish, late thirties maybe, early forties at the oldest. White, with a blonde buzz cut. Neck tattoos. The left side of his face was covered by a nasty-looking rash. Acne? Birth mark? No, Gus recognized it as a serious burn, like ones he'd seen in VA hospitals. There was something familiar...

"Recognize me?" the man said.

"Kwik-Mart," said Gus. He remembered now. The lonely night clerk at the 24-hour gas station convenience store out on Highway 169. Gus had been there only a few times, but he remembered the shy, disfigured attendant who never encouraged conversation, only staring down at the cash register and mumbling to customers. Then it hit him: Molly had come to the man's defense one night when customers were mocking him for seeming slow and dimwitted. And he'd written that Molly had been nice to him once, but Gus had missed the connection.

"That's right. You remember. I remember you, too. What else? Just Kwik-Mart?"

Gus searched his memory, came up empty.

"How 'bout Newfield High? Class of '95," the man said.

Again, no recollection. "Were you in one of my classes? On the baseball team?"

"No. But I seen you around school. And you seen me. But I guess you don't remember. Nobody does."

Class of 1995, thought Gus. That was Augie's year, wasn't it? "Did … did you know my son? Augie?"

"Oh yeah. I knew him."

"I'm sorry, I don't remember you. What did you say your name was?"

"I didn't. But it's Glen. Glen Walser."

The name didn't ring a bell. "Were you friends with Augie? Did he ever bring you around to the house?"

"Nah. We weren't friends in school. He was too cool for me. But I knew him later."

"How?"

"In the Army." Walser stared at him, then smiled, his eyes teasing as if waiting for Gus to connect the dots.

"Goddamn pussies, you'd think they never seen snow before," Freddie said aloud to himself. He tossed his cellphone on the bed at the far end of his doublewide trailer. "This is fucking Minnesota in fucking December, what do they expect?"

This morning at least half of the Blue Hogs had come up with excuses not to party at the river like they'd planned. It was a workday, of course, but that hadn't stopped them before from cracking open a few beers before heading off to their jobs. It was a Monday morning ritual, starting the week off right.

Freddie pulled on his leathers and headed out to his motorcycle, locking the trailer door behind him. He'd lived there in the wooded outskirts of Blue Earth for more than ten years. He could afford nicer digs, he told anyone who asked, but why live large and bring attention to himself from the law? Better to maintain the facade of a humble working stiff.

He had told the six club members who agreed to the meetup that he would stop to gas up at Speedway and score a case of beer and join them at the Dodd-Ford bridge. In truth, his gas tank was full and he already had the beer, strapped to the rear rack of his hog. The delay in his arrival was to give him time to make a quick rendezvous in the woods so he could transact some business then catch up with the Hogs. That way his club mates would be able to vouch for him if anyone later should become curious as to his whereabouts that morning. And the less they knew about his side deals the better.

He pulled his Harley off the main road, killed the engine, and coasted through an opening in the trees onto a dirt path rumored to be an old Indian trail. Deer trail was more like it, Freddie surmised. The path was damp but not yet covered with sticking snow. The trees intercepted the flakes, which dripped to the ground as they melted on the leaves. He coasted as far as he could then parked the bike and continued on foot through the dense woodlands to meet up with Chester Greenfield at the agreed-on spot. He hoped his old "buddy" wasn't going to chicken out. Chester talked big, but Freddie often wondered if he were as brave as he pretended to be. He was about to find out. If Chester came through with the ten grand in cash, he would be roped into Freddie's drug enterprise, ready to take a large delivery of pills from his Mexican source. Was it really Oxy, as promised? Or some Fentanyl-laced bullshit? Freddie didn't care.

When he entered the clearing at the old shed where they'd agreed to meet, he spied a tall stump, which seemed recently cut, and sat on it as if it were a throne. He pulled out his phone and he saw there was no signal.

"Does your mom know what we're doing?"

Travis didn't answer right away. He glanced over at Julio in the passenger seat then turned back to focus on the road ahead, the windshield wipers smearing the melting snowflakes across the glass like roadkill.

"What do you think? No way. She told me her whole sob story about Freddie and drugs, said to stay away from him. She's already gone loco over me buying Oxy from him. I should have listened to her. That lying fuck Freddie. She'd flip out if she knew we were chasing after him ourselves. She said to let Elvis handle it."

"You know what I think?" said Julio. "I think you wanted to try Oxy just to get back at her. Do the opposite of what she begged you not to. You wanted to mess with her head. I think it worked, dude."

"Fuck you, Julio. You know nothing. Anyway, you wanted to try it, too."

Julio went silent for a while, staring straight ahead. Travis regretted his harsh words and wanted to take them back. In his gut he sensed that Julio was right, that he'd taken opiates as an act of defiance against the mother who had brought so much pain and confusion into his life. But he felt a wall of enmity building between him and Julio and didn't know how to break through. Best friends since middle school, now maybe drifting apart.

"Do you believe her? About Freddie and meth and all?" Julio sounded more conciliatory, less accusatory.

"I don't know what to believe from her. I know she's had a fucked-up life. I was lucky to not be part of that shit. Elvis and Mavis are my real parents."

"You got to forgive her, *hombre*. She's your mom. She came back for you."

"Yeah. Eighteen years too late." Travis shut down any further conversation about his mother. He concentrated on the road. Julio stared out the passenger window at the curtain of snowfall. Travis choked back a sob, which rose unexpectedly from deep within. He did not want Julio to see how shredded he was inside. He hated Jeanne. And he loved her at the same time. Her voice, her smell, he could not possibly have remembered them from infancy, yet they had enveloped him like well-worn, comfortable clothes.

His reverie was broken by a speeding motorcycle coming toward them in the opposite lane. "Son of a bitch. That was him," Travis said. He pulled over to the side of the road and turned to look out the back window. He could see the receding taillight through the thickening flurries.

"Who? Freddie?" said Julio.

"Got to be."

"Turn around. Let's catch him," Julio urged.

"He's supposed to be at the bridge, like always on Monday mornings," said Travis. "So why's he going the other way?"

"Follow him. Let's find out."

Travis did a U-turn and headed back the other way, trying to keep his eyes on the taillight fading into the white haze. The two had been stalking Freddie for days, aiming to confront him for the pills he'd sold them, which made Travis violently ill. They weren't exactly sure what they would do once they caught up with him and his gang; they were young, impulsive, and not seeing more than one step ahead at a time.

"There he goes," said Julio, tracking the taillight. "Turned left into the woods. Pull over, there. Now, here."

Travis parked on the shoulder. They exited his car and walked into the woods via the muddy path.

Chester Greenfield parked his truck off the road opposite where the deer path led into the woods, hiding it under the snow-drooped boughs of a grove of fir trees. There was another car already parked by the entrance to the path. A rusted Honda. He didn't recognize it and wondered if it was Freddie's but didn't remember him having a car. He had hoped to arrive before Freddie so he could stake out the terrain and claim the first-mover advantage. He pressed his left hand against the bulge in his shirt pocket, protected from the elements by his down parka. The envelope stuffed with hundred-dollar bills was ready to be transformed from ten grand in cash into a hundred-grand worth of opiates, the salve for the pain of overlooked rural America. He knew firsthand what those miracle pills could do for a person's disposition and outlook on life. As long as one didn't take too many and get addicted. Which he most definitely was *not* doing. What other people did with them was their business.

He crossed the road, now painted white with sticking snow, and entered the wooded path. He followed the increasingly muddy trail deep into the brush before emerging at a clearing. There was a dilapidated old shed in the middle, which looked like it hadn't been occupied in years, as if it were someone's ice fishing shack abandoned far from any frozen lake. He wondered whose it was and how it got there. As he entered the clearing, he spotted Freddie sitting on a big tree stump, snowflakes collecting in his bushy beard, hands in the pockets of his black leather jacket, looking very unhappy to be kept waiting.

Pam Strich tried to keep her distance behind Chester Greenfield's truck so as not to be seen. Tomlinson still didn't know about her unauthorized surveillance of one of Newfield's most prominent citizens, so she'd taken pains to keep it on the QT. Fortunately, this was not difficult in a driving snowstorm. She could stay focused on his red taillights while remaining obscured in his rearview mirrors by the increasingly thick flurries. She was not entirely sure what she would find if she caught up with Chester, but she felt in her gut it would be a juicy story. She knew he was involved with Jack White, and maybe Jill, in sketchy real estate deals around the county, possibly abetted by political fundraising quid pro quos. There was also something odd going on between Chester and

Freddie Ignatowski, which seemed to involve motorcycle gangs and the Trump reelection campaign. Vague as it was, the mere thought of it tickled her reporter's instincts. In fact, she had not slept well in weeks, lying awake in bed trying to piece together the threads she'd gathered. Pam regretted the breakup with Cindy and missed her terribly but had to admit the distance had helped her stay sober and focused on her job.

In her reverie she almost missed it when Chester turned off the road about a hundred yards ahead. She kept driving past him, then did a U-turn a quarter mile down the road and turned back, hoping he hadn't recognized her car. She parked under the canopy of snow-covered trees behind Chester's truck, then crossed the road. Another car, a little Honda she didn't recognize, was parked near the path. Freddie's? Someone else's? Intriguing. She entered the woods, looking for Chester's footprints in the slushy mud of the trail. After a few minutes she came to a fallen tree trunk and squatted behind it, which afforded her an unobstructed view of the clearing that surrounded a ramshackle little structure. She pulled her knit watch cap down to cover her ears, which had started to sting from cold and snow. She dug her cellphone from her shoulder bag and checked the battery. Eighty percent, but zero bars.

Off to the side of the clearing she could see Chester and Freddie engaged in a not very friendly conversation. Chester pulled a thick legal-size envelope out of an inside pocket and waved it at Freddie, who grabbed at it, then Chester yanked it back and returned it to his pocket. Their voices rose. Freddie seemed furious.

After a few more minutes of this fat men's dance, Pam detected motion out of the side of her eye and turned to see two figures walking toward the clearing from the left side. Their hoods were pulled over their faces, but Pam got enough of a glimpse to recognize Travis Birdsong, star of the Newfield Reapers football team. The other one was probably his buddy Julio Cervantes. It sounded like they were arguing in hushed voices. Travis said something about "getting us lost in the woods." Were they in on whatever shady deal was going on? Or innocent bystanders? She considered warning them away but chose instead to let the scene play out. She propped up her phone on top of the tree trunk and set the camera app to video.

Freddie was about to call off the deal, much as he needed the ten grand, because Chester was being such a Nervous Nellie. He wanted to see the drugs, as if Freddie would be dumb enough to have that many pills on him out here. There were procedures to be followed. Money first, product comes after.

"You don't get the cash till I see the stash," said Chester, obviously pleased with himself, like a rapper spinning a gangsta rhyme.

Freddie heard the snap of a branch under foot, the sound dampened by the snowfall but still audible. Into the clearing strode Travis Birdsong and Julio Cervantes.

"What are you doing here?" bellowed Freddie.

"You said come alone," Chester said to Freddie. He pointed at the newcomers. "Why are they here?"

"You tell me, Chester."

"You ripped us off," Travis said to Freddie. "Those pills sucked, made me sick."

"Give us our money back," said Julio.

Freddie guessed this was no double cross by Chester. The two idiots had likely tracked him down on their own. Well, their tough luck. He reached into the back of his pants and pulled out his Beretta. "This here says fuck off," he said, pointing it at Travis.

"Whoa, chill, man," said Travis, backing away.

"What are you doing?" Chester said to Freddie "Put that thing away."

"Nobody calls me a rip off." Satisfied that he'd made his point, Freddie put the gun back in his pants. "You boys run along. We'll discuss this later. I am trying to do business here."

"Shit, Freddie," said Chester. "Is it true? Did you sell these boys bad dope?"

Now everything was falling apart. Because of these stupid morons. Damned if they'll ever get to join the Hogs. "You know what? Just forget it. Deal's off."

"Now hold on Freddie. Old Seventy-Five. Buddy."

Gus felt a melon-sized ball of dread forming in his stomach. He needed to know where this story was going, but also feared it. "In the Army? Where? When?"

"I told you I had a story to tell and you would want to hear it," Walser said.

"Did you see him … in Iraq?"

"I was with him when he died."

Gus had been full of questions for this strange character, but now was struck dumb. He tried to speak, but his throat was closing up.

Walser became increasingly agitated, his voice trembling as he rocked back and forth on the stool. He appeared to slide into a trance-like state and started talking rapid-fire. "Him and me got cut off from our unit. Outside Fallujah. It was a fuck-all mess. Hajis all around. Our hummer hit an IED and flipped. The other two guys with us—there was nothing left of 'em. Almost got my whole face burnt off. Augie was hurt pretty bad. Took some shrapnel in the thigh, bleeding all over. I carried him into an abandoned building. A barn or something, smelled of goat shit. I stayed with him. Tied up his leg with strips of my shirt. I though he was hit in the femoral artery, it was bleedin' so bad. But I stopped it. Did a real good job, even though I ain't no medic."

He paused and looked at Gus as if seeking approval. Gus still could not speak.

"I went outside. It was getting dark. I thought I should go find help. Had no radio, no nothin'. Lost my rifle. His, too. I didn't get too far when I heard a bunch of Hajis coming. Could hear them chattering in Arabic or whatever. I went back. Augie was unconscious. I tried to revive him. I don't know if he was already dead, or what. It didn't seem like he was breathing. Then the Hajis got closer, like they was searching all the buildings, house to house. I got scared. I left him. *I fucking left him.* Like a chickenshit. Crawled out a back window and ran away. Hid under a pile of garbage. *Garbage.* When I went back for him, he was gone. The fucking Hajis took his body."

He went silent for a long moment, apparently waiting for Gus to comment. Gus's insides felt like a wormhole threatening to swallow him whole.

"Eventually, next day, I got back to my unit. Was asked if I'd seen Augie. I lied. Said no. I was too ashamed. I'd run away. But motherfuck if I didn't avenge his death. I killed me so many Hajis I lost count. Did I get a medal? No I did not get a medal. You know what I got? I got my ass court martialed. Said I committed atrocities, quote unquote. Two years in military jail. How you like that? For killin' Hajis, like I was supposed to. No thank yous. Just fucked. F-U-C-K-D."

Gus didn't remember hearing about a Newfield native getting court martialed for atrocities. He wondered if it was bullshit. Or if it was one of those inconveniences the Army had swept under the carpet. At last he found his voice. The wave of grief that had begun to envelop him gave way to a surge of rage. "You knew. All this time. About Augie. And you said nothing? Never told us?"

Walser grinned idiotically, as if it were a diabolical practical joke.

"Do you have any idea how we suffered all those years, not

knowing?" Gus said, voice shaking. "Why?"

The grin vanished, replaced by a scowl. "I wanted you to suffer. Like I did."

"What about all those letters you wrote to Molly. Just tormenting us?"

"I was going to tell you eventually. I had to see if you deserved to hear the truth. Or if you were just selfish assholes like everyone else. Molly was nice. But not you."

Gus saw that he'd mishandled this whole mess from the start. He regretted his wise-ass, sneering tone, not only in his answer to Walser but to everyone. Arrogant fool, time to pay up. "What do you want with me?"

"Unfinished business. The Hajis killed Augie. But you're the reason he was there at all. He'd be alive if it wasn't for you."

"That's a lie. I tried to talk him out of it. He wouldn't listen."

"He signed up cuz of you. He was scared as shit. Like we all were. Said he wished he'd never signed up. But he didn't want to let you down. Big Vietnam hero."

"I was no hero."

"You were to him. He fucking worshipped you. Said he couldn't bear you to think he was a coward."

This was the moment when Gus decided he wanted to die. Molly was right all those years she'd resented him for not stopping Augie from enlisting. And for his affair with Cindy. How had she borne it? Why didn't she leave him? He didn't deserve her. He didn't deserve anything. His moment of atonement had come.

Walser stood, put the pistol down and reached for the assault rifle. "Now get up. We're goin' outside."

Now is when I die, thought Gus. Not in this little coffin of a shack, but in some hole he's dug in the woods. They'll never find my body. "What are you going to do?"

"Shut the fuck up. None of this would have happened if it wasn't for you. None of it. Augie. Me. This." He pointed toward his ruined face.

"Why do you need all these guns?" Gus asked, afraid he already knew the answer.

"Lotta scores to settle." He grinned.

The man was clearly insane, poisoned by rage and imagined conspiracies. Gus wondered how many more people would have to die to slake this lunatic's thirst for validation. He turned toward the door, calculating how quickly he would have to spin around and push away the barrel of the rifle with one hand and punch him in the face with the other before getting shot. He felt a stabbing sharp pain in his lower back where Walser had jammed the gun barrel into him.

"Move out. Now."

Gus opened the door. A blast of cold air and snow hit him square in the face. Was it enough to temporarily blind or distract Walser? The gun barrel pushed harder against him, answering his question, and together they walked out into the falling flakes.

Pam checked to see if her phone was recording all this on video. It was. She wasn't sure it was picking up any audio, too much wind, but it looked like a clear picture despite the snowflakes. Whatever was going on in that clearing had the makings of a great story. Freddie Ignatowski had actually pulled a gun on the star of the high school football team, if only for a few seconds. She hoped nobody would get hurt, but also hoped this might escalate into a major news event.

Freddie, Chester, Travis, and Julio were just glaring at each other, no one going anywhere, when everyone's attention shifted toward the shack. Pam turned to see the door had opened and out walked Gus Peterson, face bloodied, with his hands up like he was being arrested. When he stepped a few yards into the clearing she could see another man walking behind, face obscured by a hoodie pulled low, holding a wicked-looking assault rifle against Gus's back.

"Whoa, dude!" shouted Travis.

"What the fuck?" said Freddie.

The man with the gun stopped and surveyed the situation. "I said come alone!" he screamed at Gus. "Who are these people?"

"They didn't come with me. I swear," Gus said. He turned to face the man, who raised his rifle and aimed at Gus's face.

"Go ahead," said Gus. "Shoot me. Get it over with."

Pam saw another figure slowly entering the clearing from the other side. It was Elvis Birdsong in blaze orange, carrying a shotgun. This was beyond absurd, she thought. Was the whole town going to show up? Elvis was obviously trying to be stealthy, walking gingerly through the accumulating snow, slightly crouched.

It didn't work.

"Drop that gun, or I shoot this old man," the mystery man said to Elvis. "Now."

Elvis stood up straight and paused, as if making a calculation. He exchanged glances with Freddie and Chester. Then saw Travis and Julio, and his face fell, as if frozen in shock and grief. He tossed his shotgun into the snow.

While the shooter was focused on Elvis, Gus had taken a few more steps, opening a gap of several yards between them. Chester moved over quickly and stood in front of Gus. "You want to shoot this old man, you gotta shoot me first," he said.

The man pointed his rifle at Chester's head. "Don't think I won't," he said.

Elvis shifted his position slightly and the shooter turned his attention in that direction. Freddie moved into the center of the clearing and stood shoulder to shoulder with Chester. He pulled his pistol out and aimed it at the hoodie. "You're gonna have to shoot us both, motherfucker. You think you can do that?"

The man turned back toward Freddie and Chester, a look

of panic on his face. He turned again toward Elvis, then back to Freddie. Everyone froze for a long moment in a standoff.

Pam almost screamed when someone tapped her on the shoulder. It was Deputy Joe Morton. He put a finger to his lips to quiet her. "Stay down," he whispered and moved carefully around toward another angle into the clearing. Pam watched him enter the space, coming up behind Travis and Julio, out of the shooter's line of vision. He whispered to the boys and they both dropped to the ground, exposing Morton with his sidearm gripped in both hands aimed at the mystery man. "Everybody freeze," he said loudly but calmly. "Nobody here needs to get shot."

The shooter turned toward Morton, then back toward Gus, hidden between the two ex-football linemen. "Bastard!" he screamed. "I said no cops!" Two quick bursts of his rifle echoed across the clearing, startling like firecrackers on a summer night, muffled slightly by the wind and snow. Chester Greenfield fell back, clutching his shoulder, and knocked Gus over, landing on top of him. Freddie fired his pistol, hitting the shooter in the arm, causing him to drop his rifle. Morton fired a single shot, hitting the man in the thigh, sending him to the ground grabbing his leg and screaming in agony. Elvis rushed in and kicked the assault rifle away. Morton pulled the shooter's arms back and cuffed him. He examined the man's wounds then grabbed his radio and called for the paramedics.

Elvis and Freddie bent over Chester and pulled him off Gus. "Chester's bleeding bad!" yelled Freddie.

"Gus, too," said Elvis. "I think he got hit in the shoulder."

Pam turned her phone video off and leapt over the tree trunk and dashed into the clearing to get closeup photos and interviews.

"Do something," Morton yelled at her. "Go get help. Call 911."

Pam stood off to the side, dumbstruck by the tableau. Eight people scattered in snow-covered woods by the river. Three men on the ground, shot. Blood stains in the snow. The smell of cordite and a wisp of gun smoke still in the air, now blowing away in the wind.

"Go! What are you waiting for?" yelled Morton.

Pam jogged through the woods back to her car. Cellphone service restored, she called 911. She was told the paramedics were already on the way. As she pulled onto the road, she saw the flashing lights of the EMS truck in her rearview, and drove away toward the *Clarion* office, already writing in her head the lede of the weirdest, wildest story she would likely ever witness.

January

Cindy Smith decided she would buy the flowers herself, as Gus had got in so late the night before and she thought it best to let him sleep. His flight from California, diverted through Phoenix then Detroit, was delayed several hours, and by the time Cindy picked him up at Minneapolis-St. Paul International and drove them back to Newfield in a snowstorm, it was after midnight. Gus had complained of all the "rigmarole" in the airports over some flu bug from China.

When she returned from the florist, Gus was up and about in the kitchen, putting water on for coffee. She let herself in with her key, as she had been doing every day for the month since Gus decamped to Palm Springs to recuperate from his gunshot wound. He needed someone to look after his place while he was gone, and she was more than happy to oblige, tired as she was of her tiny apartment in town. "How did you sleep?" she said.

"Not so great. Still having trouble finding a comfortable position in bed. Damn this shoulder. Now I'm gimpy up top to match my gimpy leg."

"Let me make you breakfast. I loaded up the fridge yesterday. We got eggs. We got bacon. We got toast."

In no time they'd settled back into the comfortable friendship that had grown in the wake of Molly's passing. Cindy had made good on her pledge to look after Gus, making almost daily visits to the Peterson homestead. After the shooting, she moved into Augie's old room, where she had lived so many years ago. Gus was in the hospital for several days. He was lucky. The bullet went right through his shoulder, missing heart and lungs by only a few inches. Cindy nursed him for a few weeks over the holidays, with help from the Bergs and Larsens and Birdsongs, until he received an invitation from his brother Marcus in Palm Springs. Gus jumped at the chance to put two time zones and many degrees of latitude and Fahrenheit between himself and Newfield. The warm desert sun apparently had done him good, although when Cindy met him at the airport, he looked thin and frail, notwithstanding the healthy tan.

The bullet that hit Gus had first gone clean through Chester Greenfield with enough force to pass through two men and lodge deep in a tree trunk. Chester was lucky, too, even though he took two bullets in the shoulder, one that passed through and one that struck the thick wad of bills in his pocket, apparently deflected just enough, according to the surgeon, to avoid any vital chest organs. Pam Strich's articles in the *Clarion* described how an envelope stuffed with cash, supposedly ruined by a bullet hole and copious globs of blood, mysteriously disappeared sometime between the scene in the woods and Chester's arrival at the ER. Pam had told Cindy that if a drug deal was about to go down before the mayhem ensued, any evidence of it had vanished. Freddie and Chester denied knowledge of any such transaction. Travis and Julio kept changing their stories about why they were in the woods that day. The sheriff's department, weary of the whole bizarre affair, let it drop. Deputy Morton received a commendation; out in the woods tailing Elvis and Freddie, he instead stumbled upon and thwarted a possible mass shooting.

Glen Walser survived his wounds to face charges of

kidnapping, possession of illegal firearms, assault with a deadly weapon, and attempted murder. He was awaiting trial in the county lockup. Cindy opined that Walser likely would get off on an insanity plea and end up in a mental hospital. Gus said he couldn't argue with that. He also said he could not find it in his heart to hate the man, only to pity him. The harrowing story Walser had told him about the day Augie died filled him with sorrow and regret. He was glad to finally learn the truth about his son's death, that it was honorable, in battle action. He also knew he would be haunted to the end of his days by the thought of Augie dying in war just so he could please his father. Walser's account of panic and fear in the face of imminent death brought back buried memories of his time in the jungles of Vietnam, from which he never expected to return. He, too, had been scared, terrified actually, and wondered if he would have done anything different than Walser had he been in the same situation.

After breakfast, Gus suggested it was time to pick up the flowers and head to the cemetery.

"I already got them. When you were asleep," Cindy said. "They're in the truck."

"Won't they freeze out there?"

"Nah, it's warming up. Snow's already melting, it's supposed to hit forty today. They'll stay fresh in the cool air."

"How does it look? The grave."

"Real nice. I go almost every day. New flowers get put there all the time. They look pretty in the snow."

"Who's bringing flowers?"

"You know. Just people."

After Cindy cleared the dishes, they went out to Molly's truck for the trip to the gravesite. Cindy drove. She suggested that afterwards they swing by the VFW, where the "three amigos," as she now called Berg, Larsen, and Kugelman, were waiting to see him. "That would be nice," he said. He'd missed those guys, he admitted, even Kugelman.

Gus asked her to fill him in on the doings of the last month. He said he had tried to avoid any news from Newfield while basking in the desert, slurping margaritas poolside. His only connections to home, he said, had been watching the Gophers win their bowl game and the Vikings lose in the playoffs.

"I was thinking," she started. "I could stay. If you want. I like it out here. Maybe take up gardening. We could open Mollywood next summer."

"That would be okay with me."

"Brandi, too?"

"I'm not much of a cat person."

"You'll learn to love her, I promise."

"What about your job?"

"I'm quitting. I've had enough of bars and alcohol and drunks. I need to do something more wholesome with my life. Pam has shown me the error of my ways."

"How's she doing? She's a big star now I hear. Wrote all those stories in the paper."

"She's good. Still sober, after five months. I'm proud of her. I was worried she would leave for a bigger job, but she says she wants to stay, for a while at least. That makes me happy."

"I thought you two were on the outs. Broke up."

Cindy was unsure she wanted to talk about that now, so she said nothing for a moment. They drove past snowy fields in silence. It was a beautiful sight, the landscape. Gus confessed to Cindy how much he'd missed the Minnesota winter while baking in the desert sun, skin turning brown and brittle, mind slowly becoming addled by too much tequila. He said he did not want to turn into his shriveled brother Marcus, who after his wife died moved from Rapid City to Palm Springs and decided he was gay, at age seventy.

"We're back together," she said finally. "Sort of. I think. I'm not running for mayor after all, so there's no conflict for me to date a reporter."

"Not running? Since when?"

"I'm backing Elvis for mayor. He's going to win, too. Jill White is not running for reelection. Word is, she and Jack are selling the dealership and moving to Florida."

"You and Pam back together, eh? Maybe she could come live with us, too."

"You old goat. You'd love that wouldn't you? Like having your own pretend harem. Or like one of those Bible thumpers with multiple wives."

"Just a thought."

"Anyway…"

Cindy revved up the gossip machine and filled the remainder of the drive to the cemetery with a nonstop narration of all things Newfield:

"Freddie Ignatowski wasn't charged for shooting Walser. It was ruled self-defense, based on Morton's account. But his drug dealing caught up with him. He was busted several weeks later taking delivery of a massive amount of Mexican opiates. He's out on bail awaiting trial, and Chester got him a high-priced lawyer, but he's probably looking at twenty years.

"Rosalita Greenfield was getting ready to leave Chester well before the shooting, then actually did move out after she got wind of the attempted drug deal. But she went back to him once he got out of the hospital. Out of pity maybe. They're planning to sell their share of the farm—Chester's already been ousted as manager—and take a long vacation in Costa Rica, where Rosie's family is from. Unclear if they'll ever come back. That Bikers for Trump rally he was planning fell apart after Freddie's arrest. Chester swears he's done with farming and politics and just wants to sit on the beach all day.

"Jim Tomlinson and Jeanne Birdsong are still an item. Jeanne has moved back into her parents' house and has reconciled with Travis. Jim is over there all the time. Travis says he's going to community college this summer to bring his grades up so he can get into State. He has a football scholarship offer, but it's contingent on his academics."

Cindy stopped talking for a moment, needing to take a breath. "You know about Jeanne, right?" she resumed. They were paused at a stop sign. Cindy turned right.

Gus shook his head. "No. What?"

"She's writing 'Dear Molly' now. Isn't that perfect?"

Gus smiled. "I thought Jim killed off the column. Glad he didn't."

"Mavis," Cindy continued, "is expanding the café into the empty storefront next door and adding a dinner menu. She's taking on Maria Elena as a partner, and Miguel is going to work the front of the house as a sort of maître d.' How cool is that? They're upset about Julio. He wants to get a motorcycle and join the Blue Hogs. They shouldn't worry, though. The Hogs say they are out of the drug business. Get this: They're teaming up with Elvis's militia to form a citizen anti-crime patrol. Apparently, they were drinking beer together the morning of the shooting, heard the shots, raced to the scene, and bonded over the experience."

"Where are you going?" Gus, caught up in Cindy's breathless storytelling, only now noticed that she was pulling into town, not heading out 169 to the cemetery.

"Just one quick stop. It'll only take a minute." She entered the streets around the town square and parked the truck in front of the *Clarion* storefront.

"What are we doing here?" Gus said.

"C'mon, get out."

He obeyed. Jim Tomlinson came out the front door to greet them. Gus extended his hand to shake but Jim grabbed him into a bear hug. Pam Strich and the rest of the staff followed, clapping and taking turns hugging Gus. Cindy sidled up to them, holding in her arms a bouquet of flowers, a mixed assortment in a vase.

"Why here?" Gus asked, looking confused.

"That's why," said Cindy.

They turned to look at the big front window of the newspaper office. Under the curved, gold-stenciled, Gothic lettering announcing, "The Newfield Clarion, estd. 1921," there hung inside the glass a large, framed portrait of Molly Peterson as she looked forty-five years ago. The red hair. The green eyes. The wise and mischievous smile. Under the picture was an array of flowers. More flowers were placed on the sidewalk outside the window where the snow had been shoveled aside to accommodate a sort of perpetual shrine. Someone had written on the window with lipstick, "Dear Molly, Always in Our Hearts."

Gus fell to his knees and wept.

Acknowledgments

The town of Newfield is a figment of my imagination but is inspired by the beautiful small towns of southern Minnesota, a state that remains close to my heart. Many thanks to the kind citizens of the Gopher State, too many to mention, who patiently received me during my travels researching this book. Special thanks to Ed Thoma of the Mankato Free Press, who helped me grasp the lay of the land in the region, and Horace Thompson for his insights into the business of farming. Any errors are mine alone. The community of writers in Southern California continues to be a crucial source of inspiration and support, as is my circle of readers and allies including Omolola Ogunyemi, Charles Harper Webb, Laura Belfiglio Gold, J. Ryan Stradal, Don Cummings, Chip Jacobs, Mick Flores, David Bolton and Chris Allen. My journey to published author would not be possible without the wisdom and guidance of editor/adviser Ivy Pochoda and agent April Eberhardt. I'm grateful to Lisa Kastner and her team at Running Wild Press, especially Kelly Ottiano, Emir Orucevic and Evangeline Estropia, for bringing this book into the world. Finally, to my wife Rhonda Hillbery, soulmate, writer, book lover, native Minnesotan, this is for you.

About Running Wild Press

Running Wild Press publishes stories that cross genres with great stories and writing. RIZE publishes great genre stories written by people of color and by authors who identify with other marginalized groups. Our team consists of:

Lisa Diane Kastner, Founder and Executive Editor

Joelle Mitchell, Licensing and Strategy Lead

Cody Sisco, Acquisition Editor, RIZE

Benjamin White, Acquisition Editor, Running Wild

Peter A. Wright, Acquisition Editor, Running Wild

Resa Alboher, Editor

Angela Andrews, Editor

Sandra Bush, Editor

Ashley Crantas, Editor

Rebecca Dimyan, Editor

Abigail Efird, Editor

Aimee Hardy, Editor

Henry L. Herz, Editor

Cecilia Kennedy, Editor

Barbara Lockwood, Editor

AE Williams, Editor

Scott Schultz, Editor

Rod Gilley, Editor

Kelly Ottiano, Editor

Carolyn Banks, Editor

Evangeline Estropia, Product Manager

Kimberly Ligutan, Product Manager

Pulp Art Studios, Cover Design

Standout Books, Interior Design

Polgarus Studios, Interior Design

Learn more about us and our stories at www. runningwildpublishing.com

Loved this story and want more?
Follow us at www.runningwildpublishing.com, www.facebook/runningwildpress, on Twitter @lisadkastner @RunWildBooks

RUNNING WILD

RUNNING WILD PRESS